Cherry Pit Pie

by Bill Connelly

DORRANCE
PUBLISHING CO
EST. 1920
PITTSBURGH, PENNSYLVANIA 15238

Dorrance Publishing Co
585 Alpha Drive
Pittsburgh, PA 15238
Visit our website at dorrancebookstore.com

ISBN: 978-1-6442-6648-9
eISBN: 978-1-6442-6668-7

Dedication

This book is dedicated to my father and my oldest sister, Lauri. My father taught me nearly everything I needed to know about living. My sister taught me everything I didn't want to know about dying. I miss you both.

Prologue

(Nora's last cry)

Although the contractor is offensive and crude, it is only in appearance. His work is thorough. His demeanor is that of a gentleman. But his body odor and hygiene habits have cost him. He has lost many a job bid and has heard the whispers from potential clients. He has witnessed the laughter when they had thought he was gone. Unshaken by the shallowness of others, he moves on. Appearance indeed has cost him, but not this time.

She had seen his work, and by way of a friend had heard of his fair price. These, although good reasons, are not the qualities that attracted her hire. Jim Leary is grossly obese. And in a hot August sun will not hesitate to remove a sweat-soaked shirt.

The house was built in 1800 and nearly complete in its remodeling before they had bought it. Perched on a hill overlooking the surrounding farmers' fields, it is truly a magnificent structure. Nine-foot-high pillars support the wrap-around porch. Equally as high windows stretch from floor to ceiling in all of its twelve rooms. The hardwood floors themselves reflect years of living, while gumwood trim softens the look in all its imperfections. The house was picturesque in country living. Quite simply, home.

Nora stood in the kitchen performing the meaningless task of a dishwasher. Warm water trickles from faucet to sink. Unfocused, she stared and listened. Outside she could see Jim Leary's truck. It was parked askew, half on the lawn, half on a stone driveway. The hammer pounds, then stops. Pounds then stop. An electric saw cracks the hot afternoon air. To the left of the parked truck, barely visible from Nora's view, is the foundation of the old barn. Nine years have passed since Aaron, her husband, had knocked it down. "Better to knock it down in a controlled manner, " Aaron said, "Than have it fall and kill someone." As Nora thought then and so many more times to come, Aaron knows best—even at the immature age of twenty-one. Now the weeds have their way with two-hundred-year-old stone, and mice are sure to dwell in its cracks. Pound then stop, pound then stop. All the while her hands perform their lackluster labor.

"Mom," Kevin said. A quick spoonful and breath. "Maa...om," with a full mouth of cereal, more impatience and volume in his tone. Nora snapped from her daze and then turned twice, first the water to the off position, then her body towards her only son.

Sitting at the kitchen table, Kevin munched away at Frosted Flakes. If unattended, Kevin would consume the entire box. He flips the pages of a magazine, much too fast to read and much too fast to comprehend. Nearly thirteen, he shovels large spoonful's, one a top the other, never seeming to suppress his tremendous appetite. An inch shy of five feet tall, slender in build and with jet-black hair. He is a handsome young boy, and his mother is proud.

"Yes Kevin" Nora replied.

"Ah... I need a ride on Saturday... Would that be like all right?" Chomp, chomp. "You weren't... " chomp "going anywhere, or nothing were ya?" Kevin asked.

The corner of Nora's mouth twitched upward ever so slightly, and a smile barely emerged before she answered. She gazed at her only child and felt love. She marveled at the pace in which he eats and grows. And she wondered, in solemn thought, what would she do if not for him?

"No... I'm not going anywhere," Nora said. " Where do you need a ride too?"

Kevin gulped another spoonful and swallowed. His eyes bulge in disbelief at his mother's question; his eyes also make direct contact with Nora's as he turns his head and says, "Ma I told you yesterday."

And before Kevin can finish, Nora said, "Yes, I'm sorry." She clenches her fists as if to discipline herself and continues. "What's going on, on Saturday? I'm sorry Honey I forgot."

Kevin stands from the table and begins to close the cereal box top with his right hand while coordinating the left in screwing on the milk's top. If he were to perform either of these functions separately, both tasks would be done more efficiently. But he is young. The lessons of patience have to be learned over time. A long time.

"Practice," he says. "Coach Tillman wants us to kick butt this year, and since most of us guys are new, he said now is the time to get stronger"

"Tillman, is that swimming or basketball?" Nora said.

" Swimming," Kevin says as he begins to walk in the direction of the fridge. "Coach also says that... " He leans, returns the eighth of an inch of milk remaining in the jug to an open space, and closes the frig door. "That...um." Kevin looks down the long hall. There, in a huge silhouette behind the screen door, is Jim Leary. Jim taps on the screen's edge, audible to no one but himself.

"That guys at the door," Kevin says, changing his train of thought.

Nora, intent on listening to what Kevin, is saying takes a moment to understand, just as she realizes the subject has changed.

"Mrs. Mills," Jim says. Taping slightly harder, producing a double knock. One from his callous knuckles making contact with the door and one from door itself rocking open and closed, tapping on its own weathered frame.

Nora, wiping her hands on a kitchen towel, passes Kevin. As she does, her left hand touches his back, and her right hands him the towel.

"Excuse me a moment, Honey." Nora said.

Making her way down the long hall, she too can see the enormous man's outline through the full-length screen door. The hallway opens to a formal dining room. A beautiful mahogany dining set and hutch furnish the comfortably sized space. A large, six-foot opening to the front foyer divides these two rooms. Sliding-wood doors that escape into walls are always left open, a never-closed pocket door. The front door has been the primary entrance since Nora and Aaron had moved in. Previous owners used the side door; the landscape and sidewalk directed you right to it from the driveway.

"Nonsense!" Aaron says. " A spectacular door such as this pointing towards the front of the house deserves to be in use." He was right. The door held tight years of white paint. Determined, with choking chemicals and elbow grease, they had released its natural beauty. A full three-inch thick, black walnut access. Now swung completely open, awaiting a welcomed cool breeze.

The closer Nora had gotten to the silhouette of Jim Leary, two bizarre things occurred that day. One: Jim had stopped knocking because he could clearly see Nora approaching through the hall. But as Nora walked the floor of the dining room, she became the silhouette, and Jim became the clearly seen one. He raised his hand as if to salute, in an attempt to shade the sunlight from his eyes. It was of no use. There was no sunlight under the porch roof, only light. Jim had to have cupped his hands and pressed his round, full face flush with the screen to have seen Nora's perfection just one foot away.

Nora is thirty-four years young. She ages slower than time itself. Her hair is shoulder length and strawberry blond, as natural as her last salon visit. She is quite strong for her size. Although she has almost always been five- and-a-half-feet tall, she has not always weighed 128 pounds.

In all of western New York, no two contrasts stood a screen's thickness apart. Thus, being the second bizarre occurrence that day.

"Yes Mr. Leary, how may I help you? Nora said. Her tone was polite and inviting. She stood with her arms crossed, very aware that she had removed her bra. Though a cool breeze was unlikely, she was self-conscious and insecure of erect nipples, and of course, her looks. Her eyes walked from his chest to his face. Just as she marveled at Kevin's enormous appetite, she marvels at this man's enormous size.

"Yes Ma'am" Jim begins. " It looks as though I'll be wrapping things up on Friday. We've been really lucky with the weather. Three weeks, just like I said. "He moves his saluting hand to meet his other. The tips of his fingers dance and fidget while he speaks. His eyes dart from ground to her shapely image.

"Ah... I'd like to go over the warranty, if that'll be all right Ma'am?" Jim continued. "Not that I think you'll need it. This vinyl siding is great stuff. All you have to do is hose it down if it gets dirty." Jim, almost embarrassed, abruptly stops. In his mind, he has feared, and preaches to himself: *Your only bad habit Jim Leary is rambling on an on!*

"But we can go over all that on Friday, if…if that's all right with you Ma'am?" Jim's voice had quieted and slowed down after his inner voice had told him to shut up. He stands there before her, a little nervous, a little edgy. Repeating the things, he had said in his mind, wondering if they had sounded dumb, or worse, unprofessional. Beautiful women make all men feel this way. Fidgety fingers, fidgety eyes. Jim feels his chest beginning to tighten, just as it occurs to him, *I should have said something about the money.*

"That will be fine, Mr. Leary," Nora says. "And I'll be sure to have your check. Will the balance be as we agreed, or did you run into troub…?"

"No no Ma'am," Jim excitedly interrupts. "There was no trouble at all." He sighs the sigh of relief. He is glad she had brought up the money. He is not a poor man, but the timing of acquiring this job was right, and he needed the cash.

"Those eavesdrops weren't rotten at all. It's hard to tell from the ground, ya know. During the estimate, I just like to cover myself. You just can't tell in this line of work. I remember a job…"

As big Jim Leary forgets his minds preaching Nora returns to gaze and stare. She looks at his arms and thinks, *they are as big as my thighs.* And she looks at the folds and layers of fat. The sweaty, tanned body with speckles of white vinyl saw chips. And she can see faint lines of untanned flesh circling his breasts.

"So, the guy says. Look, I'm not paying for that." Jimmy rambles on and on.

"His tool belt, which holds his hammer and nails" Nora had thought, "It's huge! There's two clasps; it must have an extension." And she looks at his face, where the fat at his jowls jiggle as he talks. And a droplet of sweat takes the long journey from forehead to cheek, from cheek to chins. She stares, unaware of his story, her thoughts drifting. Is it possible? Was I once that fat? How on earth did he love me?

"How's everything look?" Jim asks.

Nora snaps from her daze. Caught off guard by his question, she struggles rapidly for the correct words to say. She's embarrassed, and if anyone else other than Jim was within earshot, they would hear it in what she says next.

"I'm sorry. Excuse me?"

"How's it look? The siding? You haven't said if you liked it," Jim said.

"Oh ...aa..." Nora replies. Shaking her head very slightly from side to side, as if to clear the cobwebs from her mind.

Jim, still in his unaware ramble, says, " I mean it looks kind 'a plain, nice! I mean, but you can't even tell from the road its newly sided, which is good I suppose, if that's the look you're going for. Durable, that's for sure. You won't have to paint it—definitely low maintenance."

"It's fine, Mr. Leary," Nora says, raising her voice an octave, trying to both slow him down and understand all that he's said. "You've done a wonderful job. It really looks great." Gathering her composure, she softens her tone, smiles, and looks him straight in the eye. Then it hits her.

Jim is relieved at her approval. He deeply breathes in air with pride of a job well done. He smiles for himself. All men seek the approval from the women they stand before. He still cannot see her face, but her smile can be felt. And before the deep breath escapes his massive lungs, as if a light bulb flashed on above his head, his mind's voice screams, *You are rambling on an on you fool! Blah blah blah blah!* Jim drops his fidgeting hands to his side. He begins to backstep away from the door, swinging his arms like an embarrassed young child.

Nora's smile abruptly stops. Not for Jim's recent actions, but for Jim's recent words. "What did you say?" Nora says.

Jim is a bit confused and almost wondering, *Did she here my thoughts? You are rambling, you fool.*

"Excuse me, Ma'am?" Jim says.

"That last thing you said. Something about paint?" Nora said. Lifting her hand from under her armpit, rubbing her index finger and thumb softly, trying to entice Jim's ability to remember what he had said.

"Oh... um, you won't have to paint. Low maintenance, definitely low maintenance," Jim says.

"Yes, low maintenance," Nora says very slowly, in a whisper barely audible even to herself.

" Yeah, well that will be all. Thank you Mrs. Mills. Thank you," Jim says as he scurries off the porch. Still uncomfortable and still insecure from his rambling display.

"Yes...low maint..." Nora says, tapering off and hardly aware that big Jim Leary had left. Nora backs away, almost in an unconscious state. Instinctively she closes the large walnut door. She makes her way from the foyer to dining room. She looks as though a startling revelation has overtaken her thoughts. At the start of the hall, which leads to her awaiting dishes, Kevin stands. Now his arms are crossed, and he taps his foot as if impatient. But impatient he is not. It has been a long time since he's seen his mother so distant. He is concerned, but more so, he is a preteen boy. His own needs come first. He snaps his fingers just inches from his mother's face, like the awakened hypnotist, Nora blinks alert.

"Ma!" Kevin says.

"Yes, yes Kevin," Nora says before he can respond.

"You were saying Mr. Tillman, the swim coach?" She continues to walk slowly, motioning with her body' language. *Follow me to the kitchen, Boy*, it says.

Nora leans against the counter in front of the sink. Her back is to the window with a mirror image of its earlier view. Kevin had followed, but only to the edge of the hall. Gliding his hands into his pants pockets, he leans on the cased, door-less opening.

"Coach Tillman is pushing us hard this year," Kevin says.

"Yes, you said that," replies Nora.

"Well, he's counting on us new guys to do really well, and ah..." He stumbles for the right words. As he thinks, he ponders not just the right words and not just the right way to say them. He stumbles because he cares for his mother. For a moment, he considers her reaction. For a moment, he considers her feelings. He witnessed the dazed look just moments ago. He remembers the zombie-like walk and blank stares. *But it's been so long*, he thinks. And he tells himself, *She's stronger now*. His instinct whispers., *But what about today?*

"Kevin, for goodness sakes. What?" Nora asks again, with the tone of a mother's inquiry.

"Coach wants me to start running," Kevin says. His look is that of guilt. He waits with abated breath to see her reaction and hear her response.

"That's it?" Nora says. She does not blink. She does not crumble, as Kevin had thought. She simply asked if that was all.

"Yeah... Well I..." Kevin says. " What about Dad?"

Nora never wavers. Her voice is monotone and calm. She slowly moves her hands from the tile counter's edge to her beautiful, shapely woman hips. Standing completely erect, she looks him directly in the eyes.

"Kevin, if you would like to run, it is perfectly all right with me," Nora says.

Rocking his body from the wall, never removing his hands, he stands in bewilderment. His instinct had warned him to worry. A gut reaction suggests cause for alarm. His instinct had lied. He quickly discards his concerns. Removing his hands from their pockets, his relaxed palms face the ceiling before coming together. He claps softly, creating no sound.

"Great. And there's no problem Saturday, with a ride?" Kevin said.

"No problem at all," said Nora.

She watched as he shrugged his shoulders and left. She had stood hard as a rock as he pondered his thoughts. Nora knew what he was thinking. Soon he will not be so easily fooled. His instincts had not lied, and there will be a day when they're not so readily discarded. Nora knew this because, *After all* she had thought. *He is Aaron's son as well.*

Nora turned and faced the sink. Her hands returned to the counter's edge, and her head hung, as if too heavy for her thin neck to hold. All of Kevin's questions and concerns raced through her mind. She had the look of an exhausted prizefighter, minus the dripping sweat. Slowly, with deliberate breathing, she returns to her role of dishwasher. Again, the warm water trickles. Again, she views the outside world. Pound then stop. Pound then stop. Nora remembers the conversation she had with Jim. She remembers as it begins to intertwine with emotions. *Low maintenance,* he had said. *Coach wants me to run,* he had said. It plays in her head like a broken phonograph. She stares, in a trance, as she holds back the tears. *Be strong Nora. You cannot run from this* echoes in her thoughts. Pounds then stops. *The list,* she thinks. *It's nearly complete.* And as she takes a deep breath of self-reliance, she sighs. She starts to feel as though all will be right. That she has grown. That Nora Mills is forever in control. Then big Jim Leary walks into view, and Nora bursts into tears.

But she cries the cleansing cry. She cries the sobering sob. She was lost but now is found, and with his strength, Nora Mills—only thirty some years young—cries for the last time. Ever.

Chapter 1

(Aaron's Way)

Standing before the garage sale deal, Aaron prods and tucks. The bedroom is lit from the last remaining sunshine of the day. He holds his chin erect while his hands adjust and tighten the knot of his tie. *Dresser with a mirror, twenty bucks*. He thinks. *You can't beat that*. Aaron pops to attention to inspect what he sees. "Not bad," Aaron states aloud. As he fastens the only dress watch he owns to his wrist, he begins to whistle, *Here comes the bride*.

Aaron was born and raised in white suburban America. Chain link fences separated equally-sized yards, each house identical in architectural design. Aaron once thought that if he were to wander into another house by mistake, the only way he would know it was not his own was by smell. He of course believed his house had no smell at all.

Butch and Gloria had brought Aaron home in the winter of 1960. His father was a truck driver all of his adult life. He smoked filter-less cigarettes and drank Genny beer. He was a large man in size, but at times short in character. Butch also loved to play games. Everyone, including Aaron's brother and sister, called him Butch. Everyone except Aaron. He simply referred to Butch as dad.

Gloria portrayed the typical mom. Family meals at the table. Laundry on the line. She never worked outside the home, living in an era that considered her "just a house wife," which suited Mother just fine. To Aaron, there were no two greater parents in the entire world. He was an unexpected child but a welcomed addition to the family tree. The day Aaron came home all had changed. But mostly for Jared.

Jared was ten and Malisa eight as they waited on pins and needles to welcome the new baby home. "It's a girl, jerky Jared," Malisa had teased.

"No, it's not! Wait and see." Jared refuted, motioning his arm to punch. Instead of forcing a flinch, which Jared had hoped, it merely forced Malisa to stick out her tongue.

Butch had turned even this event into a game. He had teased the children for months and joined in on the guessing game in the latter weeks of Gloria's pregnancy. He had wished and hoped right along with Malisa that it would indeed be a girl.

"I won! I won!" Jared screamed, his arms all the while waving around with excitement. "I finally won." Jared had felt as if this was his only victory in all of Butch's games. Perhaps it was.

Malisa had the look of a poor loser as she leaned in for a peek of her new baby brother.

"He's ugly," she said.

But although she was quite bitter that day, Aaron and Malisa went on to share a normal brother-sister relationship. About ten years of teasing and disgust, about five years of silence and ignorance of the other's life, then sibling love and respect. Normal.

Jared, however, had felt as though Aaron had saved his life. He vowed to protect him. He would teach Aaron all that he knew. The only separation these two boys had was in age. He would love him as much more than a brother for nearly nine years.

"Nora," called Aaron. "Are you almost ready?" The concerns that they'd be late accompanied his tone.

Down the hall two doors on the left, Nora leans inches from the bathroom mirror. Her right butt cheek straddles the porcelain sink. Her body is twisted, and her face holds an abstract shape. Her young, taunt skin does not need the makeup she applies.

"Ten minutes!" Nora yells. "Is Kevin awake? I want him to sleep for the sitter."

Aaron makes his way from the dresser to bedside. There, just inches from her side of the bed, a white bassinet cradles his pride and joy. He creeps to the edge and peeks inside. Kevin lies on his back, giggling and twitching, emitting baby sounds.

"Come here you little rug rat," Aaron says, lifting Kevin ever-so gently from the comfortable bed.

"Son, lesson number one in the great game of life," Aaron says. "Women, are never ready on time." He makes no attempt of baby talk as he carried his son from the room.

At each of the halls' ends are bedrooms. The master, of which they had just left, and a guest room or fourth room is currently unused. The hallway has no windows and is considerably darker. Aaron reaches for the light switch like a blind man finding his way. Before he throws the switch, he does something that's all Aaron. An action that might be defined by some as peculiar. Without thinking, but something that required much thought, he looks closely into Kevin's eyes just as the light flashes on. He monitors his pupils like a doctor. He watches as they quickly contract, shrinking to nearly a pen point in size. Satisfied with a normal response, he continues to walk to the bathroom, where Nora is waiting inside.

Aaron Mills is no doctor. Nor is he remotely qualified to be one. The man is a thinker. Always aware of action, reaction, and surroundings. A perspective on life that's part inbreeds, part taught. He is slender in build and strong. His face is heavily scared from adolescence's acne. And on his right arm is a birthmark as round as a coke can, located where a man might put a tattoo. He never considered himself different, although most that had met him or knew him did. To Nora, there was always something to learn about this mystery man.

Days after they had moved into their new home Aaron had walked by the phone and picked it up. He had paused for only a moment and returned it to its hook.

"Who were you going to call?" Nora said.

"No one," answered Aaron.

"Did you hear a ring?" Nora said, knowing full well the phone had not rung.

"Uh...no, did you?" Aaron said.

"No, but I'm not the one that picked up the phone," Nora said, somewhat perplexed. She's not even sure he's aware that he did it from his reactions and the things he has said. There's a slight pause in the air, a moment of imbalance, as Nora motions with her eyes and facial expression to explain yourself Aaron.

"Well," He paused for a second, and there was a look of complete seriousness in his face when he said, "Every minute the phone doesn't ring, there's an indication it could be broke."

"Ha...What? This is a joke, right?" Nora said. But as she said it she also knew it was not. Nora could see he was not kidding, and though their marriage was only six-weeks old, she could tell he was serious. "I mean, he's right." She thought, "If the phone doesn't ring, it could be broke. It's just weird. I mean, he walked by the phone without even thinking or knowing he was doing it, and he tested it. Checking to see it was all right."

In the years to come, Nora would witness more of Aaron's ways. And at times she would think he was quite strange, but when she thought about it, when she labored to think further ahead—something that came so natural to Aaron—she knew Aaron was right. The man was always right.

"You see if it doesn't rin..."Aaron begins to say.

"Yeah, I get it. You're weird. I married a mad man," Nora said, joking with a loving tone to her voice.

He smiled at Nora and felt honeymoon love. Now standing in the doorway to the bathroom, nearly a year later, he feels exactly the same. Honeymoon love.

The bathroom door is closed as Nora views her entire self in the full-length mirror attached inside. She looks up and down the reflected image, shifting and smoothing all the parts of her evening gown.

"Almost ready?" Aaron said with a light tap on the door.

"You can come in," Nora said.

Aaron opens the door slowly, being careful not to hit Nora if perhaps she's standing too close and careful not to lose his grip on his precious son.

"See Kev, just like I told you—never on time," Aaron said, whispering to his inattentive son. Walking in, he sees Nora standing as far to the back of the small narrow room as possible. The look on her face tells him the joking is over. Aaron, with complete concern and compassion in his voice said, "Honey what's the matter?"

Nora stood perfectly still with her arms draped to her side. A moment ago she did not like the view from her vantage point. She rarely liked the reflections from mirrors. Now, she thinks, "This is a sight I would much rather gaze at. This image requires no adjusting at all. The perfect pair." Her face, however, said something else. Her face clearly said the things she was thinking while staring at herself.

"Nothing," Nora said.

Nothing. A word that carries more weight between the sexes than love. Few couples, if any, can ever get past the multitude of meanings from the answer to a question as, *"nothing."* It can mean as much as everything or as nonexistent as the word itself. In the case of Nora Mills, nothing in fact means something, and it's Aaron's obligation to draw it out. He will not accept nothing as her answer, for if he did it would only add to an already festering problem. To Aaron, it would then be something, and to Nora, it was already everything.

"Honey, please what is it?" Aaron said. His concern is quite genuine as he walks towards her with open arm.

Nora's eyes begin to water and turn blood-shot red. To give an explanation now would go unheard. Her breathing would be choppy and irregular, her lips would quiver uncontrollably, and the words themselves would not sound like words at all. Nora is aware of this familiar feeling and chooses to hold her husband tight. She has no intention on breaking down. Although her feelings may be irrational, her thought processes remain intact. She has no desire to redo all her makeup after laboring for an hour to get it right.

Aaron rubs his wives back gently, only stopping to pat it like a burping baby. He's giving her time to gain control. He listens carefully to her breathing pattern and makes a judgment on when he can persist.

Nora keeps her face buried in Aaron's chest, being careful not to smear makeup on his clean suit. She can smell Kevin just inches from her face. *Even humans can identify their young by smell*, is the strange thought that enters her mind. The muffled sound of Aaron's heartbeat and the smell of her young son begins to relax her.

"You don't want to go to this wedding, do you?" Aaron said softly.

Nora just shook her head from side to side, indicating no on Aaron's chest.

"Too early to leave the baby with a sitter?" Aaron inquires.

"No," Nora whispers. "That's not it."

"Well," Aaron paused. He would continue to say what he was thinking, and he would mean every word. But he knew it was not the right thing to do. Certain functions, when families are concerned, you simply must attend. Weddings, funerals, graduations... a list begins to form in his head as he continues to say, "We could not go. We could say the baby wasn't feeling well. We were worried, or...

"No," Nora interrupts. She truly appreciated the suggestion, but she also knew they simply must go. "It wouldn't be right" she said. "They both came to ours."

Aaron is still compiling a list of all gatherings you must attend. But in the foremost part of his mind, he is quietly concerned with Nora's distress.

"If she has no anxieties with leaving Kevin with a sitter," He thinks. "What could it possibly be?"

For most people these two thoughts would consume all of their consciousness, but Aaron finds even stillroom for one more. Again, he wonders why the second-floor bathroom window, which he is standing in front of, has frosted glass. Clearly no one could possibly see in at this level. He begins to remember the peculiar events of the first time he saw this bathroom, how strange it was he did not notice the frosted glass during his inspection, and the image plays like a motion picture in his mind.

The realtor is walking towards the master bedroom, speaking of its size and "wonderful space." Nora is following, not intent on listing to what he is saying, but thinking about the color changes she would make if in fact they decide to buy. Aaron walks behind in guided tour, playing the caboose in the miniature train. He shakes his head up and down, saying things like, "That's nice," or "Yes, I agree," all the while absorbing every detail he possible can. As the realtor passes the bathroom, he nonchalantly motions and says. "This is the second bath." He never stops in his desire to show off the magnificent master bedroom.

Aaron leans in, quickly glancing over the room. Tile floor, cast-iron tub, adequate lighting, and there, the item that drew his attention from the rest of the room. Eight to ten inches above the porcelain pedestal sink, attached to the tile wall, was a plastic cup and toothbrush holder. The fact that it was not exactly the right shade of green to comply with the rest of the room did not faze him. The fact that it was on the left side of the sink, rather than the right side, which would have been the more logical choice, also did not faze him.

"Remember, more people are righthanded," Jared had said while teaching a young Aaron to defend himself.

The number of toothbrushes is indeed what diverted his analysis of the second-floor bathroom. He had met the widow that owned the house just moments ago.

"My Ernie and kids are long gone," she had said. "Ten years now."

So why are there six toothbrushes in the holder? He had thought, and as he rubs Nora's back, Aaron turns for a look at a plastic cup and toothbrush holder. He says, "Are you feeling any..."

Simultaneously Nora says, "I'll be fi..."

Both had arrived at the same point in time where silence was uncomfortable. They chuckled at the exchange and laughed even more when they realized what the other had said also at the same time. This simple chain of events lightens the mood considerably.

Nora lifts her tearless face from Aaron's chest; a labored, half-hearted smile is all she can muster. Aaron looks back in his wife's eyes and returns the smile. A moment ago, he was very concerned, but now he knows all is well. Although their marriage is young, he knows his wife very well. She is moments away from explaining all.

"You know my past. It's all coming back, I'm getting fat again!" Nora said.

"Honey, you're not fat." Aaron said.

"It's true," Nora continued. "I haven't lost a pound since Kevin's was born. The weight's just not coming off. You've seen the pictures; you saw what I looked like. Aaron, I'm fat and getting fatter!"

"Nora, I'm telling you, you're not fat!" Aaron insisted. "And Kevin is only a couple months old. It's quite normal for women—who are nursing I might add—to retain some weight after childbirth."

"I can hear the lewd remarks already," Nora said.

She squishes her face and points her finger as she tries to mimic a fictional someone from tonight's reception.

"Look over there at Nora Mills. What a shame, she's really putting on the pounds," Nora said, her voice higher in pitch as she mocks with tone and body language.

What Nora had said was in part true. Aaron had seen photos of Nora when, even to his loving eyes, he could not believe what he saw. She had grown into a fat child. A very fat child. Something that Aaron had not witnessed for himself. Nora had moved from an outside county to finish her last year of high school, and it was there they had met. The first day he had seen her, she was quite skinny and very attractive. No one had known of Nora's past. And it took a full eight months of dating before even Aaron had gained her trust for that dark secret.

Although Nora's mocking of tonight's guests was exaggerated, that too was in part very true. Some of Aaron's family members would talk. Not about who she is. Nora was well-received in to the Mills family. They would talk more just because she is. For some, being insensitive or backstabbing was their nature, and they would criticize and talk regardless.

"Look at me," Aaron said, insisting on her complete attention.

"You don't know what it's like, Aaron," Nora said, almost pleading for understanding.

"Nora, look at me," Aaron said. His voice was calm but insisting attention.

"What. I'm here. What is it?" Nora said, looking directly in to Aaron's eyes.

"You are the sexiest, most attractive woman I have ever seen in my life, and I don't care what a bunch of hen-pecking, jealous ninnies say. I love you and need you, and that's all that matters," said Aaron.

With this direct, decisive, true-to-the-heart message, Nora's mood softened. His compliment was comforting. It felt good to hear such passion in words he made her believe were true. She held tight the love he blanketed her with; it was warm and comfortable, like an old quilt.

"But it's easy for you," she said softly.

"No buts," Aaron said. As he kissed his wife on the forehead, Kevin let out a scream.

Nora's assumption that it was easy for Aaron was the farthest thing from truth. He did not experience obesity; however, he had experienced the cruelties of adolescence. The monkey that road his back was acne. Unlike added weight, there was no diet he could attempt. There were no clothing techniques he could practice, and there was nowhere he could hide. All of which Nora had tried. The world would see his face whether Aaron liked it or not.

He had matured early in life, tasting all the phases of boyhood earlier than most. G.I. Joes and the fascination of dissecting frogs had passed long before his peers. And Aaron had liked girls when his friends still thought they were gross. He grew fast because Aaron was Aaron, but he was pushed to excel because of Jared. It only stood to reason that acne would come early, as he was the first of his class receiving the crude remarks. Most of what his classmates would dish out, Aaron could handle. His unique outlook on life and the guidance of an older brother gave him an edge. But on the same page, he was human, and at times the name-calling or rude innuendoes had stuck, sticking like flypaper to his subconscious and working on insecurities to bring him down.

Aaron had understood Nora's inner voice reminding her of her weight. He would catch himself listening to his own on occasion. But there was one difference that gave him confidence to suppress it. There was one difference he had that combated his insecurities head on. He had learned it from Jared, but it was Aaron himself who would ultimately have to carry the load. Aaron Mills was a runner, and the open road did not drain his strength—it drove his strength.

He was young to start such a grueling exercise regime. But at the age of eleven he needed something. Aaron's acne was worse than ever. An awkward time which made him feel isolated or very much alone, even in a crowd. His hormones were propelling him into manhood, confusing his thoughts and blistering his face. And the realization that Jared was gone hit very hard in the summer of 1971. Jared's advice to run came on the day he had left for Vietnam.

No one had said a word for a full twenty minutes on the drive to the Greyhound bus terminal. The six days Jared was allotted came and went all too quickly. Now, entering the city limits, everyone began to feel a little edgy. Jared had finished his basic training in Fort Brag, North Carolina, and it was there he would return to board a plane for Thailand. The air in the wood-paneled station-wagon was stale. Butch had crushed his last cigarette in an overcrowded ashtray moments ago, and the lingering smoke blurred everyone's vision and clung to clothes, as well as their lungs. Jared and Aaron sat in the backseat with Butch of course driving and Malisa and Gloria filled the front. Outside the weather was damp and cool. A misty spray from passing motorists was forcing Butch to turn on his wipers every minute or so to clear the windshield. Buildings getting larger outside, tension growing larger inside.

"How long will it take you to get there, Honey?" Gloria said. Her voice was shaky, and it was clear that the finale goodbyes would force her to cry.

"Oh...I don't know," Jared said. " About twenty hours I expect."

"Twenty hours on a bus!" Aaron said in disbelief.

"No, stupid!" Malisa snapped.

"Don't call your brother stupid," Gloria exclaimed, slapping at Malisa half heartlessly.

"No, on a plane. The bus ride is only to Fayetteville. The plane will take me to the war," Jared said.

Gloria gasped and raised her hand to cover her mouth.

"It's not a war, Jared," Butch said in a challenging manner.

But the argument would go unchallenged. The Rochester Greyhound bus terminal had just come into view, and everyone's attention was drawn to it.

Jared would gladly have argued his point if not for the distraction. He had changed, and although Butch was the last in the family to have noticed, he had noticed just the same. Basic training had given Jared confidence. He was stronger, both mentally and physically. The boy—now a young man—was ready to fight. Aaron had seen the change on Jared's first day home.

Butch was teasing Jared about his short military hairstyle and mocking with "Yes sirs" and "No Sirs." Aaron had noticed Jared's reaction to the teasing Butch that he stood tall and erect, unshaken. His eyes hardly blinked, and he never left eye contact with Butch. The air around him said, "Butch, you're acting like a child," and the teasing did not shake him. Not like in the past.

Buses were lined close to the concrete and glass building, all parked at 45-degree angles. Some were left running, emitting smoke to already polluted air. Signs directing available parking informed Butch as Gloria navigated, pointing in this direction and that.

"All the buses look the same. What if you got on the wrong one? Then maybe you wouldn't have to go," Aaron said, both thinking wishfully and pleading for possibility.

Jared reached over and ruffled Aaron's hair into a mess and said, "I'm afraid I have to go, Buddy."

Aaron looked into Jared's eyes and smiled as Jared looked back. He truly loved his older brother, but he was only eight. Wishing he did not have to go was the only way he knew to say I love you. For the rest of Aaron's life, it was this moment he looked back on when thinking of Jared's goodbye. He had wished he told him how much he loved him. A direct verbal, unmistakable message with words—not some childish wish. He just didn't know he would never see Jared again.

They all entered the building, reading more signs for direction on where to go. Ultimately, they sat at chairs that were all connected facing the bus that would take Jared away. Glass-paneled walls stretched from floor to ceiling separating the noise and toxic air from outside. They all watched the duffel bag of Jared's belongings get loaded in compartments on to the bus. Aaron remembers thinking that you couldn't even tell that those panels could be removed and that all busses must have secret hiding compartments. He would later check his school bus for hidden doors, banging on riveted seams and pushing on nuts and bolts, hoping to release some secret hatch. For the first time, Jared looked nervous—almost anxious— to get the journey started. Across the loud speaker a crackling muffled voice announced, "Bus 410 to Fayetteville, North Carolina now boarding."

Butch was the first to stand after all had digested the loudspeaker message.

"Guess that's me," Jared said, standing and holding his arms out to receive his mother for a goodbye hug.

"You be careful," Gloria said, holding back tears, hugging her son almost to the point of pain. Butch stood at her side, rubbing her back for comfort, preparing to catch her if she were to faint or become weak with grief and fall limp.

"I will mother, I will," Jared said, somewhat choking on emotion from the tender moment of goodbye.

"I love you Jared. I love you so very much," Gloria said, running her fingers though his previously wavy blond hair and kissing his face only the way a mother can do in a public place.

Butch moved in closer to his eldest son and his wife, reaching with his free hand he began rubbing both of their backs. Malisa and Aaron stood and slowly moved in close to the three-way hug taking place before them. A slender black man with the same destination opened the glass door leading to the waiting bus. City sounds overtook the quiet terminal lobby and faded only as the door closed in a vacuum seal. The cool October air whistled and washed over the entire Mills family, leading to goosebumps and shivering shakes until the warm indoor air covered them again. Neither Aaron nor Malisa joined in on the group hug. Aaron stood to Jared's left directly behind his father as Malisa stood to Jared's right directly behind her mother. Malisa's arms were crossed as she balanced all her weight on one leg and foot, cocking her hip with exaggeration. She tapped her weightless foot as if inpatient or embarrassed, although feeling neither of those emotions. Aaron swung his arms from front to back; they scraped his narrow body and gently producing a shushing sound. His sky-blue eyes blinked twice as often as needed to keep his tender pupils from drying out.

"If there's trouble, you stay clear of i…" Gloria sobbed. Again, there was a pause of quiet still as everyone digested the word "trouble."

As Jared sucked in the air for speech to reassure his mother he would indeed be careful, Aaron spoke up. He was starting to feel left out, and he was desperate to get involved.

"If there's trouble, run!" Aaron said, with the excitement of a good idea in his tone.

Jared instantly took this advice for what it was. He had known Aaron wanted attention, and Jared understood that his eight-year-old brother's concerns and advice were just that. Eight-year-old concerns and advice.

Butch however did not understand an eight-year-old's advice and swiftly glanced over his right shoulder, instinctively snapping,

"You can never run from your troubles Aaron."

The kind of advice Butch had always barked. One-line words of wisdom that were more at home on bathroom walls or bombarding the CB radio airways on any giving truck-driving day. Hundreds of short, to the point, Confucius type jumble Jared, as well as the rest of the Mills family was forced to endure, comprehend and follow, as they grew under the roof Butch so graciously provided. Most of the time, Butch's advice was sound and true. But it was Jared who resented these comments the most. He resenting the fact that they were never original. Not once, to Jared's knowledge, did Butch produce advice someone else didn't un-wit. He had felt as though he deserved more. More of an explanation, more patience, more understanding. Why does every cloud have a silver lining? When is it better to give than to receive? And why is life no fucking bowl of cherries?

"Fatherly advice needs background, " Jared had thought. "It needs explanation." And the single-most resented factor Jared had never overcome was the contradiction between so many of Butch's favorites.

Jared was in his second year of Little League baseball. He didn't like the game as much as Butch, but he was still young enough that pleasing his father was more important than pleasing himself. During a particular game Jared chooses to remember, Jared hit safely and stood proudly on first base. After two of Jared's teammates failed to advance him to second, the inning had ended. He ran to the bench, retrieving his glove to take the field. Reaching under the bench, he glanced down the third base line. Mothers and fathers scattered throughout the foul territory with lounge chairs and spread blankets. Jared searched the crowd of spectators for Butch's eyes, but he saw no gleaming, proud father. Butch looked somewhat disappointed, almost confused. And as he swiftly grabbed his glove, he made his way towards left field, deliberately running close to the makeshift bleachers of fans.

"Why didn't you steal?" Butch said, cupping his hands and directing his question to Jared.

Jared shrugged his shoulders as if to say, "I don't know," and continued to run to his assigned position.

"Nothing ventured, nothing gained, Boy!" Butch yelled, using his makeshift megaphone. The surrounding parents chuckled and laughed along with Butch as he settled back in his folding lounge chair. Later that same game, in the bottom of the seventh inning, Jared tried desperately to stretch a double into a triple. As his young body dove headfirst into the powdery dry dirt of third base, he was tagged out. The inning was over. As the opposing team cheered, Jared brushed off the dirt that clung to his legs. He clearly didn't want to lift his eyes from the ground, doing as all disappointed boys will do. Making his way back to the bench, some of the parents clapped, as did some of his teammates.

"Nice try, Jared," the coach said.

"Close one, Jay," said a nameless voice in the crowd.

"You're trying too hard to make things happen, Bud!" Butch yelled, cupping his hands as he did before.

"Better safe than sorry!" He continued. Dropping his hands from his face Butch mumbled, "Literally," audible only to the surrounding fans.

Like a spark to the fumes of fuel, the crowd busted into instant laughter. This is what Jared would hear. This is what Jared remembers. He was too young that day to put together the paradox of advice his father had belched. Nothing ventured, nothing gained. Better safe than sorry. But he would always remember. And as he grew, the one-line words of wisdom did nothing but drive the wedge between Butch and him further and deeper. With his age came his own wisdom—sometimes false, like the kind with adolescence—but wisdom to Jared just the same. He would begin to unravel the idiosyncrasies of Butch and his quotes. And he would look for the contradiction, never saying a word, never challenging the source, and letting the comments slowly stew. Hotter and hotter. Slowly, over years, coming to a boil.

Aaron's eyes had dropped as quickly to the tiled terminal floor as Jared's did to the powdery dirt. Jared, looking over his left shoulder to acknowledge what his brother had said, found himself face to face with Butch as he witnessed the exchange.

"Words of wisdom, head held in shame," he thought. But this time it wasn't Jared who was Butch's target. This time it was Aaron. And as Jared was being flooded with emotions of nauseating contempt, loathing disgust, and the sickness of what he had just seen, the liquid of life came to a boil. He glared at his father's eyes with a semi-squint of hate in his eyes. Butch turned his head and met Jared's stare no more than eight inches from his face. The phrase "if looks could kill" would have been coined at this very moment if it had not already been devised. Butch could feel, as well as see, the burning fire in Jared's eyes. And for the first time in the father-son relationship, the tides had changed. Butch was afraid of Jared, and both felt the shifting wave wash over their aura at preciously the same time. With no more than that glaring stare, Butch dropped his head, surrendering eye contact, and mumbled, "Well, don't do anything stupid and get yourself killed," removing his hug and concerns from the group.

The word killed was all the nudge Gloria needed to begin to cry. As the three backed away from each other, Jared reached with his left hand like a blind man finding his way for Aaron's head. Butch held tight his wife as she cried, releasing some of her body's weight as they walked away. Butch never looked back. He could feel the burning glare from his eldest son, and Jared never took his eyes off Butch as he walked his hands down the back of Aaron's head to his neck and boney spine. Jared pulled Aaron in close, and Aaron wrapped his arms around Jared's waist, baring his face in his sky-blue parka.

"Don't do anything stupid," Malisa said, using her mocking voice that sounded nothing like Butch but clearly was meant to. She smiled and looked squarely at Jared.

Jared snapped from his glare and returned a labored smile to his only sister. His thoughts were racing with disgust but he needed to give Malisa the caring goodbye she deserved.

He reached out with his free hand, inviting another three-way hug, but Malisa only took one step closer and grabbed his hand. They stood an arm's length apart, locking just the tips of their fingers, swinging their arms as gently as a flag moves on a breezeless day.

"Take it easy, kid sister," Jared said. And the love he had felt for her was eminent in his voice.

"Yeah, you too." She said softly.

"And take care of Aaron here for me 'till I get back," Jared said, patting on Aaron's back and squeezing Malisa's fingers, two actions that made Aaron and Malisa feel better at the same time.

"Aaron can take care of himself; you've seen to that," Malisa said.

With this, Aaron pops up. And the three exchanged looks of loving smiling and laughing. It was certainly true what Malisa had said. Jared had taken great care in the watchful eye over Aaron. And the three of them knew it. Sometimes working against the relationship of brother and sister. But Malisa understood. Jared, in Malisa's eyes, always seemed like an outsider. She didn't know why. Although Aaron was the latter to join the Mills family, it was Jared that seemed like the addition. Most times she was glad Jared had Aaron. Aaron seemed to bring Jared into the happenings of family living. And she did not want the attention Jared gave to Aaron. In part due to the age difference, in part due to their gender, siblings two years apart only become close later in life. Recognizing the importance of your brother or sister comes with time. It seems Jared and Malisa fought more than they cared, thinking back on the times growing up. And as the chuckling and laughter dwindled and then stopped, Malisa quickly jumped and kissed Jared on the cheek, turned and ran away, almost embarrassed at what she had just done.

"Bye Jared," She said, bouncing and almost skipping like a schoolgirl in love.

"Bye Malisa," Jared said, watching her easily catch up to Butch and Gloria walking very slowly away.

"When are you coming home?" Aaron said, looking up at his older brother.

Jared knelt and became eye-to-eye with Aaron.

"I don't know, Aaron," Jared replied, "But you'll be the first guy I'll be looking for when I do."

The two Mills brother's that for the past eight inseparable years hugged. Both squeezing hard with no more than body language expressing love for each other, and the feelings of separation now becoming much too real. A single tear began to form in the corner of Jared's eye. The city sounds and October air brushed over them again as another passenger opened the door leading to the running bus.

"I got to go," Jared reluctantly said.

They broke apart as Jared stood erect. Aaron slowly began to walk backwards, trying to burn the image of his only brother into his mind. Butch, Gloria, and Malisa stood forty feet away watching the separation take place. As Jared turned and walked, extending his hand for the door handle that would begin a journey he just as soon not take, Aaron plunked his hands in his pockets and came to an abrupt stop, halfway between his waiting family and his leaving brother.

"Wait!" Aaron screamed, and he ran toward Jared.

Butch, as did Gloria and Malisa, thought this was the moment the good-bye would turn ugly. Butch gently broke away from his wife, passing her over to Malisa, fully expecting to have to literally drag Aaron away. He slowly walked towards his two sons watching and expecting the worst.

Jared turned, holding the door open with his back just as Aaron reached him. Butch stopped at the precise spot Aaron had been when he realized what he had forgotten. Deep in the corner of his blue-jean pocket was a dried-up cherry pit. Aaron's good luck cherry pit.

"Jared, here," Aaron said, holding out his hand for Jared to receive the tiny pit.

"What's this?" Jared said, looking at the tiny item in the palm of his hand.

"It's my good luck pit. Well, at least it's been good luck for me anyway. I want you to have it," Aaron said.

"Good luck pit?" Jared said, not having a clue of what Aaron was speaking of.

"Yeah, you know. The cherry pit pie game," Aaron, said. "It was fixed! This is my lucky pit."

"Fixed?" Jared said, and just then he knew. Another one of Butch's childish games. Cherry pit pie.

A large cherry tree grew on the side of the garage at the Mills' suburban home. At times this tree grew wildly out of control, covering the entire side of the yard's small space. On more than one occasion the tree would need massive amounts of pruning to keep it from tearing the cedar siding or even the roof off the double-car garage. Every year there was a short window of opportunity to harvest this dark-red fruit. In just one week's time the cherries would rot on the limbs of this massive tree. The entire Mills family was expected to pick, clean, and de-pit if necessary, the huge amounts this tree would bare.

The last week of August meant cherry juice, cherry jams, canned cherries, and of course, cherry pie. Butch had made games of the laboring chores that accompanied all these cherry products. The one game that drew the most attention was cherry pit pie.

Of the twenty or so pies that Gloria would bake, one was set aside before its oven time. The children would watch as Butch deliberately pushed three pit-filled cherries deep into the pit-less-cherry-filled cherry mixture. The game began when the entire pie was devoured after its cooling time on the windows edge. The rules were simple. The one person *not* to get a pit— Gloria not included, mother never played Butch's games—lost. The penalty for not having a pit after the pie was devoured was to have to wash all the dirty dishes as the rest of the family mocked you and laughed, Gloria not included. Mother never mocked or laughed at the loser of one of Butch's games. The loser almost always seemed to be Jared. And now standing in the doorway with Aaron and his good luck pit, Jared understands why. The reason he almost always lost this particular game and perhaps all of Butch's games is because they were fixed.

"Yeah, we never ate the pit pie, Jared. Dad would switch the pies when you were not looking, and we would slip a pit in our mouths. I always used the same pit. Malisa and Dad would get a new pit every year, but I was scared you would always catch me putting mine in my mouth, so I kept that one," Aaron said, pointing to Jared's open hand. "It's good luck because you never knew. You never caught me. Pretty funny huh?"

"Yeah, funny," Jared said, as he closed his hand, making a fist. And the whites of his knuckles throbbed as the emotions that he had felt for Butch returned in his glare of hatred. Jared did not blame Aaron or Malisa for the deception, nor did he rue the cherry pit pie. He could hear in his mind's voice Butch putting them up to it. "It'll be funny," Butch would tell them. "A real gas!"

Butch stood unable to hear what was being said; the noise from the outside world made it impossible. He watched, unable to see what Aaron had given Jared. The distance made this impossible. As he began to walk forward again,

Jared turned and glared in Butch's direction. Two more steps, and Butch stopped dead in his tracks. The look screamed, *This moment is private!*

The bus driver yelled, "Let's go Son, it's time to go!"

Jared looked down at Aaron as their eyes met, and for a split second before Jared had changed from the stare of contempt for his father to the concerns and attention he was about to demand of Aaron, Aaron saw his pain. He saw what Malisa later would try to explain after the word of Jared's death. He forever would remember the look in Jared's eyes at that moment—the look of change from someone he had known so well.

"Listen to me, Aaron. When you're feeling down or you're in trouble, you know when I'm not around. Run! Do you hear? I want you to run. Butch is wrong; you were right! It will make you feel better. It will clear your head," Jared's voice was hurried. The bus hissed as the air from the emergency brakes was released. Aaron looked confused, but not from the advice Jared was preaching. He was still contemplating the pain he had seen in his brother's eyes. Jared read his brother like a book. He demanded his attention as he grabbed at his thin biceps.

"Say it!" Jared said.

"Jared, I don't have to..." Aaron replied

"Say it!" Jared insisted. It had been a long time since he had made Aaron repeat what he said. When Aaron was much younger, and his attention span was much shorter, Jared always made Aaron repeat things. But as Aaron got older, he instinctively hung on every word his older and wiser protector would say. Now it was almost a foreign language to hear this command.

"Aaron, say it!"

"Ahu... if I get into to trouble run." Aaron said.

"Annnnd..." Jared said, insisting the one part he truly wanted Aaron to say and more importantly, believe.

"And... Butch is wrong. I am right," Aaron said.

"That's right!" Jared said. "Promise you won't forget."

"I promise," Aaron said, and he touched the tip of his nose with the tip of his index finger. A silent, hand signal that meant, "I promise." One of the many silent signs they invented. And just like the repeating of Jared's preaching something they have not used in a very long time.

Jared ran to the moving bus and jumped inside. The heavy glass door shut quickly, then slowing, just before it hit its frame. Aaron took one step inside and watched his brother board the moving bus. He could see Jared walking toward the back like a drunken sailor trying to keep his balance on a ship at sea. He watched as Jared sat, sliding to the window, and clearing the fog with a single wipe of his hand. The bus changed gears and began to roll forward. Aaron watched as Jared tried to locate him standing at the glass door. Aaron was not aware the glass was mirrored from the outside, and Jared was just learning himself that he could not see inside. Jared touched the tip of his right eyelid, then his chin, his right eyelid, and then his chin again. A silent sign that Jared never knew if Aaron received. Aaron quickly returned the exact same sign as the bus pulled away from sight, unaware that Jared would never see the returned single. Butch gently touched Aaron's shoulder, awakening him from his world of thoughts that swirled inside him. They walked slowly back toward the waiting girls as Butch tried his best to be compassionate about Aaron's loss.

"He'll be fine Bud. Don't worry, he'll be home sooner than you think," Butch said.

And the very first thought that entered Aaron's mind was *Butch is wrong.* Jared said so.

"Hey, what does this mean?" Butch said, using his index finger to touch his eyelid and then his mouth.

"Oh...A..." Aaron paused. He and Jared vowed never to reveal their secrets. But before he could stop, the words were already leaving his mouth.

"See ya," he said, regretting he had told as soon as he spoke the words.

"Oh... and what was that thing you gave Jared?" Butch said.

"Ah... Nothing...Nothing Dad," Aaron said, and it was very clear he did not want to tell. And only because of the love Butch had for *this* son, he would not pry any further. For Aaron, however, this was the first building block of the wall he would continue to construct that divided himself and his father. Walls that we all build from the aliens our parents become. And even Jared's death would not make the barrier impassible forever. For in a very strange way that Aaron would not understand, he would somehow blame his father for Jared's death. It would add to its height, its thickness, and its strength, but it should have still been knocked down after the bitterness of adolescence and the maturity of young adulthood set in. But it never came down. The wall was too high and too strongly built, and the thing that sealed it forever was what Malisa told Aaron before his trip to Washington.

Well rested to be tired, well fed to be hungry, Kevin's scream was merely an outburst of attention. "Notice me!" he cried. Having no choice, Aaron and Nora most certainly did.

"Oh, listen to you," Nora said, in a voice that can only be described as baby talk. She pulls away from her comforting hug of Aaron's, extending her arms to grab Kevin. The palms of her hands face the stucco ceiling of the tiny bathroom as her fingers dance the *Give Me Waltz*.

Aaron carefully cradles Kevin as he passes him to his waiting mother. The weightlessness of his right arm tingles with a rush of fresh blood.

"That young boy doesn't weigh much, but it sure feels good to put him down," Aaron said, rubbing the life back into his sleeping arm.

Kevin, as well as Aaron's arm, is grateful for the change. A baby—like a very old man—experiences bed sores and body aches if left to lie for too terribly long. It's not the tired, worn-out joints or the stretched-out, weakened muscles in Kevin's case, but the growing pains of youth, and that inability to sit still that produce the need for movement.

Nora buries her recently cheered face into Kevin's belly. She gently shakes her head from side to side, blowing and humming repeatedly as Kevin begins to giggle and cue.

"You're such a handsome boy, hmmm hmmm, aren't you? Handsome boy, handsome boy," Nora said, cheering herself even more as her son works out a laugh.

Aaron glances at his watch as the three make their way down the staircase. Headlights from the arriving babysitter pass through the spacious house as they reach the foot of the stairs.

"This girl's on time. That's a good sign," Aaron says, making his way towards the switch that controls outside lights. He glances through a window, pushing the heavy curtain to one side with the back of his hand. This gives a full view of the driveway and walk.

"This girl Judy," Nora begins.

"Julie, Honey" Aaron interrupts.

"Julie," she says with more emphasis. "She's a responsible girl? You checked her out?"

"Yes Nora. There's no need to worry," Aaron said, turning his attention from outside to inside. "She's a nice girl. Eighteen but acts much older. You met her at that picnic last summer, the one where some people got sick from those bad clams." His tone was that he was trying to jar her memory as well as comfort her concerns.

"Oh, really. Which one was she? Nora said.

"Oh...um..." Aaron began to say, dropping his eyes to the floor. "The one that threw up on you." He continues to say, tapering off in volume, like the conclusion of your favorite song.

"What's that Aaron?" Nora asked. She is non-threatening as she smiles only to herself, hearing all he had said but insisting he repeat every word.

"The one that threw up on you," He said, looking back to his wife's eyes. He raises one eyebrow and musters a half smile of his own. Aaron now has the look of any husband that teeters on the response of any wife. They gaze into each other's eyes for what could be eternity. Each would choose these types of moments over all others among their roles as husband and wife. Easy-going compassion. Non-manufactured acts of love. Each is washed with waves of warmth from the memories of days gone by. As they walk toward the front door, they begin to laugh.

The daylight has left just minutes ago. Three moths have already found their erratic flight pattern around their false sun. When the running engine is turned off, the sound of crickets chirping and the ticking of the cooling engine is all that is heard. The young Mills family stood under the porches roof watching the younger babysitter gather her things from the rear seat.

"Bar mitzvah," Aaron said.

"Excuse me?" Nora replied.

"Bar mitzvah, do you think we'd have to attend this function if it were a Bar mitzvah?"

Nora thinks for a moment, then understands. She understands what Aaron is talking about because she understands Aaron. He had mentally compiled a list of family events or functions you simply must attend. My Aaron. Always a thinker. Strange at times, but…its Aaron's way.

"Oh… I don't know," she said. "Bear in mind I'm not Jewish, but I would say a bar mitzvah is an optional family event.

"Optional family event…hmm." Aaron said.

And although moths would not fly around the second light lit under the porch's roof, Nora could see her thinking man turn his on.

Chapter 2

(Nora Peak's)

Clouds rolled over on themselves as the threat of rain was very real. The timber frame of the old barn had the look of a skeleton against the dark morning sky. Aaron stood at the kitchen sink sipping his coffee and examining this new panoramic view.

This will certainly take some getting used to, he thought. Looking through where barn-board siding used to obstruct his view as he sips his coffee, occasionally glancing upward. He ponders if the work crew will show and if today, May 1st, will be the old barn's last.

"No Honey, try and get it in the sink," Nora pleads, trying to get a young Kevin to spit after flushing and brushing his teeth. His two-year-old smile, covered with the foam of Crest toothpaste, forces Nora to laugh while trying to instruct the uncooperative young boy. Aaron can hear the two laughing from down the hall, the first door on your left. The main bath. The morning's indoor sounds grab his attention tighter than the outdoors panoramic view.

"Daddy!" Kevin screeches, running across the kitchen floor, the tiptoe patter of tiny, excited feet. Aaron swiftly sets his coffee cup on the counter's top, extending his arms just as Kevin dives full speed and with great confidence into his father's loving arms.

"How's my Kevin boy today?" Aaron asks, not expecting an answer and not expecting a response. He swings him high in the air, then pulls him in close, tickling and blowing on the boy's sensitive neck with nothing more than a clean-shaven face. Kevin laughs hysterically, sandwiching his shoulder to his cheek, desperately trying to foil this ticklish torture. He flips his son to his feet, and Kevin runs away, passing Nora in the hall with a near-miss collision.

"Slow down young man," Nora said, adjusting her bathrobe in an attempt to conceal her size.

"Coffee Hun?" Aaron asked, already on his way to her favorite mug.

"Sure," Nora replied, assuming Aaron's observation post at the sink's edge.

"Well, what do ya think?" She continues. "Will they finish up today or not?"

She looks upward toward the threatening skies wondering, as Aaron did, if the inevitable rain will hold off.

The rain that will eventually fall on the Mills' house that day would also cover the farm in which Nora was born and raised. Less than two miles as the crow flies from where the Mills lived now is where the Teal's family farm was planted. The current owner, far less a farmer than Nora's dad, bought the old farmhouse for its size and trendy historic background. But the Teals farmed the 120-acre land all the while Nora was raised. She was an only child born in the fall of '61. But her days as "the Preacher's little girl," a nickname the locals had labeled her, were filled with tender love and watchful care.

Her mother was a strong woman. She was at home in the kitchen roasting and baking some of the finest food ever eaten as well as turning the wheel of a tractor, turning the soil for the annual planting of winter wheat. The times that Nora spent with her mother before the cancer took her away were special and true. She was nearly seven when her mother died. To this day there are very few memories of before her death.

It's strange how we choose what we recall. Had Nora's mother never passed when she was a child, her mind's eye would clearly see without such strain. Had the lymphoma not stolen from her what she had only noticed when it was gone, she would not have to labor for some of the simplest of memories. She remembers her mother but only in bits and pieces. In her mind she can see her baking Christmas cookies, one cooking sheet at a time, and can vaguely remembering her mother telling her why.

They taste better, she thinks, but that sounds foolish, so she's never sure. She remembers her mother brushing her hair. In her memory, she cannot see her kneeling behind her but can feel the gentle yet firm stokes on her dirty blond head. A daily ritual that was both a good habit and necessary in removing the snarls of a little girl's hair. Nora also vaguely recalls a conversation they had about sleeping kittens.

"Mommy why is kitty lying in the road?"

"Kitty's very tired Honey. When kittens get sleepy, they lie right down and rest." But the bits and pieces of memories seem to fade each year. *Had mother never died, I could have asked her about tasty cookies and sleeping cats.* She had forever thought.

Nora's father was also strong—physically, mentally, and spiritually. Buford Teal was nearly six-and-a-half-feet tall. His hands, when cupped together, could hold nearly a gallon of water, and his boot, shit-covered most of his adult life, could hold twice that. He was a good farmer, a better man, and the best father a young girl could have. Nora and her father where inseparable. Even before her mother's death, she would spend every waking minute glued too her fathers' side. She woke every morning to help milk the forty or so dairy cows. She rode with him in the long, hot hours bailing the sun-dried hay. Even when she was older, when her school day was finished she willfully helped with the endless monotony of the afternoon chores. She loved the life of a farm girl. But what she really loved was the closeness she and her father always shared. He filled her emotional pallet with all the colors of a loving rainbow, exercising his right to spoil "daddy's little girl."

"You're such a pretty young princess," he would love to say, though Nora was sweat-covered and farm-work dirty from head to toe. With his showering love also came his beliefs.

"God has truly made me a beautiful little girl," he'd preach, giving both thanks and praise to his almighty Lord, as well as complementing Nora one more time. Buford found strength and reason in his religious beliefs. He thanked his God when his wife died.

"Thank you, Lord, for the fifteen years of love from such a wonderful woman," he prayed. Nora would watch as he'd bless a newborn calf every spring. Or when he would look to the clouds and pray, "Please God, make it rain." At times, when the house was quiet, moments before she would fall asleep, she would hear her father ask his God for help. Help with the strain from being a single parent. Help with the strain from running a one-man farm. Help from the strain of your daughter's disbelief.

Faith was something too hard to except for Nora. She loved her father too much to have an all-out argument over what she really believed, knowing all too well this would hurt him. So she held her tongue, never revealing the turmoil of faith, or lack thereof, that boiled inside her. Unbeknownst to Nora, there were occasions that would lead Buford to pain, but like a good parent, he would not show the side that hurt. It was the side all good parents feel when their child disappoints them. Disappointments like the farmer's son that yearns for the big city lights. Disappointments like the only child having no desire to bear children of their own, or disappointments like the preacher's daughter having no faith at all. Buford could see his only child lacked the dedication to his God he would have liked. And although he would never know her true feelings regarding religion, in a strange, way he was glad. He feared the truth about his daughter's faith, and he was content with the closeness of their relationship. A ship he cares not rock.

Nora was even happier. The fact was she had no religious beliefs, and she saw the entire subject— religion, faith, God, all of it—as one huge con. *The oldest con game in history*, she had thought. The Good Book, she felt, was nothing more than a book. The translations were nothing more than someone's ideas of what had been written, and the Holy Bible was so appropriately named because Nora had felt it has so many holes in its ideologies and theories. There wasn't one shred of proof any of it was true.

The notion that if you behave yourself and do the right thing you'll be sent to a happy place, a fairyland, a heaven struck Nora to be too astounding to be true. To the contrary, if you're bad and do all the wrong things, you're headed for Hell to spend eternity in the fire pits in a fiery sea of pain. What kind of a God blackmails the creatures he created. Worship me or else! Why create something, give it a choice, then threaten it with eternal hell if it chooses not to believe? Why not simply create believers? Or don't torture the ones that choose not to believe. It simply made no sense, and Nora found it just too hard to accept.

When Nora was fifteen her father died, and if there was ever a chance of believing in any form of God, it died right along with Buford. Worshiping in God had died, but the conflict about whether he existed was born. She remembers crying in her bed asking a God she had no faith in, "Why?"

"Why take such a good man? Why take someone that does so much good for the people of this world? If you have yourself such a paradise, why on earth do you need my father?" This was her morning cry, and these were her sobbing questions. Questions that would haunt as well as remain unanswered her entire adult life. Unanswered questions for a nameless, faceless, and speechless God.

The older Nora got, the fiercer the conflict grew. If she didn't believe in God, why did she blame him for her father's death? If he didn't exist, there cannot be fault on his part. If he did exist, why was blind faith so hard for her to swallow? She was both jealous and outraged at the spiritually content. And the single one thing that outraged her the most was the endless amount of thanks.

If a very young child dies, the spiritual happy say, "Thank God that we had him for the time that we did."

But if an old man dies they praise: "Thank God that he lived such a very full life."

Or if a person is killed in a bad accident, and it is determined the death was instantaneous, the God-gabbing gurus pray,

"Thank God he didn't have to suffer."

But if the same unfortunate soul lied in a hospital bed for months suffering, then finally died, they'd pray, "Thank God he was finally taken."

How can it be both ways? How can you give thanks in either situation? Nora never understood why it was wrong to blame, why under all circumstances you had to give thanks and praise. This is the word of the Lord.

"There was no good that came out of my father's early death! And I will not thank anyone for it! Amen!" This is what Nora would preach. This is what Nora believed.

The sound of mischief beckons the alarm. Nora and Aaron look at each other, both raising their eyebrows, both stopping their actions and thoughts. Crashing noise comes from the family room where their two-year-old boy had just realized he's alone.

Aaron is gone before Nora can even set down her mug. She's amused at the speed at which Aaron runs to protect and watch over their only son, and she is translating sound into source as Aaron is discovering it firsthand. She's a relaxed mother, confident of her wisdom to bring-up, knowledgeable in her ability to raise a child. Nora has noticed some mothers show no confidence at all. Some actually seem intimidated by the demanding task. Even Aaron, she had thought, seems to make a bigger deal out of parenting than needed. But, "He doesn't get the chance to spend all that much time with Kevin, as I do, with his work and all that running. Those two things alone take up a very large part of his day."

This is how Nora rationalized Aaron's intense and sometimes jittery parenting skills. The very insecure never hear complements towards themselves, rather finding excuses why someone else doesn't do as well a job. The simple fact of the matter was that Nora was a natural—an excellent mother. Always protecting, never rejecting. A teacher of lives, weathered roads, supportive and reliable. She would push Kevin to succeed as well as push him into the limelight, all the while standing in the shadows, never once asking or expecting credit. Credit in which Nora undoubtedly deserves. The baker receives rave reviews for the homemade cherry pie, but the tree quietly is the forgotten contributor to its harmonious taste.

She sips her coffee one last time, dumping the remainder down the sink's drain. She'll rarely drink an entire mug due to its immense size. Walking across the kitchen floor, she attempts unsuccessfully to not make a sound. Hardwood floorboards creek from their age and like her mug, her enormous size. The heel of her foot slowly presses down on the first floorboard leading into the hall. She sandwiches her face together and squints her eyes, easing her weight forward in an attempt to lighten the load. The drawn-out screech of a tired old plank creeks and vibrates beneath her.

Is it only when I want to be quiet that these floorboards make so much noise? Nora thinks.

She desperately wants to hear the conversation taking place in the other room. She knows Aaron's way, just as she knows the sound of stacked toys crashing. He'll undoubtedly explain why it's best to lift each toy from the pile rather than push the entire stack to the floor. She loves to hear the logical explanations Aaron gives to Kevin as much as she loves the cute little responses Kevin will undoubtedly give to him. But Nora is no ninja. And although her prediction is accurate as to what's taking place in the family room, she is unable to eavesdrop because of her weight. Just before she is within earshot of the conversation between her husband and son, Nora remembers her dream.

Nora floats on an angry sea, hundreds of miles off a distant somewhere shore. Fish-smelling saltwater lifts and lowers her obesity as she struggles to stay above the surface. Confused and disorientated, she swivels in circles of despair, desperately searching for some sign of land or land marker. An albatross with its massive wings tucked into its sides floats effortlessly, watching Nora drift and struggle all the while staring with an emotionless glare. In the illogical madness of this drowning dream, Nora listens to the albatross's thoughts. *Pity, so young*, the voice in her mind's ear whispers. The voice itself is that of an old English schoolteacher with a thick English accent. A someone she has never met, a someone she has never heard. "Humans are so terribly careless," the bird teacher continues. "So foolishly careless." Nora stares in the black-button eye of the great bird, angered by its pompous thoughts, jealous of the adaptable native of the sea.

Her nightmare is a familiar one. She has swum these troubled waters many times in the course of her dreaming life. The ocean is always the same: Rhythmic waves she'll ride up and down, eight to ten feet in height, never splashing or cresting but just hypnotic movement and a quite repetitive tempo— all with an overwhelmingly powerful stench.

In her conscience world, Nora has always hated the ocean. She felt that we, humans, were aliens to the vast underwater world. She could never understand why some were drawn to it, and she felt men that loved the sea or spent their lives on it or in it, were strange, pathetic freaks.

"Why on earth would a person surround themselves with a surface they can't walk on or put themselves in a substance they can't breathe in?" She often said. *The two essential things, walking and breathing, sustain life*, she had thought. "You need the ground at your feet Aaron," she had argued. "You need fresh air in your lungs." But as Aaron tried to explain his point of view, she had cut him off.

"I just don't see why you're not afraid to fly," Aaron said.

"What does flying have to do with anything?" Nora snapped.

"Well with your logic, your feet not on the ground and your lungs unable to breath, flying should be off limits as well as the ocean. So, why aren't you afraid to fly?"

"First of all, I am not afraid to fly"

"I didn't say you were, I said…"

"I'm not finished. I'm not afraid of the ocean either. Why are you being such a jerk?" Nora spit.

"Why are you getting so upset?" Aaron pleaded.

"I don't want to talk about my dream."

"But all I was…"

"Aaron enough."

She had withdrawn, dismissing his lack of concern as just not being able to understand. Her dream, or its possible meaning, and her fear of the ocean were never discussed again. "Aaron could never drown. He's much too strong. He'll never understand," she concluded.

The albatross teacher and his old English thoughts were also the same. It would float while Nora would struggle. It would preach its sarcastic pity while Nora listened and angered. Even the dialogue the old bird would preach was always the same.

"Careless human, so young and very heavy. What a blooming, bloody shame."

This outraged Nora; his effortless floating, his pompous tone, his ability—if he so desired—to simply fly away. Fly far, far away.

With a mouthful of salty water, Nora spits and gasps for fresh, salt less air. The motion of the ocean turns her stomach, flopping its contents over and over, bidding its time for its inevitable journey upwards and out. Nora tilts her head back in an attempt to straighten her windpipe. She is blinded by the hot afternoon sun and closes her eyes tight. She spits and gasps as the waves carry her up and down. The teacher bird mocks her with words she does not understand as salt finds its way into the corners of her eyes, adding to the burning discomfort. She extends her massive arms outward like a child pretending to be a plane in flight. Her paddling arms tire quickly, and she feels herself getting closer and closer to the darkness of the ocean floor. The water level that was once well below her chin now find its way into her ears. The outdoor sound of stinging heat and turning waves is replaced with underwater silence as she rocks up and down on her nightmare sea. Now she is below more often than above, and the end is very near. Her thoughts muster one last act of courage before she is content to simply sink away. *One last look*, she thinks, bobbing up and down from air to sea. "One last look," the preaching teaching bird repeats. "One last look at a world with no solid ground," she continues. "Not one that can hold a fat girl at least," the bird mutters. Looking upward into the blinding sky, she begins to sink. Seagulls fly overhead, and for a moment she can hear their familiar cry. *Seagulls*, she thinks. *Scavengers of the beach*. Suddenly, with this final thought, she awakens. She violently shakes her head so as to erase the cobwebs of acceptance of death. She wails her arms violently to return to the surface some three feet away. As her head emerges, she gulps at the hot dream air. Simultaneously her thoughts rush to the surface of her brain. *Seagulls always stay close to the beach*, she exclaims silently with conviction. In her recurring dream, the swim to a beach she never reaches is always the same. The tide's current will keep the struggling Nora some twenty yards from shore. The albatross is long but gone, and it's her own mind's voice that reminds her she is weak, she is fat. On the beach, she will see three men. One is without a doubt Aaron. He stands quiet, nodding his head slightly up and down. His arms are crossed, and she is never sure if this means he is disappointed or chilled. She feels his quiet encouragement to keep swimming ashore. The second is her father. He paces back and forth, waving his hands inward to both encourage and help her conviction to survive. He's young, long before the farm life had worn him down. She imagines his voice of prayer as she swims in place to the dreams near end. The third is a stranger she will never know in her dream world. He's young—maybe eighteen—and handsome. He's always kind of transparent, as if she can see the beach's shore right through him. She concentrates on him, but she can never get a good look as she begins to awake.

"Kevin, didn't we have this conversation yesterday?" Aaron asks, once again tickling Kevin's belly and blowing bubbles of fatherly love at the creases of the young boy's neck. Nora snaps from her dream-like state. The floor-boards moan again as her weight shifts, as she exits the hall that was providing her cover. "What are you boys doing in here?" she asks, entering the large family's room. Both man and boy pop to attention for only a moment before the tickling torture returns.

Again, Nora is self-conscience of her appearance as she tries to adjust her bath robe to conceal her girth. She moves gracefully for her size and makes her way to her side of the muti-colored beige couch. The couch was a gift Nora would have just as soon not received but filling a large country home took both time and money, so when Butch and Gloria had it delivered she did nothing but show thanks. The springs and cushion compress and creak as Nora shifts her weight, adjusting the wrinkles of her robe. Aaron and Kevin wind down in harmony as all three Mills enjoy the moment of being one, a husband and wife, a mother and son, a father and his only boy, two parents and a child. Family.

The concerns of her weight explosion Nora shared with Aaron in the up-stairs bathroom doesn't seem that long ago. Although to Kevin, it's been almost his entire life. But nearly two years is more than enough time for the very heavy to regain all the weight that was once shed. Nora sits, saturated by her families love, like a warm summer downpour from large, gumball-sized drops. She will never make the connection between the two. Her feeling content and satisfaction to her own emotional needs drives her appetite to over eat. She was almost as heavy living and working on the farm with her father and only lost her weight when she lost her dad. For years she rationalized in her youth that it was simply "baby fat," and in her late teens when Buford passed, she could have thinned anyway. Not true. Her father showered her with the love she craved, as Aaron and Kevin provide today. The reason Nora started gaining her weight back shortly after she wed was the love Aaron was so good at pro-viding. Her concerns in the bathroom would prove to be valid. She didn't know why she was gaining her weight again, she did, and today she is the heaviest she has ever been or ever will be. Nora peaks.

Chapter 3

(Buffalo Bound)

The smirk on his face said it all. The walk had merely helped. He strolled through the alleys of poverty with an arrogant strut, unaware of the polluted smell of the city, unconcerned with its apparent dangers. His eyes are only focused on the swirling thoughts from within his mind, and His pace is casual, snaking his way between buildings and dumpsters and scaling fences with ease. Fences intent on discouraging the onslaught of trespassers and thieves. The smirk certainly said it all, but the walk. The walk amplified it.

He was raised a child of the city streets. And although some would argue you're still a child at the age of thirteen, there were those who would say he was not. He lived with a woman named Dotty, and for all intent and purposes, she was his only mother. She was not. The decrepit rundown house was in a neighborhood that had died sometime in the 30's. It was a place they both called home. Home, only as a word to describe a place they dwelled, for neither took pride, or like Dorothy from *The Wizard of Oz*, felt there was no place like it.

He walks, skimming his fingers across the tops of trashcans lined all in a row. The city around him awakens, beginning a new day. The sound of car horns honking in the distance echo between tall buildings. Impatient commuters travel asphalt roads to concrete jobs. A few blocks to his east, a siren screams. He stops for a listen, cupping his hand to his ear like a yodeler critiquing his art. He judges distance and direction, pinpointing its familiar cry. He is confident of its location when the smirk transforms.

"Forgive me Father, for I have sinned," he said, smiling and mocking his concerns. Each hand holds the other as he grabs at his heart, a dramatization not worthy of an Oscar. The thought of his own humor forces him to laugh. He pauses at the last can in its row, and for a moment—just a split second—you would say he might have just come to grips with the magnitude of what he had done. Bam! The moment is gone as he smashes his fist to the trash can's lid. Feeling both laughter and pride, the young killer runs home.

Dwayne Cunningham arrives at the back door of his home just as the police arrive at the front door of his work. He prepares himself for a day of rest as the investigation begins.

"Jesus, who the fuck would shoot a priest?" Jack said, the third homicide detective to arrive at the scene.

"What's the matter Jack, not buying the obvious suicide theory?" Number Two replies.

"Gimme a break asshole. What do 'ya got?" Jack said with impatience in his voice and a dab of "don't insult my intelligence" in its tone.

Twisted and cold in the confessional's small space is the Reverend Frances Case. Blood, brains, and skull chips decorate the wall in a remorseful pattern to the reverend's right side. He is slouched in a sitting position with his head cocked to his left, an exaggerated position no doubt uncomfortable if in fact he were alive. A powerful blast to the head is both the apparent and obvious cause of death. His preaching rob is blood-stained and thread-barren. It is a garment he has most likely owned some good many years. Intertwined through the fingers of his left hand is the rosary he would fidget and fuss, all the while the confessor lied. Its tiny cross and cheap beads hang inches from the floor. A single drop of blood hangs from the feet of the sacrificed son. Across his lap and very loosely held in the right hand is a forty-five-caliber revolver. A single spent cartridge rest in the turret, its mission complete, its purpose fulfilled.

Flipping open the note pad in a similar fashion to Captain Kirk requesting to be beamed up, Number Two reads the itemized notes he had written just moments ago.

"Francis Case, age sixty-one. Been the mission's priest for about a year. Tuesdays and Fridays he keeps the church doors open all night in case some troubled youth needs special guidance," he rolls his eyes and continues. "Apparently the good Reverend was warned this was a bad neighborhood, but he said he was doing it for the children," Number Two said.

"Who found him?" Jack asked.

"Ahh... a Miss Amy Fielding, a volunteer, puts out the free coffee for the local wino's. She says she noticed the body as soon as she walked in. The door was open, Jack."

"To the booth?" Jack said in disbelief, pointing to the confessional's door.

"Yeah... the guy that did this is pretty sloppy," Two said, looking from his notes to the stiffening corpse.

"Or stupid," Jack whispered.

Dwayne was neither sloppy nor stupid when it came to murder. It was simply his inexperience due to his youth that caused such carelessness. He had thought long about the day he might have to kill. Fantasizing of a shoot-em-up, gangster-type show down where he always prevailed. Although this was his first, he had prepared himself for killing. Strange as it may seem, he would even follow strict guidelines or rules for crime.

Stealing someone's life is no different than stealing goods, he had thought.

Rule number one: Never take from the less fortunate. He was in fact ruthless, and he considered himself a good thief, but he would never, never take from those he felt couldn't afford it or those he felt didn't deserve it. And deserving was just how the Reverend Case applied to this rule.

He had also felt it was foolish to steal something you didn't even want, which was something he had witnessed among his fellow gang members.

"If you can't sell it or use it, why take it?" He would say to any of his disobedient friends that would listen. Rule number two: Don't steal just for the sake of stealing. Image is nothing, survival is everything.

He had succumbed to peer pressure, but only for a very short time. Smoking cigarettes, drinking beer, and the taste of his first joint; all were done for the sake of approval. But it didn't take long before Dwayne felt this behavior to be foolish. He was only ten years old when he was asked to peddle drugs, and it was his response to that encounter that outlined his personality to the area thugs.

"Fuck you, I ain't no chump. No one's making money off my back," he had said.

Simply put, he's more the leader than the follower, the manipulator than the manipulated, a crafty matador patiently wearing down the aggressive bull. But the difference between Dwayne and most others was he would perform in an empty coliseum. Dwayne would never look to the stands for applause or approval. He was a loner in that regard. A loner in the world of crime.

Most people have said at one time or another, "I don't care what other people think." To acknowledge that other people will think suggests your concerns. Most people care a great deal what other people think, and it's at that very minute they're preaching they don't care that they care the most. Not Dwayne. He has never said he cared or didn't care what other people think. Because he has never cared for other people.

His values and lifestyle were really no different from everyone else's—or so he believed. He grew and watched as the adults in his world stole when they could, lied when they needed to, and ran when they had too. He was a student of the ghetto. Should the young be blamed when the lessons they learn are wrong? Wrong to whom? Good or bad, black or white, to judge is to perceive. Dwayne simply strived to be the very best he could be. The best at lying, the best at stealing, and today he would give running a try. He was one of the best. But of course, this meant the worst that society as a whole had to deal with. The incredible adaptable human.

His mother was a prostitute that took little precautions. She was an attractive woman until the drugs and lifestyle wore her down. Barely a teen and insecure, she was an easy target for the area pimps. Long dark legs attached to a firm, full buttocks. And a young, girlish smile with full lips and large breasts should have reflected confidence. It didn't. The overpowering inner voice, the sense of being nothing more than a faceless nigger in an overcrowded city brought her down. She had no father figure to remind her she was daddy's little girl; only a slick-talking pimp filled that empty void that all little girls need to hear. When the pimp had her hooked, so was her fate. The heroin that controlled her lied more than the insecurities of her own self-worth. And the lying drugs that comforted a deteriorating life had finally taken it.

Dwayne was only five when his mother didn't return home. He has no memory of her or the time they had spent together. For Dwayne there was always Dotty, and in fact, there is only one memory he has of the days there were before her. With any luck, those memories will fade because the good Reverend Case won't rape little boys any more.

Washington D.C.'s low income housing projects were only two miles north of our nation's capital. The contrast between the White House and clean streets of Pennsylvania Avenue to the dirty alleys and living quarters of the projects are too numerous to mention. But it was there that a small act of humanity, or so it seemed, took place in the summer of 1972.

"Boy! Quit that cryin! Where is your mama?" Dotty said from the crack between her chained door and its metal frame.

She recognized the young child sitting in the darkened hall of the projects' fourth floor. She had seen him run these halls with that same young child's energy, and she remembers seeing him play in the streets near an opened fire hydrant on a hot July day. She also knew of his mother's habits—more than she could remember her name. But it's only now that she realizes it's been at least two weeks since she's seen him last or seen his mother for that matter. Why is it we only notice the absence of others upon the reckoning of a familiar face?

Dwayne just sat and sobbed, looking up at the giant of a woman before him. The whites of his eyes under his pupils were tearful and large.

"Boy! Can you hear me talkin'? Where is your mama?" Dotty insists. She Looks down the dark hall, first to her left, then to her right. Her view is limited to only a few feet, and in her mind, she doesn't trust what she can't see. Looking down at the boy in his grief, she shakes her head from side to side. Her lips and jowls clench in disgust as she begins to mumble.

"God damn sonoma bitch. It ain't my child. Why in the world would, I don't care..." Her mumbling will go unheard to anyone but herself as she slams the door in disgust.

Dwayne's head and hopes snap back from the slamming door. His stomach growls to the point of pain as he drops his head to observe his lap. His young thoughts are still mulling over what the large woman had said.

Can I hear?" Of course I can hear. I hear just fine, he thinks. He wonders about the kind of question that has confused his thoughts. Perhaps his young mind wants to forget the other question. Perhaps he doesn't want to think about the possibilities that could exist. Blocking out the unpleasant is something he's grown accustomed to. He shivers with the very thought of...

The sound of chains and latches vibrate the heavy wooden door before him, clashing and clicking from the very top to its very bottom. If Dwayne were to try to count the amount of locks on the large woman's door, he would lose track after seven. Dwayne Cunningham, age five, cannot count past seven.

Dotty opens the heavy door as the two smells collide: the hallway's unclean, stale, almost musty stench and the simmering poor man's stew just a few hours old on her electric G.E. range. She is rushed and nervous as she extends her welcoming arms trying to entice the young child along. She will barely take a half a step outside the comforts—or as in the case with Dottie's paranoid mind—safety of the apartment she calls home.

"Come along now Boy, times a wastin'" Her voice is softer than its previous tone, but the undertone of fear and concern is both sensed as well as heard by Dwayne.

He looks up at Dotty leaning back once more against the poorly lit hallway wall. His legs as well as his arms are criss crossed and the lack of blood flowing through his gluteus maximums will contribute in his decision to move. He has stopped mulling over her previous question on his ability to hear, just starring in wild wonder,

"Should I trust this unknown face, or should I fear it." He thinks.

A crossroads in such a short life is just another one of the tragedies he will have to endure. A tragedy that on the surface seems secondary, after all his mother has been gone for ten days. And this crossroads tragedy at a casual glance does appear insignificant. He hasn't eaten in three.

We all experience the decisions in the course of our lives that will lead either to happiness or despair. Points where we must decide which course we will charter, which road we will navigate. How we make these decisions are based on the expectations we perceive will happen. Weighing out the pros and cons or trying to rely on a previous experience are the tools we'll use to direct our decision. But how many of those decisions at the tender age of five did you make? For most a parent or loved one was always nearby making those crossroads nonexistent. A child needs direction from those they love and trust. They simple can't be left to decide their fate or rationalize what's best. There is no previous experience to compare or rely on, nor is there the ability to weigh out the pros and cons. This situation is a perfect example. Dwayne may consider whether he should enter this strangers' home, or trust the unknown woman in the door, but the final decision on whether to except Dottie's seemingly harmless invitation will be the smell of food and the fact his ass hurts. A monumental crossroads tragedy.

"Dimmit boy I don't often leave this here door open long." Dotty said, as the concerns for her own safety were beginning to overcome her thoughts. Her eyes darted from side to side, constantly aware of the move less shadows from beyond. She feels both confidant, on what appears to be an abandon child sitting before her, and cautious, the perfect distraction for the evils of the outside world to infiltrate. She is seconds away from closing her door and her concerns.

"I am a hungry," Dwayne said, as he stands and picks at his buttocks with his left hand.

Dotty may be a hard woman. And she is certainly the non-trusting type. But the image of this young child standing before her, picking at his numbing butt, blinking large puppy dog begging eyes is more than her cold heart can ignore. This image, even at the ice-cold age of fifty-one, will melt her. She feels an unfamiliar muscle contract on the sides of her jiggling jowls as her arms find their way to the sides of her large frame. She stands like a super hero minus the waving wind-blown cape.

"You're a hungry, are you? " She says, as her voice rings as soft and non-threatening as a kindergarten teacher.

Dwayne shakes his head up and down vigorously indicating yes, his response is instantaneous to her question, as if his growling empty stomach controlled the answer he wanted to send. He never removes his eyes from the hero standing before him and he notices the smile that had cracked on the supper woman's face.

Although Dwayne will spend the next twenty or so years with this woman he'll refer to only as "Nanny" he won't witness another smile, nor will he remember the genuineness of this one. And for Dotty, she'll spend the next twenty or so years with a child she'll call "Boy" never feeling the mother like instincts to nurture and protect as she does at this moment, nor will she, concerning him, flex the unfamiliar muscle again.

For the past eight years Dwayne's routine has for the most part remained unchanged. Sleep from sun up to early afternoon, check with Dotty on any errands she may want him to run and hang out near street corners, questionable public parks and abandon buildings. Considered a night person, Dwayne takes this description of himself to the extreme. Sleepless by night, restful by day. The perfect mole.

He enters their home with the reminisce of his previous performance glowing about him. The killing, quick and true, just as he had planned. The lies that lead to its success, cunning and manipulative, he's proud of its creativity. And of course, the joke, he surprised himself with its timing and its humor but mostly it's irony.

"Forgive me Father.... ohhh, that was the best." His mind flops over and records.

Could this be the happiest day of Dwayne's life? He's not sure. Most times of joy are short lived at best. He remembers a quick score on some stolen goods, easy money, that made him feel good. Or his friend's misfortune with an aggressive security dog, he still can't believe Tito shit his pants. He laughed pretty hard at that one. But aside from those two items he can't remember feeling this good, at least in the last month anyway. Though he may reflect on the regularity of his happiness, right now he simple doesn't care, he feels good and that's all that matters.

Now seems to be all that matters with most teens. Now is as far into the future most dare to explore. How do I feel? What do I need? When do I want it? All would, could and should be now for the selfish adolescent. Now is why some try drugs. Now is why some steel or lie. The consequences of now are hardly considered to the young teen. Now in itself suggests no concern for later. And for some teens later turns out to be much too late. A lesson Dwayne will eventually learn, the consequences of now, later.

The distraction of happiness evaluation and demon elimination is enough for Dwayne to overlook two of the three inconsistencies entering their modest home. Item number one, an unlocked door. Highly unusual for Dotty, but even more so for Dwayne not to have notice. Characteristics that define each for who they are. Dotty and all her locked doors, Dwayne and his cat burglar personality trying to unlock them.

Item number two, the sound of silence. Also, unusual, also unnoticed. For like Dwayne and the regularity of his nightly rituals, Dotty too, was mercifully predictable. To paint Dwayne the nighthawk for his life style defined by time, then equally so Dotty mocked the humming bird. Busy, buzzing, always rushed to get all that needs doing, all of course before eight AM. Nowhere lived a woman with so little to do that need doing all within the first three hours of her day. A day of food preparation, food consumption, and of course television watching. Game shows, soap operas, local and world news all needed to be watched, but more importantly heard. Dwayne always knew Dotty was home when he heard that television scream.

Physically not having to unlock the door and not hearing the regular sounds in his home environment had just started to filter from unconscious to conscious. Then the third inconsistency alerted his senesces. Smell. Unlike the trivial tasks we perform without thinking, like unlocking doors. Or the attention we would normally give a blaring television, instead of listening to our thoughts, like murder and how well it transpired. Smell is the one sense we really can't control. Hearing, seeing, feeling, and even speaking all come after our mind decides what to be conscious of, but our sense of smell works in reverse. Smell tells the mind, "We've smelled this before." Smell stimulates the mind before the mind is aware of its presence. Or as in the case of Dwayne on this particular morning, the lack of it.

He was always hungry after a night of prowling, and his stomach looked forward to the fresh-cooked meal Dotty had prepared in her mornings rush. It was this sense of smell that warned him that the door was unlocked. He smelled the TV, which was not blaring from the other room. It was smell that told him no food was cooking, although he stood in the kitchen looking directly at the pot-less stove. Dwayne smelled fear for the first time as goosebumps raced up the center of his back like a cool gust of wind on a sweat-soaked body.

"Something is wrong," he whispered as he fumbled for the knife lodged in his rear left pocket.

Now all his senses are alerted to danger and his mind twists and turns erratically in wild wonder. Guilt pounces on his swirling thoughts like a cat on an unsuspecting mouse. And with the guilt comes the *how's*. How did they know it was me? How did they get here so quickly? How in the fuck will I get out of this one?

He creeps past the doorway that separates the tiny kitchen from the even smaller pantry. Bed sheets hung with thumbtacks hide shelves on his left and right. These were home for all of Dottie's cans: canned corn, canned beans, canned potatoes and tomatoes. Cans of this and cans of that.

Cautiously he leans and peeks into the living room where Dotty spends the majority of her days. His heart pounds to the beat of the anticipation of violence. His knuckles are bleach white from the death grip he has on the only weapon clenched in his left hand. Now his vision confirms something is definitely wrong. Dwayne couldn't hear the television's droning sounds because the television's gone, and gone are the piles of junk Dotty once claimed were her "possessions." The electric space heater she would keep close to her tattered reclining chair—gone. A magazine rack/end table/slash reading lamp—gone. Knickknacks of ceramic, non-salable garage sale junk—gone. And mail. Piles, mountains, and heaping unorganized stacks of Dottie's mail. All gone.

Dwayne's body relaxes as he stands erect. His mind tries to comprehend the image before him. He looks confused as well as stunned as the feeling of being small washes over his previously pulsating body. He doesn't remember being abandoned at the age of five. For if he did, this might explain why he feels so small. And feeling smaller than his usual self could be the room's new open look. Every realtor knows the best way to sell a tiny home is to empty it. But smaller than ordinary or being less than his ordinary self-floods over Dwayne every time he knows he's alone. There is no doubt; all his senses are working properly. He can hear it, he can see it, and he can smell it. Dwayne Cunningham is alone.

He walks into the open living space breaking the knife in half and returning it to his rear pocket. He looks down at the old faded carpet scuffing his foot on the time seam he stands on. Dirty flattened fibers to the left, cleaner fuller fibers to the right. His foot swipes over the lively, less-traveled carpet hidden by unmoved furniture, then back to the deathly well-traveled carpet exposed to the traffic this room has endured. A carpet seam that only develops by time. Time seams. The entire room was blanked with time seams.

"What the fuck..." He mumbles. Searching for the reasoning for all this empty space. His mind returns to the hours before—before this empty shell of a home. When he had gone out for the evening, at about a quarter to midnight (seven plus hours ago), every item was in its place. The couch was there. He turns his head and looks at the empty spot. The television was there. He turns his head and looks at that empty spot. And her chair, her mail, all those little bits and pieces of junk. He extends his arms like the Virgin Mary stamped on a locket so many wear; all of it was right here. He looks around the entire room as his arms collapse down to his side once again. All he can say is, "What the fuck?"

Dwayne and Dotty had moved to this house from the projects shortly after Dotty had found him hungry in the hall. It was time for Dotty to move on, and finding Dwayne was a good excuse. She was at the time preparing for another move anyway, and as she watched the young child over-indulge himself with poor man's stew, she came up with what she later called, "a damn fine idea."

"Sit your ass on that there chair, Boy," Dotty said, pointing to an old limegreen, metal-backed chair.

The apartment was cluttered and dimly lit, but Dwayne was glad to be in there rather than in the lonely, darkened hall.. He scurried and sat at the chair Dotty had pointed out. His attentiveness looked as though he was an obedient child, but his eagerness to sit at the matching lime-green table meant he was that much closer to having some food.

Dotty labored as she walked the exact path the younger boy scurried. She carefully maneuvered around the table and chairs, positioning herself directly in front of Dwayne. To her back were the stove, sink, refrigerator, minimal counter space, and a handful of cupboards, all sandwiched into a tiny little space—the kitchen. She slid the chair out from under the table's surface—a distance of at least three feet. She carefully placed her left hand on the chair's back side, gripping firmly and giving it a little shake to check its stability. Her right hand laid flat on the tables' surface as she slowly lowered herself into a sitting position. The chair creaked and screamed at the added weight, and when she was finally settled, her butt checks hung well off both sides of the chair's cushion. After a few grunts and groans, she spoke.

"Where's your mama, Boy?" she said, fluttering the top segment of her garment just above her massive breasts. The act of walking the small apartment's length and sitting at the kitchen table seemed to have exerted her.

Dwayne just sat and stared at the woman before him. He would have much rather played question and answers after his stomach was full, and getting his stomach full was all he was able to think about. The look on his face told Dotty he was not listening to what she had said.

"Boy don't you know where your mama's at?" Dotty asked once more.

Dwayne's eye dropped to his lap. Perhaps he didn't want to think about the whereabouts of his only mother. Perhaps his young mind would rather not indulge in those uncertainties. He contemplates the question at hand but can only speak of the thing he's certain of.

"I'm hungry," he whispers, almost ashamed to admit it. As the words slowly and quietly leave his mouth, he raises his eyes and head to see the big woman's response.

"Very well, you eat first Boy," she said as to suggest the questions would follow.

Dotty Washington is a large woman. She is neither fashionable nor attractive, wearing bed sheets for makeshift dresses. Her eyes are as brown as her skin, and she remembers all too well the days of racial war. To look at this antiquated woman, your thoughts would conclude she's someone's great grandmother or a harmless senior citizen in need. A conclusion of illusions. Dotty herself most times believes this lie. She's a mover and a mumbler, and if you were to translate the stories she mumbles as she carelessly walks about her day, it would suggest unbearable adversary she's had to endure. But the truth—something very alien to Dotty—the truth reveals she's lazy. Completely uninterested in a hard day's work. Naive to the concept of well-earned pay.

She is in fact a mover, and she is no doubt a mumbler, but mostly she's a paranoid taker. Constantly searching for the eternal free lunch. Her jobs have been far and few between, she only once held a steady job for more than a month. At best, her work is sloppy and irresponsible. She will undoubtedly retire the unemployment queen. Queen of the social systems the givers invent. Queen of the welfare state America has become. Queen of all the takers. Food stamps, government checks, and low-income subsides all find their way to Dottie's purse. Stir in frequent moves, add a pinch of false ID's, and Dotty successfully keeps all her police—imaginary as well as real—at bay.

As she prepares a bowl of stew for Dwayne, that fine idea is born.

This child could very well be mine, yes sir. My daughter has fallen from the grace of God, her thoughts transpire. *The devil himself has taken her away.* She begins to imagine the conversation she will have. A conversation that with her determination and persistence should get her one more check from the social system.

"No Ma'am, I don't know who is the father. No Ma'am, she's been gone for months."

Dwayne just watches as she prepares the food he so desperately needs and wants. Dotty just mumbles the incomprehensible conversation that's taking place in her mind.

"Of course, I have her identification. I have her picture ID right here."

She places the bowl in front of Dwayne as her thoughts of another scammed-check swirl within her. *We'll have to move.* She looks down at Dwayne as he gobbles his stew.

Her idea is to play the victim of her imaginary daughter's irresponsible behavior—an idea that's really not that much further from the truth. Dwayne's mother was a prostitute and a heroin attic, and she has, although unwillingly, abandoned this child. Dotty would simply tell the tale as though Dwayne's mother was her daughter and she desperately needs financial help for his care. *Time's a wastin'. This'll be easy enough,* she concludes. *A damn fine idea.*

Snapping out of her dazed and consumed world, she stands towering over the boy as he nears finishing his first helping.

"What's your name, Boy?" Dotty asks in a sinister and conniving tone.

"Dwaymme." he answers with a mouth full of stew.

"Dwayme?" Dotty asks.

He swallows the mouthful of stew and sniffles at the dripping snot that's about to run down his nose. His stomach happily accepts the offering as a burp begins to fester within his chest.

"Dwayne, my name is Dwayne Cummingham," he says, meaning to say Cunningham. He quickly returns to devouring his food.

"Well Dwayne Cummingham, my name is Dotty, but you call me Nanny, you understand me Boy?" she said, again placing her arms to her massive sides like a superhero without the cape.

Dwayne finishes the last spoonful of poor man's stew and holds the empty bowl up for Dotty to see. The burp that was festering found its way out as he belched with relief.

"Burghhhp."

His eyes, the way he held the empty bowl, and the long pressure-relieving belch told Dotty he wanted more.

She took the bowl and painstakingly walked the short distance to the simmering pot. She carefully filed the bowl to its very rim and labored as she walked back to the waiting child. Before she set down the second helping for him to enjoy, she made her point very clear.

"You call me Nanny, you understand me, Boy?" she said, holding the food just out of his reach. This action told Dwayne all he needed to know. The stew in that there bowl, the shelter this apartment provided, even the watchful eye this large woman could give, all came with a price. And right now, it was time to pay.

"Nanny," he said.

"Good boy," she replied, setting the bowl on the table directly in front of him.

Time seams and empty spaces. Murder and the irony of the joke. All flew around his head like a barn swallow protecting her young. He just stood there, his arms dangling at his side, wondering what had happened. Wondering what he will do now. Just him and this empty room. Alone in a vacant house, isolated in a barren world. A chill races up his spine, shivering his body as well as his thoughts, and the demons of being alone, which he had thought he had killed earlier this morning, begin to take hold.

Dwayne hates to be alone. It's the very reason he takes his night lifestyle to the extreme. The pain and suffering of being molested at such a young age robbed him of more than just his innocence. At night, when you close your eyes and it's dark, you're very much alone, and every night when he lied in bed drowning in the darkness, he was alone. He was eight years old when the nightmares came. The demons that haunted him in his sleep all took the appearance of Father Frances Case.

Children can block out the unpleasantness they endure at times much better than adults. But in most cases, sooner comes quicker than later, when the demons come crashing back. For Dwayne, he was still very young, and the crashing came in the form of his sleep, possessing his time of rest. As he grew older, he feared the darkness, to the point of near-neurotic behavior. Closing his eyes at bedtime only opened a dark and frightening place. Places where he was very much alone. When he was eight he began to lie awake all night long, and the only sleep he got was in the brightness of day. Then and only then would he sleep, staring at his lamp as it spun as the day's light filled his room.

Above him the ceiling's support joists creaked. Old timbers covered with plaster and lath and many, many years of added paint whined like a thirsty kitten. He turned his head as well as his attention towards the noise, looking upward at the tongue and grove ceiling.

The house was a small, three-bedroom colonial; two very small bedrooms upstairs with an ineffective sharing closet system dividing the two rooms. Downstairs there was a fairly good-sized bedroom just off the family room, were Dwayne now stood. The room up the stairs and to the left was unoccupied and filled to the rim with junk. Junk that Dotty insisted on saving. Junk that Dwayne was constantly asked to carry up the stairs and put away. The room up the stairs and to the right, the one directly above Dwayne, was Dwayne's. It was the room Dotty stood silently in as soon as she heard the kitchen's back door slam shut.

Once again, with cat-like reflexes, Dwayne removes the knife from his left-rear pocket. Also, once again his heart begins to pound. But this time, almost sensing the danger is no real threat; the pounding is less severe as he cautiously walks to the foot of the stairs.

"*Without a doubt,*" he mumbles. "*This is one fucked up morning.*"

He places his right foot on the bottom step as his right hand rests on the banister's head. His left-hand hangs to his side limply, gently holding his Stiletto imitation. Dwayne's thumb and index finger carefully cradles the duel-sided blade. His weapon prepared for flight.

"Who's there?" he yells, as the pounding in his chest jumps one or two more beats.

"Boy is that you?" Dotty answers.

"Nanny?" Dwayne replied, completely confused.

For Dwayne, this morning's bizarre events have just taken another turn.

The killing—something he's never done—was certainly strange and new. The unlocked door—he doesn't see that very often—at home or anywhere else for that matter. The pot-less stove, the noiseless television and all those time seams. All of it, the whole crazy morning, just keeps getting weirder and weirder. And now this. Dotty *upstairs*. This has got to be the strangest of things yet.

In all the years they have spent here—nearly ten—Dwayne has never seen Dotty climb these stairs. In fact, during the early years, these stairs and his room were the only safe haven from the strict back-of-the-hand discipline Dotty would try to enforce. Dwayne learned early on that Nanny isn't very fast. If you can get around her and make it to those stairs, you're home free. No way she can climb these stairs, so he had thought. But what is she doing up there now?

"Nanny?" He questions again.

"Listen up, Boy. Get up here and help me with these things," she barks, reaching down to pick up a night lamp that sat beside Dwayne's mattress on the floor.

Within an instant, Dwayne is up the stairs and standing in the frame of his doorway. The knife he had held ready for flight was returned to his pocket as he had raced up the stairs with ease. There, was something he'd never witnessed before— Dotty standing in his room. She was holding his bedside lamp under her massive right arm.

"Where the hell you been Boy, time's a wastin'," she said in disgust.

"Wh... At..." Dwayne mumbles as the palms of his hands face the ceiling.

"We gotta' a get a move on Boy. Any of these here belongins you want?" Her eyes take a lap around the room as she continues, "Where the hell you been?" She takes in a half breath and snaps, "You want this here lamp, right?"

Dwayne's mind is flustered, just as Dotty had planned. The multiple questions, the barking of commands, and even Dotty knew the sight of her being in his room would confuse him. All were intended to cover the truth. A truth she is now trying desperately to hide.

"Nanny, wha…what's going on?" Dwayne pleads.

"We gotta' a move Boy. Now is there any of these here belong' in you want, other than this here lamp?" she says, extending her right arm slightly to get him to look at his favorite lamp. Another element of confusion Dotty masterfully adds to the mix—Dwayne's favorite lamp.

That morning in '65 when Dwayne learned how to say Nanny and Dottie's "fine idea" was born was also the last time Dwayne would set foot in the apartment he was raised in. Dotty knew it wouldn't be long before the authorities would inquire about the missing whore. She knew she would have to move fast to avoid police confrontation.

If his mothers found dead, they'll surely come lookin' here, she had thought. *And if they start poking their noses around here, they'll surely be askin' questions at my front door*, her paranoid thoughts would conclude.

But this time Dotty was dead right. The police would come knocking two days after they had left. And she was right about Dwayne's mother also. Although she had no proof the woman was dead, in Dotty's mind, anyone missing for more than a week is "dead as dead," as she would so often say.

As Dwayne happily devoured bowl after bowl of poor man's stew, Dotty began to pack. He sat and watched as Dotty clumsily moved throughout the small apartment packing item after item in weathered cardboard boxes, stuffing two suitcases that looked as though someone had discarded them years ago. And just as his stomach was reaching full capacity, so was the amount of belongings Dotty could carry.

She stood in the small doorway that divided the kitchen and living room. Again, her massive arms were perched at her side.

"Boy, I was just on my way out," she said calmly and matter-of-fact like.

"Do you want to go home now?" she asked, raising her left eyebrows and tilting her head slightly to the right.

Dwayne just sat and stared at the large woman before him. "Home?" he thought. "I don't wanna go home." It was ten long days he had spent locked in that apartment down the hall. It felt like eternity. especially when the food ran out on the seventh day. And the noises had frightened him; the ones during the day just outside his door and the ones during the night just outside his window. During those ten days there were many a times he wept himself to sleep. It was only because of his starving stomach that he would even attempt to unlock the huge door. He remembered his mother's command: "Honey, don't ever leave the apartment!"

Home, no sir. As he sat and stared at Dotty, he did not answer. But even more so than his inability to speak was his lack of desire to return home.

"Listen up here Boy. You caught me at a time when your Nanny was movin' on. Now you're welcome to come along, and I'll tend you. You understand me, Boy? But first we gonna check'n see if your mama come home yet. I won't lie to ya boy. I don't think she's ever comin' home. But we'll check, ya here? You wanna come along? Or you wanna stay?" she said, as-a-matter-of-fact-like.

Dotty held out her right hand so as to entice the young boy's decision. It was completely unnecessary. Dwayne knew his mother was never coming home. And though his tiny mind thought no further ahead than the moment at hand, he also knew he would follow the large woman no matter what.

As Dotty scoured the boy's apartment for the last ten days, Dwayne again just stood and watched. Dotty quickly (as quick as Dotty's capable of moving) checked all the room's hiding places for cash or anything of value. The three small rooms that made up the entire living space were a mess. In one corner of what would be the only bedroom in the apartment, there was actually no bed. In the mess of a room was a child's mattress, a filthy pillow, and a lamp, all conveniently tucked in the corner. A makeshift child's room. The lamp is what caught Dottie's eye.

It stood about a foot high, cylinder in shape, and about six inches in diameter. The base was genuine artificial brass with eagle-foot-claw-like legs and decorative carvings. The top matched the bottom in design, with an eagle at its perch; it was like a hood ornament in size and design. The cylinder, or lamp's shade, had a picture of a mountainside landscape—waterfalls and pine trees, some even set ablaze in a miniature forest fire somewhere in the distance, and a snowy mountain peak all wrapped itself around the lamp's entire shade. When the lamp was plugged in, the cylinder would slowly spin, and some of the scenery would appear to move. The waterfalls looked as though they were running. The forest fire looked as though it was burning. And some but not all of the big fluffy clouds in the sky looked as though they were drifting. This part of the illusion on the lamp was the element Dwayne loved the most.

The lamp—though magical in Dwayne's young eyes—was not magic at all. A separate cylinder spun on the inside of the lamp in the opposite direction of the outer cylinder. The transparent parts in the scenery were replaced by the striped colors on the inner shade. The red, white, and blue of the fire, clouds, and water all appeared to move. For Dwayne, it was his magic lamp.

This lamp was the only item Dotty felt worthy to steal. Dwayne had never requested his magic lamp that morning in '65. And Dotty had never asked the child if there were anything he would like to have from a home he would never see again. But the lamp, his magical lamp, would later comfort him when the demons of being raped came crashing in. He would stare at the moving pictures and slowly and calmly find sleep. Even now, a hardened criminal. Even now, a mouthy teen. Even now, an apprenticed murderer. He loved that lamp, and Dotty, masterful in her ability to confuse Dwayne, knew it.

"Dwayne! Do ya want the lamp or don't ya?" Dotty snapped.

"Yeah, yeah, I want the fucking lamp already. Where we are going?" Dwayne said, snapping himself out of the confusing state Dotty had masterfully placed him in.

"Buffalo," she said, brushing past him as she made her way toward the stairs. "And stop cursing."

"Buffalo?" he questioned, "where the hell's that?"

Dotty paused at the top of the stairs as Dwayne turned and looked at her. He stood in the doorway to his room. Her plans had changed ever so slightly in the last twenty minutes or so, but her crafty ability to lie on the fly took complete control.

"New York, Boy. Buffalo is in New York." A truth.

"My sister is there, and she plans to give us a hand." A lie. Dotty in fact has no siblings.

"We will go to Buffalo and make a fresh start." A truth.

"I'm glad you're finally here..." A huge lie. She had all intention of leaving Dwayne. Of course, after she scoured his room for valuables.

"...We really have to get going." A truth, she concluded, as she painstakingly started the long journey down the steep stairs.

Dwayne whipped his left hand through his greasy, black hair, his fingers slightly apart like a makeshift comb. *Buffalo*, he thought. *Now is a good time to leave*. He spun around in excitement for a quick last look at his room. His measly belongings he had no intentions of taking were ever so slightly out of place. You see, Dwayne was wrong about Dotty, how he had thought she was never in his room. He was wrong in his assumption that she could never have climbed those stairs, and wrong was his faith that she would never do anything to hurt him. In fact, she had just tried to rob and abandon him.

But that was all well and good as he slept on the bus ride, Buffalo-bound. He may have been wrong about Dotty. But more importantly, Dotty was wrong about Dwayne. She too, in her blind faith, thought, *He wouldn't do anything to hurt me*.

Chapter 4

(Pebbles in a Pond)

Some of the universe's connections are not very obvious. They clearly overlap with oblateness, slapping the world in its apparent ignorance with opened eyes. Astrologists, for example, connect random stars in our star-filled skies to unleash stick drawings. Like a giant connect-the-dots drawing book, we are led to believe that some naked woman is pouring water from an ancient vessel somewhere in the heaven's skies. Aquarius. Or a handled saucer pan and its smaller brother hang in the night air *dipping* darkness, both big and little. These imagined connections, even well documented from their creation, are accepted without debate only because of their duration and the generations that have pass. However, some connections are obvious. It is easy to see the similarities in siblings from the same parents. Even if these two children do not share the same gender or age features and personality traits make identifying these connections obvious. Another example is father and son. A man's son might grow and never take on the carpenter trade his father learned and loved his entire life. However, the son might enjoy programming and building inside the synthetic brains of a computer in much the same way. Connections both obvious and not so obvious happening at the same time. These ringlets of water in a pond when a pebble is dropped ripple their way to the edges in a rhythmic wave of symmetry. But when a pebble is dropped at the other edge of the same pond, eventually the ringlet waves meet. The water ripples in unison no longer as the two collide. This inevitable collision plays out in the universe without anyone aware of the pending clash. Like father and son growing to tackle different trades but building in all the same ways, the universe's connections are both obvious and unpredictable at the same time. Aaron and Dwyane are every bit of this unpredictability connection. In fact, they are only nine months apart in age. They are so much the same but so very different, and the collision course they are on has the same odds as that of the team with the worst odds of winning the championship series. The same can be said for the fragile Nora Mills and the fat Jim Leary. For them, the dots in a random sky filled with stars have no more the right to draw a little or big dipper than a coin flipped that lands on edge. However, the coin in the rarest of flips does land and balance on edge. When it doesn't, the universe laughs. When it does, we explode in bewilderment and laughter.

In 1960, Butch is promoted with a new trucking route. Promoted only in that it is different than the route he had traveled the past six years, day in and day out. The monies, or lack thereof as Butch would complain, is nearly identical. The difference being that the time on the road is longer, as well as the distance the big rig wheels turn. Thus, it is more money, but it means more time and miles. Butch and Gloria are celebrating their tenth year as husband and wife, and truth be told, as of late things could be better between them. Mother is eight-plus months pregnant with Aaron and Jarred—now nine—is no help around the house at all. Malisa, only six, is a little mother hen, for her Gloria's real house duties are her play duties. But let's be honest. When your six-year-old offers to help and tries to do so, it really means more work for mom. Thus, when the promotion came for Butch, in Gloria's eyes this meant more work for her on top of the twenty-pound globe she carries around under her bed-sheet-sized shirt she used to call her waist.

"Now?!" Gloria questions in disgust. "Now is when they want you to take the South Carolina route?"

Butch, although a couple cans short of a six-pack mentally most of the time, knew his pregnant wife's reaction to his "promotion" would be less than congratulatory. He had in fact delayed telling Gloria nearly a week until hours before his first run.

Like all men who know what is to come when they talk to the always-right wife, he dreads the conversation to come and thus waits until the very last minute. Butch joked one time to a co-worker in an exchange that amplifies this very situation. Butch asked, "Is a man wrong in the woods if his wife is not there to tell him so?" Butch had shared this with his truck-driving buddy as they both chuckled at the joke.

"Gloria, what do you want me to do?" He responds. "If I don't take the fucking thing now, I might not ever get it offered to me again."

"Jerry knows I'm eight-and-a-half months pregnant right?" Gloria states, referring to the dispatcher Jerry Hobbes, Butch's drinking buddy, boss, and sharing jokes companion.

"Yes, of course he knows, but there is nothing he can do," Butch continues. "That little fucking weasel Benny has to have his appendix taken out or some shit like that. I don't know. Jerry asked if I took the promotion. Now he can keep Benny from getting his route back if and when he ever does come back. Jerry said the little prick might not even survive the operation. Look I'm not…"

Gloria stands and listens to the bullshit she knows is spewing from her husband's mouth. She has no clue if what Butch says is true and if she ever called Jerry or Benny or anyone else at that dive of a trucking company to confirm his story with the people Butch works with, who lie for one another like faithful brothers in arms. What choice does mother really have? Butch is the sole provider for her growing family. Another argument on top of the constant arguments—for example, about how Butch treats Jared—will do nothing to help their troubled marriage. And Gloria is worried about this baby-to-be. If it is a boy, she is terrified Butch might even treat this one worse. Mother never understood completely why Butch didn't seem to care much for the eldest boy, but she thinks it has something to do with the math.

"All right Butch, go," Mother interrupts. "It will be fine. If the baby comes when you're gone, the baby comes when you're gone." Mother hangs her head like a prize fighter who just learned she lost fifteen rounds by decision. Butch stops talking and walks toward Gloria for a hug. A step and a half away, Gloria, knowing what her husband intended to do next, turns and walks away. Butch is crafty and always knows when he gets his way is the optimal time to shut up. Also, he knows mother is a sucker for the hug. Hugs, however, as well as anything else from mother, have been very far and few between as of late. Butch is both emotionally as well as sexually frustrated with one simple stroke of mothers hug less turn. Six sleepless hours later he is in his truck heading South on a new run. The law states he will need to stop in Washington or after ten hours on the road. In the years to come, the only time Butch will do so on his new promotion and trucking route is at a truck stop near D.C, A truck stop he is well aware of that is littered with prostitutes Benny always claimed were well worth the twenty bucks spent. Unfortunately, eight short days later when Butch returns home, he is no longer sexually frustrated. However, he is in fact home for his son Aaron's birth.

Dwyane Cunningham has fit into the criminal elements in the city of Buffalo, New York like a fish to water. He is very clever and good at stealing and misleading others and has only been arrested a couple of times. Like Dotty, he lies about nearly everything, and the ghetto slum projects they live in are really not much different than D.C.—only a smaller version of the same thing. Smaller in size, equal in crime. Dottie's health is not good, and Dwyane is rarely home and never notices or cares. The relationship between these two had deteriorated the older both get. Dotty is losing patience for the insubordination of Dwyane and his attitude, and Dwyane is seeing clearly now her true feelings for him and that she is a con woman. A relationship built on deception and mistrust will crash and burn eventually. Shortly after arriving in Buffalo, that process started to unfold. It took years, but in the end, neither really cared for the other, and in those rare occasion their paths crossed in the apartment, neither said much to the other. Dwayne is now twenty-six, and Dotty is all of seventy-seven and aging—as well as dying—faster than any seventy-year-old normally would.

Dwyane is sleeping in his bedroom with the door closed on a mattress on the floor. It is nearly two in the afternoon, but the bedroom is completely dark from the spray-painted window and the dark blanket acting as a make-shift blind that hangs from nails on the frame's edges. The only small light is a Christmas-bulb, clear nightlight on the wall closest to Dwyane's head. It is a much brighter light in all the darkness, and when the bedroom door is completely open, the light that stays on all the time is not even hardly seen at all. Dwayne, even though a hardened criminal and professed tough guy thug, is still afraid of the dark—a disorder that has been with him all his life. Dotty creeps the door open a crack and peaks inside. She is crafty and can tell when this young man is truly sleeping or faking it. She desperately wants to check the top dresser drawer for cash but needs to be very careful not to wake the warden to the dresser's contents. When Dwayne arrived home early this morning, he seemed very happy and in good spirts. Dotty takes this to mean that the criminal scored big last night. If that is the case, Dotty thought, then now is the best time to skim something off the top. Dwayne, like most thieves, is terrible when it comes to counting out the exact amount stolen the night of the crime. The goal after the theft is to escape, count the take in a safe location—or as in Dwayne's case, Dotty knows so well—don't bother to count it at all. Stolen money or items have little value to anyone. When you work hard, save your money, and finally buy what it is you wanted and saved for means that the item will be treasured and taken care of. However, steal it, and it has little to no value at all. The takers never learn this lesson. They spin their wheels thinking that what they take becomes theirs, but in reality, the items never really becomes theirs at all. Something you claim as yours that never was yours in the first place never becomes yours and has little value. There is no value or honor when you steal something as opposed to working hard to obtain it. Fathers teach this lesson to their sons. But Dwayne did not have a father, only Dotty to teach what she knows, and Dotty is about to steal from Dwayne as he sleeps. The door creeks as she pushes it a sliver at a time farther and farther as it opens. Floor boards do the same as she slowly tries to slip inside the darkened room. Afternoon daylight from the hallway cascades a perfect stream of light across the floor inches from Dwayne's face. Dotty is very careful not to let the open door's light touch Dwayne's face as she creeps farther and farther inside. Dotty has lost a considerable amount of weight since that day that the two were Buffalo bound. Her weight loss is not due to eating healthy and exercise. No, hers is a deteriorating aging process from years of bad living. She doesn't know it today as she creeps in to steal once again, but a year from today she won't even be around. She is inches away from the dresser when Dwayne breaths heavy and rolls over to adjust and comfort his sleeping body. Dotty closes the door completely, as quietly and with the same care as when she opened it. She stands in silence in what is now a very dark room looking at the Christmas tree bulb illuminating Dwayne's hardened face. Slower than how she had opened and closed the bedroom door, she slides the top drawer to the dresser towards her sagging breast. There is no noise in the bedroom except for the heavy breathing of the sleeping thief. Without looking inside the drawer, she slides her hand slowly around the drawer's insides. Her hand brushes against clothing that is either socks or underwear or something altogether different as her mind's eye searches with only touch for a stack of cash. Finally, in the drawer's corner, she feels for the first time what brought a smile to Dwayne's face and the explanation for his cheered spirts when he returned home early that morning. Unfortunately for Dotty, this stolen item has little or no value to her at all. She is appalled at Dwayne and his lifestyle even more now than before she crept into his darkened room. She thinks to herself that she has stolen more from the givers in the world without said item and sees neither a need or purpose for a loaded gun. For Dwayne, however, this is the last gun he will ever own. The first, of course, he had left on the lap of the rapist priest back in D.C so many years ago. For Dotty, the con is her theft style of choice and people that use guns get guns pointed at them more often than not— bizarre wisdom that holds truth that not all can or will understand. Dotty creeps out like a ninja as silently as she crept in and thinks to herself that the risk was not all for not. Now she knows Dwayne has crossed over into an even more sinister world of crime. He did so and has been in it for a couple years now but hid it well when and if he ever came home. She had the opinion that he was a crook; she never diluted her thoughts on this or made excuses about his behavior. However, now she thinks getting him to leave or her slipping away in the dead of night might not be such a bad idea. She decides to give this some thought. She will process a plan that she believes will be beneficial for both Dwayne and her if all goes according to said plan. *Crafty, manipulative, and brilliant,* she thinks, as a new con is born. What she does not know at this point is that when Dwayne awakes and leaves the house, he never returns. Her diabolical plan needed be executed, and when she learns of

Dwayne's future and what is to become of the sonless son she really never cared much for to begin with. A week later she is in his bedroom once again, rummaging for valuables as Dwayne cries with terror in his mind, in darkness forever as a prisoner of a life of crime and murder.

The day Aaron was born was a cold November day in Western New York—as cold as any winter day the state has. Oddly enough, a couple of months from now, a groundhog in Pennsylvania would declare an additional six more weeks of winter to an already harsh one. Jared plays in his room with plastic army men joined at the feet with even more plastic. The army fantasy the ten-year-old boy plays with is narrated in his head as well as quietly aloud on the bedroom's carpeted floor. Malisa too is in her bedroom playing. She is only eight and her fantasy of choice is a tea party with stuffed animals and Barbie dolls. Gloria is in the laundry room setting cycles to spin or cold water only. She has been having very light contractions all day, and the intensity will come on suddenly and unexpectedly. Butch has been home now for a day and a half and is expected to go on another run when the call comes in. This usually can be anywhere from two to twenty-two hours, but he is rested and ready, watching television with both eyes closed. Mother lifts the laundry basket that contains the clothing that has just exited the dryer. The warm air surrounding the basket cascades on mothers' belly and face as she groans at the basket's weight. A sharp pain follows, and for a split second she nearly drops the clean cloths. She pauses, holding the basket while standing in the laundry room's doorway. In front of her is the basement entertainment space that Butch insisted the basement needed to be. To her left is the bar that Butch almost never stands behind entertaining friends that never come. On the wall directly behind the invisible entertaining Butch is the exhaust fan leading to the space under the breezeway. All of this goes unnoticed because mothers' pain has just jumped from a race car in idle to a race car running in the red. Gloria sandwiches every muscle in her face, closing her eyes tighter than any normal eyes shut. Still holding onto the basket of clothes, she screams under her breath in a voice that only she can hear. The contraction seems to last a full minute or maybe two, but in reality only seconds of pain is felt. When it subsides, she gently bends awkwardly forward with all of the soon-to-be-born Aaron's weight nearly tipping her over, and places the basket on the basement's floor. She stands erect and places both hands on her back as she stretches to stand.

"Butch!" Mother screams upstairs. "Butch, it's time!"

One eye opens as Butch, reclined and comfortable not watching T.V., comprehends the words that are now reaching his ears. He takes a very deep, deliberate breath and fumbles with his right hand to find the oak recliner handle that will collapse the foot part of his chair. Pulling the handle while straining ab muscles never used and pushing his feet to the floor all in unison, he sits erect. He scratches the top of his head with the same hand that was previously pulling the oak handle. His mouth is dry as he wets his lips and wonders if the Genny beer can sitting to his right on the end table has anything left inside.

"Butch!" Mother screams loud enough for everyone in the house to hear.

"What?" Butch answers. "I'm coming," he yells in return, then finishes with under his breath, "What's the big hubbub bub?" A question that is not intended to be answered.

"It's time!" Mother follows up and yells.

"Time for wha…?" Butch states, only now understanding what is about to unfold.

Jared and Malisa come out of their rooms and meet at the top of the stairs at the same time. Both pause for a second and start to descend simultaneously, almost stepping on one another. Jared yells, "I'll get the number!" and Malisa screams while running behind her older brother, "No! Jared that is *my* job!"

The number, of course, is that of the Sands across the street. Young Becky Sands has agreed to watch Jared and Malisa in the event the young Mills baby is on the way. There was no such agreement on whom would get said number, but this was something all brothers and sisters fight over, regardless of a predetermined agreement. In fact, "getting" the number that was scotch taped by the rotary dial telephone mounted on the kitchen wall was not even necessary. The number needed to be right where it was to call the teenage Sands girl. Butch reaches mother in the basement near the basket of clean, warm, clothes at the same time Jared and Malisa fight over who will rip the number off the wall near the phone.

"Okay, here ya go…" Butch said, reaching with both arms out to mother as careful as a nurse hands over a newborn child. "Easy now, Gloria. Take your time," Butch adds as they find their way to the foot of the stairs, looking up. It is these moments when Butch can seem so loveable and trustworthy, and it is these moments that led Gloria to fall in love with him. He is a strange man, mother thinks. He is a brut with stupidity and vulgar nonsense in one breath and then a perfect gentleman and caring husband the next. She will never figure Butch out, yet she will stay her faithful self until his passing.

The stairs are navigated with the caring help of the husband's hands. Mother's contractions continue to worsen all the way to Saint Mary Hospital, where Aaron will be born. Eight pounds eight ounces with about two full hours of hard labor and the Mills family is two children plus one. They had three possible names for the child to be. Kelly if it was a girl and Aaron or Barry if a boy. When mother looked at her youngest son, she said, still dripping in labor sweat, "He looks like an Aaron to me." Butch, of course, had no say really and in truth did not care. He pressed his proud parent checks against the window of a room filled with babies and puffed his chest with pride. The name mattered not, and to see Butch standing there, you would have thought he endured the two plus hours of hard labor. For Butch even forgot all about the game he created as he stood looking through the glass. Back home, Jared and Malisa waited, pregnant with anticipation of the revealing of the baby's gender and who would win. Jared, of course, would go on to win and was in fact the only Mills family member that thought the child would be a boy. Even though mother did not partake in Butch's silly games, she did feel as though the child felt a lot like Malisa insider her and thought it might be a girl. Butch and Malisa also thought it was a girl, hence the single name. All agreed Kelly would be a Mills, thus mother was shocked when the doctor announced the child to be male. That night Jared laid in bed looking out his only bedroom widow as snow gently fell. His arms are crossed behind his head, and he is still beaming from what can only be described as a "Jared win." The wind howls outside as the thoughts swirl in this young boy's mind.

"I have a brother, "Jared whispers to only his poster-covered bedroom walls. "I'm an older brother to Aaron now," He concludes in a whisper. And the weight of what Jared just said out loud sets in. "I have to show him everything," Jared says, drifting to sleep as the snow continues to pile up outside. A small, welcomed pebble drops on the edge of Jared's pond, and the ripple effect that would join these two brothers in love will soon collide in peaceful harmony.

Dwyane awakes after the creeping Dotty exits his room some few short hours later. It is roughly 4:15 in the afternoon, dinner time to the rest of the world, but for Dwayne it is breakfast time. He stretches, standing tall and erect in his still-darkened bedroom and scratches at his chest and butt. He has this sickening feeling that someone was in his room but passes it off quickly and quietly as it hits as nothing to worry about. His jeans from two nights before lay bundled up in a pile of other clothes that need washing; he pulls them on. His left-hand plunges deep in the front pocket to check and see if the roll of bills are still there. Satisfied that all our accounted for, (Dwayne has only a rough idea the total) his mind flashes a silent movie when he and Cheet'O split what they looted two nights ago. The shirt he slept in is the shirt he will wear, and he walks to the dresser's edge and opens the top drawer. A quick shuffle through some socks and underwear and he has in his hand the new toy he acquired during his heist. A 9-millimeter polished, chrome, stainless-steel handgun made by Tarus with the weight of quality bounces in his left hand. It feels good, he thinks, and the staggered rounds inside the clip will ensure that even if he misses his intended target, he will have plenty more rounds to fly off as he sees fit. He slowly closes the dresser drawer and starts to play out the movie of two nights ago in his head. An abandoned house on Carter Street was just one of many in that dying neighborhood. Cheet'O, Dwayne's partner in crime the last year or so, said that this house was being squatted for a drug dealer in a low-level gang. Dwayne and Cheet'O staked out the house and watched as the buyers and sellers came and went and waited for the opportunity to strike. In a high-level drug distribution house, the house itself is owned by someone. A low-level drug distribution operation house is used and left behind almost nightly. Unfortunately for Buffalo's dying city, there are plenty of streets like Carter Street to choose from if you know what to look for. Buffalo has been dying slowly for a long time. The steel industry was once its bread and butter. However, Chinese steel became so cheap, the steel mills and unions of Buffalo suffocated themselves as unemployment grew. Crime also grew, so for Dwayne and Cheet'O, business was good. Another anomaly in a low-level drug gang distribution operation compared to a high-level one is the fact that there are times—small windows of time at night— when no one is actually in the house being squatted. This is the opportunity Dwayne looks for to rummage the house as fast as he can and steal what has worth. Did Dwayne learn this tactic from Dotty? Not directly, but in a subconscious way, he was indeed taught. Dotty was careful; Dwayne was careful. Dotty took little risks; Dwayne took little risks. Dotty would rob the hand that fed her; Dwayne would steal from his friends and co-criminals if he knew he could get away with it. Cheet'O never met anyone like Dwayne, someone so careful and patient when it came to crime. Dwayne didn't "need" Cheet'O but would use him just the same. Like pebbles in a pond, the rippling waters start to merge.

Confident the house was empty, the two criminals struck. Cheet'O stood close by the house outside, hiding in the dark of night's shadow. Dwayne quickly and quietly used a butter knife to jimmy the back-door's lock open and crept inside. Dwayne taught Cheet'O to bang his fist on the side of the house with one sharp blow if anyone was in the area or heading to the house. Like a well-trained combat veteran, Dwayne assesses the room quickly and quietly for any valuable hiding spots and takes anything and everything that has worth. The tops of kitchen cabinets, backs of old televisions, and lamps with large wooden bases that are hollowed out for a stash are all checked as quickly and quietly as possible. Nothing, and the hair on Dwayne's neck begins to stand erect. *This is taking too long*, his mind whispers as he looks feverishly from room to room. He had entered the house from a backed-in porch of sorts. Piles of garbage littered this small space. From that room, he then steps into the kitchen, where he checks the tops of all the wall cabinets and the only two working drawers (Working meaning the only two drawer spaces that actually had a drawer). That room led him to two choices: down the hall to a bathroom on the right or bedroom on the left, or the living room where a bedsheet-covered sofa, an end table and lamp, a non-matching coffee table with beer cans and cigarette butts littered about it and an old console television set were the only items in the room. Dwayne did the living room sweep first then headed for the only bedroom. Nothing. As he left the bedroom, he poked his head in the bathroom for a quick peak: toilet and tub, no shower curtain, and a bath vanity with no doors on the front of it. Discouraged, he swears in his head, and for a split second he hears the voice of Dotty in his thoughts telling him not to cuss. As he turns to walk back to the kitchen, he recalls a friend that told him he always hid his shit in the tank of the toilet in a secondary bathroom that did not work. Light from an idea light bulb flashes atop Dwayne's head as he turns around quickly and enters the tiny bathroom. He removes the porcelain lid to the disgustingly unclean toilet and looks inside. At first glance, clean water and the workings of a commode flusher system with rusted chain and a black, odd-shaped floating plastic ball is all he sees. Holding the top with both hands, he starts to return the top when something catches his eye. Setting the top down on the seat less toilet, he plunges his left hand into the tank and fishes around with his hand. He feels and grabs at the hockey-puck-shaped item that caught his attention as the said item smooshes in his hand and dissolves. *What the fuck?* he questions in his mind as he again feels the drippings of discouragement fall down the back of his mind as the blue dye and water from the toilet tank drips from his left hand. At the very same moment, a sharp thud is heard from the watching shadow eyes of Cheet'O, his partner in crime. "Nothing, fucking nothing!" Dwayne concludes as he shakes his hand dry; it is slightly colored in blue, wet muck, and he heads for the kitchen with some giddy-up in his steps. Ready to leave through the back-porch door he had entered, he glances at a silver, once-clean vent hood above the space a stove would fit if there was in fact a stove in this kitchen. His mind made up on leaving, and his mind's conclusion that this was a risky fucking waste of time, he notices something about the silver vent hood that looks out of place. The screen where the cook's vapers would exit the house (if there was a cooking stove beneath it) was clean. Everything else was covered in grease—old grease from years of not cleaning after cooking. The vent hood underbelly was dirty and greasy; the plastic light bulb cover to the right side was greasy and dirty; the exposed left-side light bulb was covered in grease and was dirty. *So why?* Dwayne thinks as he passes by. *Is the vent screen clean?* he asks himself in a microsecond. Turning quickly as he answers his own question, he rips the clean vent screen from the hood, and like the toilet bowl plunge, he fishes for what is inside. A brown paper bag and a polished 9-millimeter hand gun is removed almost as fast as the clean screen hits the floor. But the screen wasn't clean at all. It had the appearance of cleanness because whoever returned it to its non-concealed hiding position inadvertently put it back upside down. The other side of the screen was as greasy as the rest of the vent hood. The squatter, stoned drug dealer that is entering the front of the house as Dwayne exits the back did not notice the error of his ways. He soon finds out, but when he does, Cheet'O and Dwayne slip into the night covered in darkness, preparing to split the take.

Cheet'O laughs hysterically from both the successful take and from the story Dwayne tells him about why his hand is now dyed blue and splits the cash. The laugh they both share will be short-lived after the stupid fucking Cheet'O repeats the blue-died hand story with some of his friends later that night. Back at the house on Carter Street, it does not take the world's best detective to understand what took place in the burglarized house in their absence. Someone rummaged in the bathroom and checked the toilet tank for a stash. Then that same someone left blue-die, hockey-puck-shaped toilet-tank cake residue on the hallway floor and the greasy vent hood and ran off with the drug dealers stash and gun. The question that only now needs to be answered is, "Who the fuck stole the stash and has blue-die-stained hands?" Street talk, stories, and rumors spread like wildfire in the hood and within a couple hours, the drug dealers had a name to hunt. Lucky for Dwayne, he did not return home that early morning and stayed with a mutual friend of Cheet'O and himself inside his shitty apartment. Had Dwayne went home, two thugs waited with loaded weapons ready to ambush Dwayne outside the project's front entrance. Only the one thug knew of Dwayne Cunningham and could identify him had he walked by—the very same thug that listened to Cheet'O open his stupid, fucking mouth bragging of the stolen goods and the blue dye story. This weasel had a name and reputation for talking too much, and he and Dwayne did not like one another at all. His street name was Snot. This was not because he had nose-dripping issues. Snot talked too much, and when he was accused of doing so, he replied, "It's not true. I didn't say nuff'in." He had to say this line so much and when doing so, when he spoke, where the "s" is at the end of the word "it" came out sounding like it was at the beginning of the word "not." Thus, the sound, and mocking listeners would hear and repeat back to this blabbering moron, Snot. Hence the name. Dwayne stayed clear of him and had words with him shortly after moving to Buffalo. He even reminded Cheet'O on more than one occasion not to repeat anything they did or did not do regarding crime (or anything else for that matter) in front of Snot. However, like most with half a brain, Dwayne could not control Cheet'O or anyone else when not in earshot distance and remind them to keep their fucking trap shut. Dwayne had left Cheet'O the night of the crime and headed straight to Armando's place with a twelve-pack of Miller Lights. Dwayne liked Armando, even though he was related to Cheet'O. Armando probably would have never repeated what they had done, but Armando rarely did anything criminal in nature and had a good job that he liked. Dwayne respected that about Cheeto's cousin and spent a good part of his nights, randomly, in his company. Unfortunately for Dwayne, his fate was doomed because of toilet water and Cheet'O. However, fortunately for Dwayne, the two thugs waiting for Dwayne to return home two nights after the theft went unnoticed because Dwayne rarely used the front entrance. It was only late in the afternoon when leaving that the chase of Dwayne running from the hunter thugs would begin. A chase that ended in a crash. A chase that would end in confused shooting, and a chase that would leave two brothers from a different mother sprawled out on route-33, bleeding and clinging to life. Pebbles in a pond rippling toward one another.

Chapter 5

(Assassinating Birthdays)

The sun, although bright and shining, provided little heat this November morning. It rarely did so late in the month, but as the days get shorter, its appearance—if any—is a welcomed warmth all on its own. Mother prepared for the busy afternoon affair as Aaron buzzed from room to room with excitement of this special day as well as energy only a young boy of four can feel. He plays with toys that undoubtedly will be replaced after today's gift-giving ceremony, all the while anticipating and building higher and higher the expectations of the party to come. From the toy box to the floor of his room, from the floor to his box-spring-less bed, and back again. He is nothing less than a humming bird soaring from feeder to feeder.

Gloria and Betty Crocker begin the cakes preparation as Aaron enters the room. "Ma, is Billy Parknner comin'?" he asks, skidding to his knees and tucking tiny feet under an even tinier hiney.

"Yes Dear, I've told you three times already. Billy Park*er* will be here," she said, emphasizing the "er" in Parker.

"Billy Parkner's my bests friend, Ma," Aaron said, rolling his Tonka truck back and forth in his left hand, never removing his eyes from its make-believe tracks in the kitchen carpet, and never hearing the answer his mother has repeated.

"Yes, Aaron I know. Now try not to make a mess. We have a lot to do to get ready for your party," Gloria said, mixing measured ingredients of love, as only a mother can bake, for her youngest child.

For Gloria, the times between today and four years earlier have passed all too quickly. She ponders as she gazes down at Aaron in his Tonka truck world, *Each year seems shorter and shorter. It's nearly 1964 already.* She softly shakes her head from side to side in a "tisk tisk" fashion. *Where does the time go?*

For Aaron, four years have been nothing short of a lifetime. Every day a new adventure. So much to see and do, so much to find and learn. The days pass by in slow motion as the weeks take months to unfold. And the months— if you had to wait a month for something like a birthday party—at this age, the month would never pass at all.

Aaron's count down to this Friday's birthday bash began earlier in the week, somewhere in the hours between Sunday and Tuesday. He would hold his right hand at attention, then with deliberate and complete concentration, point to each finger (starting of course with the index) and count off the years he had lived. "One, two, three..." Then he would pause, look to see who's watching, and with a smile of excitement, with his ability to count to four and his anticipation on becoming four, he would screech, "Four!" as his whole-body jerks upward—an action you could only describe as a jump, if in fact his tiny feet had left the floor. The boiling point to all his expectations came at dinnertime, the very night before his big day.

"Pass the mash," Butch mumbles over a mouthful of Oh No Meatloaf. Mash, meaning mash potatoes, and pass, being a polite as a trucker can be, meaning "Gimme, gimme, and make it snappy. " No meal ain't complete without meat and tatoes," he said, accepting the bowl from Jared sitting directly to his left.

It was Malisa that came up with the name Oh No meatloaf, however it was Butch that pointed it out and made it stick. Once a week for as long as anyone could remember, meatloaf was in the Mills family meal rotation. And when someone would ask what's for dinner, and mother would say meatloaf, Malisa would stomp her foot in disgust, shrug her shoulders and whine, "Oh nooo, meatloaf!" Complaining, in part due to her little girl nature, but mostly in part to the fact she didn't like meatloaf, it was almost a comical routine that played out week after week as the family evolved. Who's on first? What's for dinner? Oh no, meatloaf?

The silverware chatters as everyone comes closer and closer to having their fill. An outside observer would see nothing more or less than a typical suburban family of five. Mother and father at each of the table's heads, the children poised in positions established long ago.

Aaron sits to Butch's right as Jared, directly across from Aaron, sits to Butch's left. Malisa is seated at mother's left alongside Aaron, and directly across from her is the only empty seat in the house. Most of the time, the larger portions of the meal found their way cluttered in front of the empty seat. It simply made good table sense. But it also made good table sense for Jared to become the designated waiter. Pass the peas, pass the tatoes, and pass the mash. All were directed to Jared, whether you directed your request to Jared or not. Consequently, Jared's meal was always interrupted, but for now Jared didn't mind, and it wasn't until years later that he would even notice, and it wasn't until years later that he would start to mind.

"Ma do you think I'm getten a G-Joe?" Aaron asked.

"GI Joe, stupid," Malisa said, pushing peas and meatloaf around her plate as she gives the illusion that she's eating her dinner.

"Don't call your brother stupid!" Gloria snaps, with an indication that she is going to strike, raising the back of her hand.

"Ma, I want a G-Joe like Jared's," Aaron continues, completely unaware of Malisa's insult and oblivious to his mother's response.

"We'll just have to wait and see, Honey," Gloria said, with a sweeter more caring tone.

Aaron wiggles in his seat with excitement. His eyes are glazed over with the thought of receiving exactly what he wants, which is what his young mind has concluded will happen as his head nods yes ever so slightly up and down.

"I'm gonna get a G-Joe like Jared's," he surmises, speaking aloud but talking only to himself.

"Don't count your chickens before they're hatched, Son," Butch says, using his fork to point at Aaron with a gesture that sends his message home.

A moment elapses before Aaron computes what his father had said, or more accurately, doesn't compute what his father had said. His face holds the stare of confusion as his simple-minded thoughts flip flop what he has heard.

Chickens? I'm getting a G-Joe like Jared's. I don't care about no chickens, he thinks, and he is seconds away from dismissing what his father has preached when Jared speaks up.

"He means like what Mom said. Just wait and see," Jared said, looking directly at Aaron, then slowly looking up toward Butch, all without moving his head and just rolling his eyes.

His instincts to explain things to his younger brother were more overpowering than his instincts to survive. He saw the confusions on Aaron's face, and he was quite aware the risk he was taking by helping to defuse it. Butch never said he didn't like the closeness these boys have shared, but it was something everyone could feel. He was jealous of the respect Aaron so eagerly gave to Jared, and it was easy for him to blame his eldest son exclusively for it. As soon as those words of clarity and compassion left Jared's mouth, he was regretting he ever spoke them. And although it was a small comfort for Jared to see Aaron plainly understand what he had said, by shaking his head up and down and then returning to his meal, it didn't help his own situation.

Butch turns his head slowly to his left, staring directly into Jared's eyes. His mouth begins to self-pick food lodged between his teeth. The high-pitched screeching sound from sucking trapped meatloaf free rings louder in his own head than to his family gathered around him. Jared's eyes find their way back to his plate as he to begin the practice of eating illusion.

"Well Jared here seems to know an awful lot he's not telling," Butch said with sarcasm as thick as the mush that's developed on Malisa's plate.

"Jared! Sit up straight, your father's talking to you," Gloria said, trying to both intervene the inevitable attack and become involved in the dialogue that's about to transpire.

"Why don't you tell us Jared what I mean to say," Butch continues, reaching for his cigarettes that are always close by. Tension begins to fill the dining area air as Butch circles his prey like the great white shark. Jared sits and stares at his plate; his mind races for a suitable response. There is none. Butch's insecurities about his relationship with Aaron are much too close to the surface of his thin skin. Regardless of Jared's response, Butch will strike. Again, like the great white, because even if it's not hungry, it cannot ignore an easy kill.

"Well? What exactly do I mean to say?"

"Um... I don't...know"

"You don't know. You seemed to know a minute ago."

" I.... ah..."

Jared fidgets both mentally and physically. Though his thoughts scramble in confusion from the attack at hand, he finds room to think of Aaron. Jared wishes he was anywhere but here. He wishes he were alone, just simply left alone. And it's this wish, being alone, that includes his brother. Jared's idea of being alone always includes Aaron. Aaron is in Jared's definition of being alone.

"You ahhh what?" Butch says, mocking the speechless boy in front of him.

"Butch, do you want me to save the rest of this or just throw it out?" Gloria interrupts. She points to the bowl holding the remainder of the mash potatoes. She has begun the clearing of the table, a task she will undoubtedly do alone, concentrating leftovers into Tupperware bowls.

Butch holds his smoking hand up. His cigarette balances between his index finger and his middle as he shakes his hand slightly, indicating the number one.

"In a minute," he says, giving clear direction with his tone—butt out!

He pulls his filter-less crutch into his lungs with a large deliberate drag. Pal Malls non-filters has been his brand of choice for as long as anyone can remember. He had started smoking when he was eight, hocking smokes where he could, but it didn't really become a steady habit until he was fifteen. It was then that he noticed something about people and their cigarettes. Some folks had 'em, some folks didn't, and the ones that didn't bummed from the ones that did. Unless of course you smoked something no one wanted to smoke. Pal Mal non-filters were as harsh a smoke Butch could find. Although they took some time getting used to, he found most folks wouldn't bother to bum one, and if they did, they only did so once.

He exhales his smoke in Jared's direction in an attempt to spark a response. The billowing cloud surrounds Jared's head as he squints his eyes to escape the smog.

"What's the matter Boy, cat got yo..."

"Ma, can I get chickens?" Aaron says, completely unaware of the tension he's defusing and oblivious to the attack the fearless shark has begun.

Malisa and mother laugh out loud, and even Butch chuckles slightly after comprehending what Aaron had said. He sat there as the minutes ticked by, thinking about birthday wants. Boxes wrapped with pretty red bows., cake and ice cream all you can eat, GI Joes, and of course chickens, and they all intertwined in his simple four-year-old mind. He liked chickens, he had thought, and his request to have some seemed perfectly normal. After all, tomorrow is his birthday.

"Haha…What a dope. Can I be excused?" Malisa said, removing herself from the table before Gloria had a chance to answer.

"No Dear, you cannot get chickens," Gloria said, smiling and looking deep into Aaron's eyes. He always made her laugh, and she loved that most about him. "Malisa I want you and your brother to clean that room of yours, do you hear me?" Gloria said to the exiting girl. "Jared, do a good job in there, do you understand me? Now hurry it up." Jared quickly removes himself from the clutches of the shark's jaws, and Butch almost says, "Sit down, I'm not done with you," but doesn't.

"I wanna help! " Aaron screams, pushing himself away from the table's edge.

"Aaron," mother says, snapping her fingers to get his attention. "Wipe your mouth, you have something."

"I wanna help, Ma."

"You can help. First wipe your mouth."

She points with her index finger toward the left side of his chubby-cheeked face. Aaron grabs the clean triangle-shaped napkin from under his plate's edge. He wipes his face quickly and inefficiently, barely removing the debris stuck to his face. He looks up to his mother, shaking his head vigorously up and down an eighth of an inch.

"Okay, you can go now," she says, smiling.

He crumbles the clean napkin and sets it carefully on his plate.

"Wait fer me!" he yells, running up the stairs. Thumpty thump, the sound of happy feet.

Gloria and Butch look at each other and sigh. Their sigh simply says, "Kids," in a way that all parents say, either out loud or to themselves. It's not a bad thing, just the space that lies between a child and an adult. Uncharted space in a galaxy of a mature world. These sighs say, "To be young and carefree. To have all our needs and wants handed to us." These sighs envy what they had as they realize those days are forever gone. "Kids," we sigh, rolling our eyes and suggesting that they're foolish. But who out there wouldn't want to be the fool again?

"I swear Butch, they're just growing up so fast," Gloria said, returning to her table-clearing chore.

"Just put all that stuff into that one bowl. I'll take it with me tomorrow for lunch."

"All of it in one? That's disgusting Butch."

"Hey, just kill it and grill it Babe. Anyway, I gotta eat on the road if I'm gonna make it back by Sunday."

"Do you have to drive straight through? I hate when you do that you know."

Butch crushes his cigarette into the scraps of his plate. The sizzling sound of the butt hisses to a stop.

"Babe, you know I have to if I wanna be back in time for Aaron's party. I mean, Jesus Christ I'm already gonna be two days late as it is." Butch said, standing and unbuckling the pressure that's developed around his waist. "Hey, you get that army guy like I told ya? I want ya to keep that one aside. That's the one I want to give him, you hear?"

"Yes Dear, I got it. He's gonna be very disappointed tomorrow. Are you sure that's the one you want to give him?" Gloria said. Her tone was to suggest some rethinking on Butch's part. Mother didn't need credit for a gift when she gave. The giving and happiness it gave was all she ever needed. Mother understood what it meant when they said, "It was better to give than to receive." Butch however, did not.

"Yes! Are you crazy? You heard how he goes on and on about that thing..."

"GI Joe."

"Yea yea yea, whatever. I wanna be the one that gives it to him. By him havin' to wait a couple more days will be even better. Jesus Christ Gloria don't fuck this up. Everyone knows wine's made fine through the course of time."

With his words of wisdom still echoing throughout the room, he makes his way to his favorite chair, but not before turning on the evening news.

There, he and Pal Mal will criticize Walter Cronkite and the idiot programmers at CBS until he eventually falls asleep. Gloria scrapes and combines, not without some criticism of her own. She thinks in total silence, *The big jerk shouldn't use that truck-driving gutter-mouth in this house, wine before its time...*

Then, quietly aloud to no one but the flies on the wall, she whispers, *Yea yea yea, Butch, whatever* as she alone finishes the chore of clearing the dinner table.

The electric buzzer of the stove's timer alarms mother that the cake is done. She and Aaron were just finishing the breezeway's decoration when the buzzer had rung. Now it was time to remove the cake (provided that it passed the toothpick test), let cool, and then switch from decorating the breezeway to decorating it.

The breezeway was the one room in the house Gloria had thought twelve boys could least destroy. Some had referred to it as a mudroom, while others called it the TV room, after of course, the family's second television was bought. But the Mills, like most in the neighborhood, referred to this cozy living space as the breezeway. It was a nine-by-twelve-foot room that separated the garage from the original door that lead to the driveway. The builder had designed all the houses in the track to be very similar, while the garage and room that connected itself to the house was the homeowner's own lay out. Some built a one-car garage and a large breezeway, while some like the Mills built a two-car garage and a small breezeway. Some built their room as wide as the garage, giving the house a much bigger appearance, and still others chose a smaller size with recessed doorways and windows, which gave the two structures a broken-up or separated look.

Trees and shrubs or the color of your house was really the only difference among all the homes in this newly built track, but the breezeway and additional garage made your home unique. What you did with this space made your family unique. For Jared and Aaron later that day, the breezeway, and what *they* did, made their relationship unique.

"It's ready!" Aaron screams, dropping all that he's doing and running the short distance from the breezeway to the kitchen.

"No! No, don't...ohh," Gloria said, as the ribbon Aaron was supposed to hold falls to the floor and unwinds.

"Maaa its ready!" He repeats, standing in front of and peeking through the stove's glass door. The distance he stands from the oven is a good two feet. He remembers being told when he was younger—barely two "Don't touch, hot!" and there has never been an ugly incident that warrants such caution now. However, Aaron has always been careful when it came to heat, even to the point of over-cautious behavior. Anytime he passed by the stove, moving from kitchen to breezeway or vice-versa, he would cover his cheeks with the palms of his hands. It was a humorous behavior for the family to watch, since the stove was located alongside the door between the two rooms. But Gloria and Jared speculated on his curious habit. "His face is the closest thing to the heat, seeing as how he's only a foot-and-a-half tall."

"Maaa!"

"I'm coming, I'm coming already," Gloria says, doing her best to salvage the mess her son had left. She enters the kitchen to see Aaron in his comical stance: tiny, cute hands squished tightly against chubby cheeks, eyes opened wide with excitement, and his feet dancing in place with the urgency the situation demands.

"I swear Aaron, you're going to explode from excitement if you don't try and calm down," Mother said as she reached for oven mitts her husband so graciously had given her on their seventh wedding anniversary.

"Now stand clear, Honey. I'm gonna open the door," she continued, as the heat and aroma of freshly baked cake fills the room with a welcomed wash.

Aaron runs from the kitchen screeching with excitement. His party is ever so close, and all the good things that were promised are less than two hours away: presents wrapped in colorful surprise, games like pin the tail on the donkey how many jellybeans in the jar? And of course, his friends Eddy Pretko and Tony Maleto, the two McKenna boys David and Ronny, Tommy Backus and Ray Pasagno, and one of those Horton's. Aaron was never really sure which one was his friend. There were so many so close in age, he didn't know which one he always played with or which one it was that he liked. Then there were the Eggleston's, Keith and Mark, and who can forget Billy Parker, Aaron's "bestest" friend in the whole wide world. Everything he had waited for was coming together. Everything that he had thought about for the past week-

and-a-half was near climax. And it would have been his greatest day to date had the phone on the wall never rang or the shots down in Dallas had never been fired.

The first call came to the Mills' home about an hour after the fatal shot. Although the two events were in fact separate from each other, they held the same devastating effects. One to a nation that was excited and hopeful, balancing on the edge of great things to come; the other to a young boy of western New York, also excited and also on the edge of great things to come.

He stood on tiptoes at the family room's picture window, watching and waiting, vaguely hearing the phone ring somewhere in the background of his mind. His thoughts are focused, zeroed in on the one thing that's consumed him and that one thing only.

"They should be coming any minute," Aaron said, repeating what his mother had told him moments ago.

Gloria stands at the opening that divides the two rooms. Her right hand holds her small waist as her forearm crosses her stomach. Her left hand covers her mouth, as if to prevent something from going in, or as in the case of all bad news, something from coming out. Her eyes are large and tear-filled as she leans to the wall's edge. Mother will forever remember this sight. Aaron standing on the tips of his toes, watching and waiting for friends that will never show. And it's this view that she will describe every November 22nd when someone asks, "Where were you when Kennedy was shot?" She is about to muster the courage of informing her son, when the phone rings again.

"Hello." Her voice is pale and uninviting.

"Gloria? It's Rose. I take it you heard the news."

"Hi Rose. Yes I heard, everyone's been calling."

"I'm sorry, but I think you can understand if Billy and I can't make it."

"Yes, yes of course, I, ah...I don't think it would be right to have a party."

"How's he taking it? Billy's pretty upset."

Gloria slowly turns around, bringing her left middle finger to the front of her teeth. She would have bitten her nail had she not broken that habit some time ago. It occurs to her that the faint crying she's been hearing in the background is little Billy Parker, and a large lump develops in her throat as she notices Aaron standing and starring at his mother squirming on the phone.

"I. Ah," Gloria starts to say as she looks down at Aaron and deep into his puppy dog eyes. He senses something is wrong. He's young and has no perception of time, but he's no fool, and he can plainly see the troubled look written all over his mother's face.

"Look, Rose, I gotta a go." Her voice is shaky as the thoughts of disappointment swirl through her mind. Her eyes never leave Aaron's as she blindly fumbles to hang up the phone. And the words she'll use to let down her son sound shallow and without reason as she flip-flops them over and over in the corner of her mind.

Then, there's Aaron. Young, perceptive Aaron. Moments from crying Aaron. Happy fuck you birthday, Aaron. He stands and stares as his mother kneels before him. He listens as she explains, "This man, the president, he's very important."

He listens to all her reasons why tomorrow, Saturday, is a better day, and he wonders why someone who's shot in Texas can stop him from having his birthday party. Especially when he doesn't even know what Texas is? Through all the reasoning and all the explaining, all Aaron really hears is that no one's coming. No games, no presents, no friends, and that's when he bursts into tears. That's when Gloria tries to hold him, and that's when he runs to his room.

What Gloria tried to explain, Aaron could never understand. How can she reason with this small child of four? How can she make the unfair seem rational? Everything she heard herself trying to explain she herself imagined hearing. Everything she heard in this imaginary state made no sense at all. The president is very important. Okay, so what's a president? He's a good man; he runs the country. If he were so good, why'd they shoot him? Some people are just bad; they don't do the right thing. Oh, you mean like people that promise little boys birthday parties?

Mother too could not hold back her tears. He had run to his room in an attempt to hide from the truth, and when he did, she collapsed from her erect kneeling position to her emotionally-drained kneeling position. His disappointments, his inability to understand, all of it pushed her toward the floor as she wept. Mother felt his pain. All mothers bleed when their child bleeds. All mothers cry when their children cry. And all mothers know what it's like to hurt.

Aaron's room, now cleaner than normal, was not accustomed to such crying and pain. Most of the crying these walls had heard was from boo boos or frustration—the whining crying kind of frustration, like when Malisa wouldn't give him what he wants or when it's way past his bedtime even though he pleads, "I'm not tired." But this crying, this was different. This was genuine disappointment. This cry was very real.

He laid face down diagonally on his bed. The colorful pillowcase that he had clutched became tear-soaked and snot-covered. His left leg bounced rhythmically to his wailing cries as his thoughts jumbled and swelled. This is how he spent the better part of an hour. This is how he released all that bottled excitement. And this, this is how Jared had found him.

The bus ride was buzzing with excitement of an early dismissal. Children laughed and carried on in a more rambunctious manner than normal, even for a Friday. It hadn't occurred to Jared that Aaron's party would be canceled. He, like so many of the other school children, was caught up in the moment. Some kids, older high scholars, understood the severity of the assassination, but others still wished aloud that someone were shot every school day. When Jared had entered the breezeway, he knew. And the first thoughts that entered his mind were the "*how's.*" How'd he take the news of his party being canceled? How's he holding out and doing right now? And of course, the one how that's consumed Jared his entire life: how can *I* make him feel better?

Gloria sat in the family room watching as the news slowly unfolds. Her butt cheeks held onto the sofa's edge as the television brought the images from Texas right to her hungry eyes.

Malisa entered the house just seconds before Jared, and although she was home an hour or so earlier than usual, her after-school routine remained the same, falling like stacked dominos all lined in a row.

Jared paused to digest the decorations that hung, all of which we're frozen in time. Paper plates that never saw cake or ice cream. Cups that never held grape punch or cherry soda. And a caricature of a donkey, hanging on the wall no more than two feet from the floor, smiling and appearing quite happy, although tailless.

He passes the stove that baked the untasted cake. He passes the spot where Gloria knelt and wept. He quickly leans into the family room, momentarily being drawn into the Zenith's picture and sound.

"Ma, where's Aar..." he said, without finishing.

"He's in his bedroom," Gloria said, raising her right arm in a fashion that is to shoe a pesky old fly.

Jared slaps at the walls that divides the two rooms. This action confirms what his mother had told him and at the same time awakens Gloria from her dazed and consumed world. He walks down the short hall facing Aaron's door, a hollow door that appears to have been slammed shut. He passes the bathroom, the first door on the right, and he passes his parents' room, the second door on the left. He stands before the door, turning his head to the right and concentrating on listening. His left hand balances in a cupped form inches from the door's knob as his left ear floats no more than a paper's thickness from the door's surface. The imagination begins.

Jungle sounds echo somewhere in the bowels of Jared's mind. The rarest of all cuckoo birds sings its familiar song far away in the distance. The high-pitch cry of the spider monkey squeals, fleeing in panic. And the sound of heat. Hot, sticky, humid heat, screams almost unnoticed. His imaginary world has placed him deep behind enemy lines in the heart of an imaginary jungle. Costa Rica, the Amazon, or even Vietnam could be the geographical location entangled within Jared's thoughts. The bamboo hut before him holds the one prisoner he must always free. As the air he breathes sizzles and bakes while the mercury reaches 115 degrees, he visualizes Aaron trapped inside. A makeshift cage of sticks and twine. Rats scurrying about trying to get a bite of young, trembling flesh. And flies. Hundreds of buzzing, crawling, disease-carrying flies trying desperately to soak up droplets of sweat from the prisoner's tortured little body. Jared's imaginary army fatigues are always the same. Multi-colored, green camouflage pants torn at the knees. Matching long-sleeved, buttoned up shirt with the sleeves rolled up to his massive biceps. The nametag "MILLS" embroi-

dered on a patch above the left breast pocket. G. I. Jared. An elite special forces expert no enemy has ever captured or controlled.

A young boy with an active imagination, soaring through the clouds of a make-believe sky. It is Jared and Jared alone that must save Aaron. It taking only seconds for him to leave the real world as he stands before the bedroom door, and as the door swings open, even less time to return.

The first steps into the small boy's room are with direction and purpose. Enter the room fluidly, side-stepping to the right. Close the door gently and step back to the left. The room itself is nearly divided in half, one side brimming with the afternoon light that shines through the west side window, the other shaded in darkness where Aaron lies askew on his pint-size bed. Jared stood and looked as Aaron rhythmically bounced a leg up and down on the edge of his bed. His crying has subsided but the pillowcase his face remains buried in is tear-soaked and snot-ridden. Jared stands tall, pausing only for a moment, bathed in the afternoon's light. He turns over the logic once in his mind, like the first pull of a cold gasoline-powered engine.

Aaron remains unconcerned that someone has entered the room. He had barely flinched when the bedroom door had opened and then shut. And the crying that has all but consumed him these last two hours is nothing more than irregular breathing. A four-year-old minute elapses before he is curious to whom it is that stands behind him.

"Happy birthday Aaron," Jared said, very monotone and almost questioning in delivery.

Aaron rolls quickly over to his backside. For an instant he almost forgets his pain and suffering. He is always excited to see Jared is home. He has grown quite accustomed to the lessons and games that follow his brother's school day. Their eyes meet as Jared walks the divided room's floor.

"Happy birthday," he repeats, this time with more care and enthusiasm.

"It's not a birthday, Jared," Aaron softly says as his lower lip puffs inward and out with every breath he takes.

"Why sure it's your birthday, Bud. Today will always be your birthday."

"It's not," Aaron replies, as his young, tearless eyes drop to his chest.

Jared understands what his only brother means when he simply says, "It's not." This child cannot articulate and describe how he feels about the party that almost was. He is unable to express the disappointment he feels from expectations never fulfilled. He understands the child because he's a child himself. He too has kept it simple when trying to express disappointments, and Jared knows all too well what it's like to be left unfulfilled.

"Aaron..." he begins to say as he sits beside him lying on his bed.

"It's not fair what happened..." The tone in his voice is that of a wise old man.

"I know, but tomorrow is just a day away," He pats at his thin, young thigh.

"You'll have your party tomorrow, I promise," Jared said.

Somewhere a clock's second-hand ticks, five, six, seven. Aaron lifts his head and looks deep into his brother's eyes.

"We can still make the best of today... You know, if you want to," Jared said.

Eight, nine, ten.

"Or"…" Jared pauses, licking his upper lip as if the idea he now has was there all along and all he needed to do was taste it. Jared is not yet fourteen, his birthday nearly two months away. However, his care and love for Aaron is parent like.

"We can sit in here and cry some more...Ya know, if you want to."

Aaron blinks twice as often as needed as he contemplates what Jared had said. He continues to look into Jared's eyes, but Jared can plainly see he is looking straight through him. Jared pats his thigh one more time as if to comfort a faithful old dog.

"What's it gonna be, Bud?" Jared asks.

"Sit in here some more and cry, or make the best of today and have some fun?"

Jared watches as Aaron's eyes return to focus. Once again Aaron sees Jared sitting before him.

"Whatever you decide, that's what we'll do," Jared said.

He skootches to a sitting position. He sniffles and wipes at the excess snot that's developed in his nose. Aaron sighs with concern when he asks, "Are you gonna cry Jared?"

"Only if you want me to," Jared said, slowly shaking his head up and down, so as Aaron is to understand what he says is very true.

Aaron again drops his eyes to his lap as his thoughts fold over and over the options that sit before him. He believes what Jared has told him because Jared has never let him down. Everything Aaron remembers Jared ever telling him has always come true, mostly because Jared is careful not to make promises to events he cannot control, but also because Aaron's memory is really only accurate to about two weeks past.

If Jared says my party's tomorrow, then my party's tomorrow, his thoughts conclude. *And if Jared says were gonna have some fun today, then were gonna have some fun today.* He wipes at his snot-filled nose one last time using only the sleeve of his left arm. Just then the thought that scares Aaron more now than even when he heard it the first time swallows his mind. *If Jared says he's gonna cry, then Jared's gonna cry.*

The genuine love he feels for his brother is displayed in the thoughts of this young boy's mind. Regardless of the disappointments he's felt in these last few hours, the last thing he wanted was for Jared to cry. This is what scared him. This is what drove his decisions, and this is how GI Jared would always win. Jared would use the love he knew Aaron felt for him to divert the pain he had felt.

Softly and with a shaky, unstable voice, Aaron speaks.

"I don't want you to cry, Jared," Aaron said, sniffling back tears and more unwanted snot.

"Well let's go have some fun then," Jared said, as perky as a cat-nipped kitten.

The mourning from the death of a party was all but over, and the smile that returned to the four-year-old's face was ear to ear. Jared too could only smile; an overwhelming sense of accomplishment glazed his face to see that the prisoner was finally free. The two boys sprung from the box-springless bed.

"Come on," Jared said. "I have something I want to show you."

Aaron's curiosity perked slightly, and the tip of his tongue protruded from between his lips.

"But," Jared continued. "It's a secret."

"Secret!" Aaron interrupts in a screeching young voice "That means you can't tell 'em."

"That's right!" Jared said. He was pleased the pupil remembered and reaching out to rub at Aaron's head. Teacher and student off on another adventure, the two bolted from the divided room's light.

Jared was six when the Mills family added the garage and breezeway to their suburban home. He vaguely remembered the work crew that constructed the enormous structure. When you're six, every structure being constructed was enormous. He remembers the arm that dug the foundation. The man that controlled it called it a Cat. He remembers the truck that poured the concrete floor, its huge belly turned and turned. The man that controlled it called it "a piece of shit," and he remembers the gray, muddy slop slowly crawling down the shiny metal shoots. Oddly enough, what he remembers most about that day is that he would be in deep trouble if he had gotten his boots as dirty as the men playing in the mud.

"Jared, you stay the fuck off that floor!" Butch had barked.

Now six years later, he stands at its two-car opening with his favorite person in the entire world.

"Step inside here Aaron while I close these here doors," Jared said, reaching for the overhead handle that just one year earlier was nearly out of reach all together. Aaron jumps the crack that separates the driveway and garage floor. His party is all but forgotten as his attention is drawn to Jared's commands.

"We gotta hide cause of the secret?" Aaron asks, never once looking to see where Jared is, just continuing to jump, like an inexperienced frog leaping from lily pad to lily pad.

"Yep," Jared replies, pulling the second garage door down its metal tracks. The oversized door springs twang and uncoil, singing their vibrating song.

"We can't let anyone see, so you gotta' do good and keep this a secret."

"Yep," Aaron says, mimicking what Jared had just said. "Secret can't tell 'em."

"Look at me," Jared orders. He stands directly in front of Aaron no more than a foot away.

Aaron freezes from his jumping world. He is well aware of the difference between casual conversation and a direct order. Not from fear, but respect, is why Jared will get his immediate attention. From his crunched up and squatted position he slowly stands erect, looking directly into the general's eyes.

"Don't tell no one about my secret hiding place. I'll take you there, but you just can't tell, okay?" Jared said, but not like the order just seconds ago. This was a plea. A plea to understand.

Aaron of course couldn't and wouldn't understand for a long time. He didn't understand that Jared needed a place to go. He couldn't understand that sometimes Jared needed a place to hide. He would never understand how Jared stood alone among his family and friends. Gloria, Malisa, and even Butch knew that Jared was different. But Aaron only saw his older brother as a hero, a someone he wanted to be, and in a strange twist of irony, Jared felt the same about Aaron. A someone he wanted to be.

"I promise," Aaron said. "I won't ever tell." He shook his tiny head slowly up and down. He clenched his lips tight as if to confirm that not a word will ever slip out.

Jared too shook his head up and down, and he was convinced the secret would not be revealed. He walked toward the garden hose, stopping only once to look around. He turned his head from side to side, checking like a cat burglar would be before he steals. There, on an old tire rim fastened to the garage wall, twenty feet of garden hose hung loosely inches from the floor. The original design of the house had the water spigot attached to the wall were the breezeway is attached now. During the remodeling, Butch had demanded it be moved to the inside of the garage. This made no logical sense. The builder had felt that the best spot was the house's back wall. This, he concluded, would be the easiest access to a would-be garden. Or, if the homeowner someday chose, a pool. The front of the house had a water spigot close to its driveway for washing cars, so the next best spot was the house's back wall.

But Butch, for no other reason than to have the final say, said, "No! I want it here," pointing to the very spot Jared and Aaron now stood.

Aaron watched as Jared removed an obscure-shaped piece of paneling that was sandwiched between the tire rim and wall. This ugly, old, puke-green piece of paneling was deliberately placed between the rim and wall some time ago. A poor man's answer to home repair. It was Gloria, on a hot

July afternoon that caused the needed repair. However, it was Butch that had answered it.

The day was humid and sticky as mother rushed from errand to errand. In her haste, as she attempted to back into the half of garage she referred to as her "spot," she inadvertently caused a chain reaction of debris that punctured a hole into the gypsum board siding. Siding that divided the garage and breezeway. This hole, about eighteen-inches round, was within inches of the tire rim that held the twenty feet of garden hose. Butch simply grabbed whatever was nearest—in this case the puke green paneling—and wedged it between the rim and wall. It covered the hole and his concerns regarding it. All that remained was the ammunition it provided in criticizing mother's driving skills some more.

"Stay right here one second," Jared said, crawling headfirst into what appeared to be a dark, bottomless hole.

Aaron just stood and marveled at what he was currently seeing. Like so many people before him, he simply assumed that paneling never moved, like a billboard that's never changed. It disappears in the landscape we expect to see, always there but never noticed.

Less than a moment elapses when the dark hole is softly lit. Aaron can vaguely see that there's some kind of space down that mysterious hole. He is unsure as to what he is looking at, and he is confused as to where Jared had gone. Jared's head and hands pop into view.

"Come on, I will help you," he said, extending his arms to guide his young follower.

"Where is it?" Aaron asks, slightly apprehensive upon advancing.

"It's okay, it's only the room under the breezeway," Jared said. "You have to hurry. I don't want anyone to see." Again Jared extended his arms, trying to entice his young partner in crime.

Aaron's reluctance to advance vanished like the rabbit in a magician's hat. He was excited about the secret Jared was sharing. Although he would only tell one person (Nora) his entire life about this secret hiding place, when he chose to do so it no longer mattered. "Jared's Lost World," is what Aaron called it. Nora never understood the term.

The crawl space beneath the breezeway was Jared's secret world. As much that it was an accident that lead Gloria to produce it, it was as much an accident that leads Jared to discover it. It was quite the adventure the first time he had crawled in that dark hole. But as time passed, it became home for Jared. A somewhere he could go. A comfortable safe haven the outside world could not infiltrate. He was both smart and careful when it came to his secret place. Smart, because he furnished it with other people's garbage. No one ever notices when their garbage is missing. Careful, because if there was the slightest chance someone would learn of his rue, he would simply stay away, sometimes for days on end.

The light he had lit before Aaron had joined him was a Superman light. A porcelain superhero lamp every kid in America at one time owned. Superman, standing in his customary stance, wearing a shiny blue leotard jump suit, a large capital "S" prominently displayed on its chest. Its left arm and would be flowing in the breeze cape broken clean off, undoubtedly the reason it found its way into the McKenna's trash. The carpet scraps that covered the dirt floor of the Sherlock's former dining room, coffee cans and old glass jars, broken played-out toys, and used up small appliance all found their way to Jared's secret place.

Aaron stood in amazement at the space and all its collectibles. The room looked well lived in, not like somewhere that was recently discovered.

"Step over there," Jared ordered as he attempted to fidget with the paneling to cover their tracks.

Aaron easily walked the crawl space erect, something Jared had never done. The floor joists of the breezeway's floor were no more than an inch from Aaron's head, but the space between them, every sixteen inches, was more than enough clearance.

"I marked the inside of this board, so I can tell when it's lined up," Jared said as he shifted and slid the paneling from side to side.

"It has to be just right, or someone could tell."

He was clever to trace the hole's shape on the backside of the puke-green paneling, and gluing two small blocks of wood within its traced boundaries made it easy for him to manipulate its position. Although it wasn't exactly as Butch had installed it, it was guaranteed to be the same time after time when he moved it. Satisfied, he turns, crosses his legs and sits Indian-style facing Aaron.

"Well, what do ya think?" He asks.

"I won't tell 'em. Not no one," Aaron said, his eyes bulging with conviction.

"I know Bud, that's good, but do you like it?" Jared said, drawing out the word *like*.

"It's a good secret, Jared." Aaron said.

The two boys smiled at one another with the smirky looks of con-man sitting at a poker table; two long time players cheating the unfortunate gamblers around them.

"I have something for you, Bud," Jared said, crawling on his hands and knees across the carpeted dirt floor.

"For me?" Aaron asked, one moment wondering why, in the next realizing it's his birthday. "What is it now?"

"Yes Sir," Jared said, digging through piles of debris and junk. "It's your birthday ain't it?"

"Yes Jared, what is it? What is it now?" he said, as his tiny fingers wiggled with excitement, perhaps flexing for the gift's unwrapping. His eyes widened as his brother suddenly stopped searching, and he leaned in a little closer. Trying to sneak a peek over Jared's right shoulder.

"Hear it is!" Jared said, quickly spinning around for Aaron to see. The erratic movement startled and surprised the younger boy, but the item that Jared held in his hand surprised Aaron even more.

Jared's voice was loving and gentle as he held out the GI Joe in his hands.

"Happy birthday Aaron," He said, holding the toy soldier in his cupped hands, passing it over, as if it were liquid gold.

"It's your G Joe, Jared," Aaron said, almost afraid to take what was presented to him.

"I know; I want you to have it," he said, "Cause it's your birthday and all." Again he extended his arms, gesturing for Aaron to take hold.

Aaron slowly lifted the soldier figure, never once taking his eyes off the priceless gift.

"Whoa," he slowly said, with more exhale than vocal sound.

It was the best gift he had ever received. His reaction just hung there like cigar smoke long after it's been extinguished. When his eyes finally lifted from his prized possession, he locked eyes with *his* superhero. Both boys held the stare of complete satisfaction. Aaron from birthday desires fulfilled, Jared from the one who fulfilled them.

"Thank you, Jared," Aaron said, pausing only for a moment for those words to settle before lunging foreword into Jared's arms. The impact nearly forced Jared over as the two boys feverishly hugged one another. Jared patted Aaron's back seconds before they separated from their emotional exchange.

"You're welcome, Bud. I knew you'd love it," he said, sniffling and wiping at his nose and face. "Now, do you want to play army?" he asked.

"Yep!" Aaron exclaimed, jerking upward in an excited, half-hearted jump.

"Careful, you don't want to hit your hea..." Jared suddenly stopped. He pressed his index finger against his lips, quietly shushing and whispering when he spoke.

"What was that?" he asked, turning his head slightly sideways trying to exaggerate his power to hear.

"I didn't hear nuffin'" Aaron said, confused from his brother's actions.

"I think it's communists," he whispered.

The imagination begins.

Jared would narrate his make-believe world as Aaron willfully played along, and the two boys would enjoy their fantasy world the rest of that fateful day. GI Jared barking orders to his one-man platoon, private Aaron, who respectfully obeyed his only higher in command. They played in a world were neither birthdays nor commanders-in-chief were ever assassinated. For Aaron, it was the end of a perfect day. For Jared, however, he would later have only one regret concerning this day.

He simply didn't listen.

Chapter 6

(The Lost World)

An asteroid the size of Kansas falls silently through the darkness of space. The ragged, sharp edges of this blistered, lifeless planet pass constellations and stars, most half its size and weight. An orbiting satellite monitors and informs a handful of Washington's elites of its inevitable flight path. In a tax-paid room, a letter is drafted to prepare the ill-fated. They never even saw it coming.

Aaron rummages under his bed, first on all fours, then flat on his belly with only his feet protruding the bed's edge. His bedroom is virtually un-Changed from the day Jared had saved him from assassination. The differences from that day to this would produce a shorter list than the similarities. Wall paint the same. Bed location the same. Carpet, blinds, and dresser all the same. In fact, old toys and even some of those items are the same.

"Maaa!" Aaron yells, the sound completely adsorbed in the mattress above his head.

"Ma! have you seen my magnify glass?" He continues squirming his slender torso out from under his bed.

He sits with his legs crossed under his buttocks and listens for mother's reply. His door is half-open and half-closed, but later in Aaron's life he would always refer to the door, as well as the glass, half-open or half-full, of course depending only on which he was referring too.

"Ma?" he repeats, only softer because now he really hears.

When Aaron thinks back to this day, he recalls how all along he had heard the crying from the other room. Before he had looked under his bed, in the back of his mind he had heard the tears and sorrow that filtered down the hall. He thinks he even heard it before he checked the shelf in his closet or the bottom drawer to his only dresser that had never held cloth. But only now when he stops to listen does he hear mother and Melissa's sobs. He walks in disbelief down the hall toward the kitchen. The day's light is fading somewhere in the West, and the hall seems darker and longer than ever before. He stops at the hall's edge and sees his mother and sister seated at the table weeping and consoling one another. On the table is the day's mail. Two unopened Mastercard bills, a colored grocery flyer educating the household of this week's sales, and of course an opened Western Union letter informing the ill-fated that an asteroid the size of Kansas has just hit the Mills' world opened. Private Jarred William Mills has died during combat in Vietnam.

Mother looks up her tear-covered face and sees, now, her only son standing at the hall's edge. The pain and loss Aaron witnesses in his mother's eyes will haunt him the rest of his life. Mother was from that day forward a shell of her former self. She would over-compensate the love she had always felt for both Aaron and Melissa. Aaron would think the love from mother had changed from something great to something unknown. He would never describe it as bad or unwanted—just different—and this confused his young mind and heart from that day forward. Even Melissa and Aaron's relationship changed. For Aaron she was still his big sister that was always there for him to converse or fight with, but now he looked and perhaps guarded his emotions in the event that maybe she would die. Thus, Aaron concluded that the asteroid had taken more than the world Jarred and he once had. It in fact destroyed all the worlds he interacted with—forever.

Gloria reaches her arms out toward Aaron and motions with all ten fingers to come to her as she explodes in even greater sorrow and grief. Aaron, like a zombie without thought or feeling, slowly walks to the mother he no longer knows. Melissa collapses to the floor of mother's feet, and she too explodes in more tears. The pain they all feel from a fucking piece of paper is more real than the life any of them have ever felt. This is the moment when all is lost.

When love, the most powerful force, has nowhere to go. When all that mattered and all there ever was means nothing, and you and every ounce of what you thought you were is gone and means nothing. You will never be the same, and whether you're ready or not, the storm of change has just blown in. He's gone, and words mother uses to tell Aaron will never be repeated or remembered. Aaron's days and weeks to follow will also be black and dark. Shock from the news has cleared his ability to retain information. Thus, his memories of the remainder of that day as well as the days that followed are bits and pieces of other people's recollections. Someone had said that Aaron had laid on the kitchen floor for hours, but Aaron doesn't remember. Someone had said Butch would later carry him to his bed, where he would sleep without a thought or dream, but Aaron doesn't remember. Some would say this is when Aaron Mills became a runner, but Aaron… Aaron doesn't know what he's become.

An optimist might say that luck was with them regarding Butch. Butch had just finished a four-day trucking run that covered some 3,400 miles. The day the ill-fated envelope was opened, he was only 47 minutes from home, or as Butch would have said if asked, "My 10-77 (ETA) is only 30 mikes." Consequently, when he did walk into his once-happy home he found all three of the people he expected to be busy living out their lives as they always do huddling around the kitchen table. He opened the door and stood for a moment in the breezeway. He spun his keys in his left hand like a gunslinger twirling his six-shooter. He looked down at the shoes and sneakers piled in front of his walking path that would lead him into the kitchen. A question that has entered his mind for what seems like a thousand times, *Why on earth can't they toss their shoes over there?* he wonders looking to his right a mere four feet from his walking path. As quickly as the question is asked, again he dismisses the possible answer as well as the idea to repeat himself to his family. Butch steps over the sneakers and shoes and stands at the opening that separates the breezeway and kitchen. Gloria, Melissa, and Aaron hardly even notice their father has just entered the room. He stares at the three most important people in his world and immediately recognizes their pain. Like his own eighteen-wheeled rig that never slowed or diverted from its chartered course when he had struck a white-tailed deer in the mountains of Pennsylvania, Butch is struck with the pain of reality. It is at this moment that Butch, the truck driving, ball-scratching, filterless Pal-Mal smoking, bad mouthed, news critiquing, steak and potato father of three does something unlike Butch. He becomes his family's rock. Maybe it's the genuine pain and suffering he sees in all that is left of their family of five, or maybe it's the guilt he will try to suppress for not loving Jared as he did the three he stands before now. Or maybe it's because we all do the unexpected under traumatic situations in our lives. Or maybe, just maybe, for Butch, it's all three. He walks to the trio of mourners and reads the opened letter. He kneels beside his loving wife and holds her with such love and compassion that Gloria is moved to even greater flows of tears. As he hugs and consoles her, he reaches down to Melissa's back and rubs it gently, turning his head in the direction of his only son. Aaron lies on the floor in a ball of pain and grief. His teachings from Jared had taught him to recognize reality. It is these lessons that have made him mature at a faster rate than most his age. But also true is that these lessons have molded his mind and thoughts to the reality of the situation at hand. *Jared is gone forever, and I will never see him again,* his young mind repeats. *Jared is gone forever, and I will never see him again,* he says again and again in his shock-stricken thoughts. *Jared is gone, Jared is gone, Jared is gone.* Over and over again he lies in his reality and repeats the lesson at hand. Jared taught this mental lesson of reality repeating just a few short years ago. Jared had said it will help you heal and act on the facts at hand, that understanding and repeating what the facts are in your head can help you conclude what needs doing to resolve or understand any situation. Jared himself used this technique to discipline himself for life's cruel inevitabilities. So, in his grief, Aaron listens once more to Jared's lesson. Once more he repeats in his mind what Jared had told him about this mental strategy to cope and to persevere. He just lies there repeating over and over in the bowls of his own grieving thoughts, *Jared is gone, Jared is gone…"*

In the days that followed, an uniformed young man visited the Mills' home to give his respects and answer any questions the Mills family might have. Butch fielded all that was needed and handled the funeral arrangements that would follow. Aaron only recalls how old the man that ran the funeral parlor was and thought how he had wished that he was the one that died and not his only brother. Other than that childish wish, he has simply very little memories from the days and weeks that followed. One unfortunate item that had stayed with Aaron his entire life was the letters. Not just the letters that came semi-regularly while Jared was in combat but the seven letters that came after Jared was dead. Four were addressed to the entire family, and it took mother twenty-six years to even start to read one. When the second line of Jared's letter read, "This war is very real," Gloria put the letter down and wept. She would not attempt to read any of it again for another six years. Fortunately, before mother herself would pass, all the letters Jared wrote were read. This action did not help mother in her loss of her eldest son, but it did help Aaron & Malisa. Truth be told, this is the only reason mother would ever suffer from one child and the loss to help another and their ability to cope. The other three where addressed to Aaron directly, and one even said on the envelope, "For Aaron's eyes only." This handwritten instruction was clearly visible right under the word "FREE" where a stamp would be needed if it was not a G.I. letter's home. Stamps were something the United States Postal Service did not need or want in the era of war. Still, letters took weeks to find family members and the same for the return letters to the soldiers in the bush. Ironically during that time, the more a civilian wrote their GI, the greater the likelihood a letter would find its way. The only letter worse than none at all for the grunt where the hundreds of "Dear John" letters that found their way to an unsuspecting Marine. These heart-breaking letters from girlfriends or wives back home informing them of an affair or pending split sent many a young man in depression and sometimes death. Jared had no such love awaiting his return other than his brother and family. Malisa, however, would learn all too late of several school girls that thought Jared was cute. But this knowledge did nothing for Malisa's grief and in the years to follow in fact made her even more sad (if that was possible?) for her older brother.

Aaron sits on his bed and looks at the three letters addressed to him alone. He knows he will open each one and read them on this day but does not know how much he will do so in the decades to follow. As he stares at the letters out of their envelopes, he notices the dates in the upper-right corners stamped by the postal service. All three are the same dates, but clearly one envelope, the one that instructs for Aaron's eyes only, looks older, more yellowed, and well-traveled. He knows Jared, he knows Jared will always start his writings with the day, month, and year in the upper-right corner of his letter. All he has to do is open all three and read them in chronological order. However, it is this thought process that is keeping Aaron from opening any at the moment.

Butch taps quietly on the door's frame leading to Aarons room. For Aaron, there is no way of telling how long Dad stood and watched his only son staring at the three letters in thought. "You okay son?" Butch asks, almost apologetic for the interruption. Aaron snaps from his gazed, overanalyzing trance and turns to look at Butch. For a very long frozen moment, neither say a word and simply look at one another. Aaron whispers, "I don't know which one to open first."

Butch for a spit second barely hears what Aaron said and almost responds with a robotic, "What," but then just as quickly he understands and says nothing. Butch gives a very slow and deliberate nod, as if to convey *Yes, I understand*, as his eyes begin to swell with tears. Aaron has yet to see Dad cry but somehow knows it surely took place frequently since long before this moment. Other than the silent nod, Butch simply taps the door's frame once more with half the strength and sound and slips away. Aaron returns to his glare, staring at the letters, which look back at him, and he begins to cry.

These quiet moments of pain between loved ones lost played out in cities and towns long before the war and long after Vietnam. Pain is something we cannot avoid. Hurt is a drink we drink until drunk on more than one occasion. We bathe in its tragedy, consume the fire of its sale, and walk until we crawl in its sorrow. It misses none of us, but this provides no comfort in the moment.

After Aaron Mills finds the courage to open each letter, reads them in succession of time written, and digests the contents from his lost brother, he develops at this very early age the idea of a list in the event of his own death. A list of instructions much like Jared's and the hidden tin under the breezeway covered with dirt. A map to such a tin was all that the coded letter for Aaron's eyes included.

Aaron would forever treasure this tin and its contents as well as wonder if Jared knew of his pending death. The date the map was drawn was April

25th. According to this date, Jared was killed in combat on May 7th. Just twelve short days between the two dates. Thus, Aaron would always wonder. It wasn't until Aaron would make a list of his own so many years in the future that he concluded that only God himself knows these dates. Preparation is something we can do, he would later think, but ultimately "over" is in the hands of the creator.

The day Aaron stared at the three letters on his bed with the brief interruption from Butch was three day ago. As the milk in his cereal bowl turns to frosted sugar he would not drink, zombies walked the halls and rooms of Aaron's house. He thinks mother was in bed but was not sure. He thinks Malisa was in the front room watching television but was not sure. He thinks dad is mowing the front lawn but is not sure. Pushing the drowned flakes around in the bowl, he decides it is time to follow Jared's map. The map is in the garage and is a crude aerial of the Mills' home, with arrows directing the course to follow. It is behind the plywood repair and into Jared's secret room under the breezeway. There the map, not even close to scale, uses dotted lines to indicate a further path that will lead to an exaggerated "X". No words instruct Aaron to dig, and no words are needed for him to understand this instruction. He recalls dialogue between Jared and himself about treasure maps and can hear Jared's words tell him, "X marks the spot to dig." Aaron recalls many of Jared's instructions and as the years passed even recalls more. Time, it would seem for these two boys, strengthened their bond and brotherhood. Aaron held tight the words he heard from his older brother. Jared of course did as well but only had one regret.

When the cereal bowl was rinsed and left in the sink for mother to wash, Aaron headed outside. The lawn mower noise he heard was in fact Butch cutting the front lawn. Butch hated yard work and in his ignorance to do it would always let the grass grow much too long before cutting it. This of course made the task at hand even more frustrating, provoking even more hate on Dad's part. Aaron was careful while heading out the breezeway door to wait for Butch to tun his back on the front of the house. Aaron would then slip into the garage unseen and slide the thin, plywood patch to enter the secret fort. Once inside, he would without thought continue to listen for the mower's strain cutting the much-too-tall grass. When the mowing stopped, he knew Butch could and would be too close for him to exit. His operation then would need to be quick and silent. In his haste, however, he forgets to grab something to dig with, so he listens for the sound of the mower to get farther away and exits the fort. He quickly rummages through some garden tools and returns unnoticed with one of Mother's gardening spades in hand. In his head he hears Jared's soft words, *Think about what you are going to do and be prepared.* Aaron realizes he did not do so this time but mentally concludes that it will never happen again. Of course, it will. He is just a boy. But he will always hear Jared's instructions, and he will always strive to do better.

Under the breezeway, he orients the map, looking from corner to corner and pointing where Jared was careful to note a heating duct and the exhaust fan that attached to the bar area in the basement. He scampers to the area with the "X" and with a deep breath dives the small garden shovel into the hard soil. The clay-like dirt is very hard and unwilling to be easily removed from years of compression. For several minutes Aaron digs and stops every once in a while to listen for the mower above. Six to eight inches down, he hears a clink. His heart races, and his digging becomes more feverish and effective. Within a minute he has uncovered the tin's edges. The tin itself was about eight inches long, five inches wide, and approximately three-and-a-half inches thick. Jared barred the tin upright on its edge. Thus, the top was along the tin's side some eight inches deeper in the hard clay. Jared did this intentionally so that the contents could not come out without the entire tin being removed from the ground. Aaron kept digging and since he became engulfed in concentration, he never noticed the mower had stopped. He wiggled the tin back and forth trying to coach its removal from the ground. Dig, wiggle, dig, wiggle. Aaron is all in now.

Above ground, Butch walks into the house and heads to the sink. In the wall cabinet to his right are the glasses and mugs. He opens the cabinet and retrieves a glass displaying a Ronald McDonald looking much too happy to be holding a hamburger. He runs the water with his left hand and waits for the water to cool. As he looks out at the back yard in disgust, he begins to fill the happy clown with cold water. He shakes his head, knowing all too well the back-yard needs cutting too, and whispers, "Shit" to himself as he drinks. Standing with the scene of the yardwork dripping down his neck he lowers his sight to the bottom of the sink before him. For a moment the cereal bowl goes unnoticed. Not because it is not plainly in sight because it is plainly in sight. Butch and his simplistic thoughts, like a grandfather clock in dire need of being rewound, stares at the bowl before concluding that Aaron is up and has eaten breakfast and is not readily around or in sight or sound. Butch looks out back once more and utters a simple, "Hmm?"

Meanwhile, Aaron has successfully excavated the precious tin. Unlike the many thoughts that stopped the young boy from reading or opening the letters, as fast as his tiny hands can, he wipes them clean on his denim jeans and back to the tin's top to pry the tin's lid off and looks at what is inside.

A handwritten note is atop several sealed envelopes. In the bottom of the tin is some silver coins, two cigarettes, Lucky Stripes unfiltered, a pack of matches never used, and a tiny glass jar with what looks like a dried-up, dead spider.

The note reads:

> If you are reading this I have instructed you to find this treasure. The only reason I can think of on why I would tell you about this is I am not ever going to come back for this myself. The only person I can think I would ever tell is you. Aaron.

From the looks of the handwriting, at best guess Jared was maybe fifteen or sixteen years old. In the envelopes that followed, it was clear that Jared had aged maybe four or five years. None of the items in the tin had dates, so a best guess was all that could be done. Thirty-seven one-dollar bills were in the final envelope as well as the eighty-five cents in change (two quarters, three dimes, and one nickel) at the tin's bottom. Another envelope explained the spider in the jar. Apparently this spider bit Jared on the hand as he allowed it to crawl about his hand and arm. He instinctively slapped at the insect when it was biting him and in doing so killed it. The letter was filled with remorse. Jared felt the spider was just doing what spiders do. He felt bad that he had killed it for something the spider had no control over doing. In the letter he said he would never kill anything again. That did not stand to be true. Two more of the envelopes were written in diary-like fashion. At the start the entries were every day but as the "diary" continued, they were further apart. There were no dates, only days of the week, written before that day's entry. Thus, there were seventeen Monday's, twenty-two Tuesdays, eleven Wednesdays, thirteen Thursdays, and only one Sunday. There was one Friday, but it was crossed out and replaced with a Thursday. Aaron's name was peppered throughout all these entries. Things Jared and Aaron had done that day. Things and instructions Jared had given Aaron to remember. However, on the day that was originally marked as Friday and crossed off, Jared had written, "Showed Aaron my secret place today." As Aaron rummaged through the tin and read some of this, it never occurred to him about that fateful day. It was only many years later that Aaron would realize that Kennedy was shot on a Friday and Jared either deliberately mis-corrected his entry or mistakenly entered the wrong day. But for Aaron. who once believed there was no dates but only years in this tin at all, many years later he concluded that there was. Then and only then did he realize how old and how long Jared was in his own world. A world Aaron would come to call Jared's Lost World.

Chapter 7

(Jared's Regret)

The bus ride, as of yet, had no delays. It was something Jared had worried about on the ride down to South Carolina. A small girl somewhere between the ages of seven and nine had thrown up. Her mother made quick of the clean-up and the driver slowed but never stopped to see if the child needed help. Jared's thoughts had wandered. He enjoyed his weeklong stay at home, but in a strange way, he was ready for war. Basic training did this to a young man. It was designed to ready a solider, and Jared took to the lessons like a duck to fresh water. He was prepared. As prepared as the studies could have made him. But never, never in his wildest imagination could he prepare for what was to come. Unlike so many of the young that had given their all for this country, he was more realistic than most. As the buses wheels droned along the open road, and the smell of cleaned-up puke filtered through the already stale air, Jared thought back. Back to the final week of basic training and the conversation that unfolded between the readied men of his platoon. Men, only described by the government's description by age. Truth be known, they were simply boys.

"I don't know about you fags, but I can't wait to kill me some gooks," An eager solider spat. He was a strong boy from a small town west of Billings, Montana. Private Patrick Frye. His comrades called him Prick.

"Fuck that, Prick. I hope we don't even see any," said Darren, An Iowa native.

"You're such a fuckin' wuss, Darrr-Win," Prick barked, throwing the rag he had used earlier that day to polish his GI goods.

"Jared said we won't see shit for at least six months," Darren rebottled.

"Fuck Jared too," Frye replied, punching just once at the bottom of the bunk that he laid backside to. Jared's bunk.

He was right about the combat and when they would see it. First, the time frame. it would in fact be months before they're off to the front lines. Training took place in non-hostile environments. Cambodia was their company's first stop. Jungle training, which would not draw enemy fire, was to say the very least non-non-hostile.

Second, combat itself; Even Prick would have a change of heart when real bullets flew his way. Or worse yet, when Darren would cry to go home after sniper fire would pierce his chest.

Yes sir, Jared was wise about war and the battles to come, but he would die just the same. It was this he was not ready for, and what Aaron back home would be forced to digest.

The winding wheels droned on. The smell of puke began to fade, and Jared drifted in and out of consciousness.

Jared walks with full gear through a maze of tall hedges. In the distance he hears Aaron's cries for help. Sweat drips down his face as he creeps forward with his rifle drawn.

"Jared, help me Jared," a young Aaron's voice cries.

His heart pounds, almost to the point of pain.

He hates this dream. In a strange way, he knows he rides the puke-filled bus to war. But in an even stranger way he lives out the dream at hand. All within the bowels of his brain.

"Jared, I'm over here," Aaron cries once more.

Jared breathes hard and deliberately as he inches forward. To his right he hears the snap of a broken twig, the sound you your self would hear in a wood with the approaching enemy at hand. To his left, the shuffling brush. Perhaps a rabbit stirred from his burrow, or perhaps your adversary wishing you dead.

Again, he hears Aaron's cries for help. Again, he hears his own heart pound with pain.

He snakes his way through out the hedgerow maze. The clouds overhead move fast and without rational speed. Dream clouds. The sweat, the noise, the cries, all start to boil as he heads closer to the maze's center.

Just then, the air brakes on the bus screeched to their finale stop. Just then, a young solider readies his rifle for fire. Just then, the enemy is clearly visible in a dream Jared would never understand. Jared awakens. Shocked as the brakes' rude awakening screams. Shocked as the rifle fires cracking the clear, dry air. Shocked as the enemy holding Aaron in the center of the hedgerow maze is Butch. Butch sitting atop a bamboo cage that Aaron is unable to escape.

The military leaves no time for waste. The 109th converged at base camp at O-700 hours. All had shown. All had thought at least someone would not. Their time was well managed. They would ready as quickly as humanly possible, then wait until they would have to ready again.

The months of jungle training went well for Jared. He was physically prepared for the endurance tests that each day would bring. His rifle skills were exceptional, especially for a young man that had never fired a real weapon until basic training. And it was easy for Jared to follow barked orders that at times made little sense.

But when things were quiet, as he lies awake in his bunk, he would miss Aaron, Mother, and Melissa. And yes, even Butch. Jared had loved his father. He was only frustrated that his father did not love him, or so he sometimes thought. Or to Jared's translations, did not know how to show it.

Like a flower cursing at the sun's violate rays, blaming the hot sun for burning off the only rain clouds in sight, the thirsty flower can't entirely blame the hot sun. Without it, it would have never grown. It was in this strange way that Butch and Jared coexisted. Jared, thirsty for Butch's love and approval, but growing just the same. Had it not been for Butch's ability to procreate, Jared would not have been at all—or so it had seemed. Melissa's theory would test this thought.

When the times of quiet homesickness bunkered in hard and fast, Jared would write a letter home. All GI's used this method of medication. In this regard, Jared was like every GI.

Dear Aaron,

I can't wait to see you again. I am sure your schooling is going well, and I hope you're still having fun with all your friends. Don't worry about me. I too am having fun and have made many friends. The other day we got to slide down a long rope into a large puddle of water. You would have loved it. Although I don't think mom would have liked how your clothes would have looked afterwards. Then last week we went into a large room and had to hold our breath for as long as we could. I didn't win the game but when they let us out I was the only one that did not puke. It was so gross you would have laughed I'm sure. Anyway, say hi to everyone there for me, and please remember all that I have told you.

—-Love Jared.

It was a simple GI Jared letter that Aaron would savior and keep to this day in a shoe box atop the closet's only shelf. All twenty-two letters Jared had written are still sitting in the Mills' home.

However, there were far more ways Jared was unlike every other GI. He never complained openly to anyone, which was something he had to endure from every GI he had ever met. At times the conditions were harsh and cruel, but Jared had felt that complaining did nothing to better the situation. Jungle patrol, trash detail, filling body bags with guts, flesh and body parts were not made better by complaining. So, although it was unnoticed, he did not do it. Why is it we don't notice when people don't complain?

Jared also differed to some degree by never questioning the logic to the mission at hand. Raid this village but let this one alone. Blow up this bamboo bridge but leave this one be. Take this Vietcong prisoner; execute this one right here and now. He did it all. To Jared it was all part of war. War he had played out in his mind nearly every day of his life. The only difference with this war was it was real to everyone else. Jared wrote home that this was in fact a real war, and Gloria would never read this line for some thirty-two years. Jared's mind's wars were very real to Jared, but others saw and heard nothing. Now however, reality to the rest of the world was Jared's reality as well. The beginning of Jared's fantasy trips to war happened when Jared was only nine.

The last day of February in 1959 was Butch's only free Saturday of the month. He had gotten in late from a three-day trip to our nation's capital. He hated the Washington run because as he put it, "Washington's roads are all fucked up." He once again, to Gloria's distaste, pulled an all-nighter. But because of it, he is able to sit at the kitchen table drawing on both his filter-less crutch and jet-black coffee. Gloria cleans the breakfast mess when the questioning begins.

"So how was the trip?" Gloria inquires. She really does not care, but the silence they have been enduring as of late is weighing on her mind.

"The trip was a trip," Butch says without thought.

"What's that supposed to mean?" Gloria asks as she turns both her attention and herself toward Butch sitting in his grandeur. A full stomach always made Butch seem proud of his existence, as if he was a Neanderthal that successfully hunted and killed his gorge-full meal.

"It doesn't mean anything," he said as his eyes dart to the floor and he scratches at his face at an itch that is not there. Guilt is what he displays. Guilt is what Mother sees.

"It obviously means something. When did you get there?" Gloria asks.

"When did I get there?" Butch replies. "Who cares?"

"I'm just asking you about the *trip*," Gloria say's sarcastically emphasizing the word trip. "Why are you so defensive?" she continued.

"I'm not defensive. I'm just wondering why you give a crap about me driving to Washington," Butch argues. He inhales long on the final drag of his cigarette and crushes it in the family-owned Holiday Inn ashtray. He continues without more thought. "I mean really Gloria what does it matter where I went when I was there?"

"Where you went? I didn't ask you where you went," Gloria said. Now her own thoughts start to flutter. She has felt the strain on their marriage for some time now. Some would call it the seven-year itch, but Butch and Gloria have in fact been married now for eleven years. This strain is the strain that all marriages go through. At some point every couple will figure out they do not need each other to survive. That the infatuation and flirting nature of a relationship anew is long past. When this realization will hit is anyone's guess. Professional marriage counselors have concluded that the seven-year mark is the most common time frame. Thus, the itch. But all couples are different. Some will feel it sooner, some will feel it later. Butch and Gloria, however, are feeling it now, and each will do things to make themselves feel whole again. Gloria will throw herself into motherhood, perhaps explaining why she will become pregnant with a child again by mistake. Butch, on the other hand, will falter from his vows. Only once, but once is all it will take for some.

"So, tell me Butch, where did you go?" Gloria said. Her voice is shaky and insinuating distrust.

"Gloria, it's my only day off I've had in a month. I don't want to spend it talking about my fucking work," he said, removing himself from the table as he walks towards the breezeway door.

Gloria would ask no more. She was an obedient wife. Never faltering from the vows, she would make. Love, honor, and obey. "I do," are the only two words she used to remain faithful on her wedding day—except maybe the second; honor was something mother felt was earned.

Butch stops in the door's frame for just a moment before continuing on. Gloria too has paused in a frozen position as the two stand paralyzed back-to-back. No words, no sounds, just thoughts, hanging in the air like a feather neither floating to the ground from gravity or sailing upward from a thermal current. Each at this still-photo moment in time wants this instant to pass. Each has grown tired of the seven/eleven-year itch and its consequences. Each will say nothing of what they are thinking. Gloria, almost certain of her cheating truck driver husband. Butch, more certain he will never pay to cheat or feel this way again.

He walks outside, laboring at the task of coat assembly. The day is clear and unseasonably warm for February in New York. It feels warmer than it is—five degrees above freezing—but it is these warmer than normal days that make northerners forget what real warm air feels like. He rounds the corner to his new garage. The structure is in fact three years standing. But to Butch, always on the road, he has only been home about one year in that time. So to him the garage needs order and straightening every free moment he has. He stands at the one open bay door and observes his only son busy in thought.

"What are you doing Jared?" Butch asks, still smoldering from the fire that burned just minutes ago inside.

"Nothing Butch," Jared says, both startled and off guard. "I'm just messing with this hose."

Jared, in his nine-year-old world, was trying to get the frozen water that crackled and creaked inside the hose to come out. He had stretched the hose out onto the garage's floor and turned the spicket on and then off to force the frozen treats out. All nine-year-old boys think icicles are frozen treats. When Butch interrupted his progress, he was checking the nozzle's end.

Butch stands and thinks as he fishes for a smoke from his jacket pocket. For a moment, he's back in the breezeway having feelings of guilt. Then in another he's a truck-driving dad that stands before his mischievous son. He pulls a smoke from its pack with an aggressive snap of his wrist using nothing but his nicotine-stained teeth. He fumbles for his Zippo as he walks toward Jared.

"You don't have that water on do ya?" he asks, a rhetorical question he knows Jared won't answer.

"Water won't come out of that hose Jared. It's too cold out," Butch murders. He's disgusted with his son, but he still feels disgusted with himself as well. He stands towering over his only son. Jared just stands and waits for the preaching to end.

"You see Boy, water freezes at thirty degrees (Butch failed science). So even if you have it on, it won't come out," Butch explains. The unlit cigarette hangs from his lips. The two just stand there, each not knowing what to say or do next. Jared was used to having his Saturdays left alone. He did what his young mind felt was best to do at the time. Mess with this, mess with that. Play here, play there. He was not used to Butch's pathetic attempts at fatherly lessons of science. And Butch, even riddled with guilt, didn't know how to communicate with his only son. He was trying to be dad, just never sure what was next. He realizes two things at this uncomfortable point. One, he has nothing of value to add, and two, the smoke he is craving is unlit.

"I tell you what. I'm gonna go inside and get my lighter. You start winding this hose up, and I'll come out and help. Okay?" Butch said.

Jared, shocked by the compassion and warm words, simply agreed.

"Okay Butch." he said.

And as unexpectedly as when Butch interrupted, in an instant he was gone, back inside. Jared started the task of winding the hose back on its tire rim. The hose crackled and creaked as he labored at the winding process. The ice inside made the hose as stiff as a rotted stick. Jared kicked and scuffed at it as it awkwardly hung on the wall-mounted tire. A lime green piece of paneling wedged between the tire and wall would eventually come free. When it did, Jared's hiding place and fantasies of war were born. Butch never did return to the garage that February morning. Instead, he and Gloria found words and themselves as well and were making love once again. Jared didn't even notice the broken promise of Butch's return. He was busy exploring his newfound imagination of war and his secret place. And now, thinking back to the day he discovered that sanctuary he called home, he has no memory of Butch ever being in the garage at all.

The day Jared died was like any other day during war. Except for Jared. The unit was instructed to advance some forty clicks south to a village suspected of aiding the Vietcong. Intelligence gave these instructions constantly. Coordinates, distance, and direction were all mapped out before the company forged onward. It seemed that Jared's unit was on the move more than most, but Jared liked it that way. Sitting around and waiting for war was something his imagination never did. So reality for Jared was a little disappointing when the normality of the real army played out. However, the reality of death—something Jared had never considered during his imagination games—was also normal for this army game called war. And right up until Jared's last breath of life, he still had no clue he was going to die.

The air was hot as the sound of distance gunshots rang out. Some of the newer grunts, Ludwig and Reed, would look in horror in the direction of the threatening sound, but the veterans knew better. The shots were better than three or four miles away and paying attention to what is transpiring around you will keep you alive much longer in the bush. They moved quietly but briskly in their intelligent direction. Their formation was a standard GI drill. Jared, like so many times before, volunteered for point, a position in the formation that made him the leader. Leader, of course, only defined by orientation of a group of men moving forward. He had, however, no say in the destination or the path they would take to get there.

The brush was thick. The heat and ants that seemed to accompany every hot day found their way to the back of your neck. This was jungle travel, but Jared made his way, giving predetermined hand commands to the men that followed. After a few hours on the move, he suddenly gave the command to stop. The entire platoon freezes on Jared's erect fist. Kyle and Dodge hunker down and ready their rifles. Brady, Shine, and the Kid do the same, but adjust their helmets for gunfire. The captain and Reed—Captain always liked a green horn—first walk out close by, kneel, and wait for Jared's next command.

"Turn the safety off your girl," the captain whispered to Reed.

"It was never on," he whispered in reply.

Jared motioned for the captain to advance to his side.

"Let's go Kid," The captain quietly said to Reed.

A few moments of quiet walk and the captain and Reed find their way beside Jared, who is leading. "What is it Jared?"

"Road, Sir. I don't remember a road in the morning briefing," Jared whispered.

The captain popped his head up for a look. Sure enough, less than a hundred yards out, plain as the sweat of his brow, a well-traveled road cut the brush before them.

"Reed," Captain said, pointing his index finger to the sky and twirling it as if to whip an upside-down cup of tea. "Come here."

The captain knew the maps they used could not possibly have every road and trail the jungle hid. But a double check on the accuracy was not a bad idea, especially due to the size and wear this road presented. Plus, a quick check on their coordinates would also prove wise. Even the most well-trained jungle men-of-war can become twisted and turned finding their way. The radio confirmed that their position had them a few clicks east. The road before them would turn hard south. The Captain concluded a short way down the road and back in the brush would both correct their position and give their jungle travel misery a break. The group forged onward.

Road wars were another formation or tactic of travel. Unlike the brush, the distance the men walked was critical. Too close and one hard attack would prove fatal for an entire platoon. Too spread out and any one member of the platoon can become isolated and ambushed. Sometimes it even happened without any one member of the group knowing. But point. Point was a constant, and again Jared choose this position in the formation. The captain and Reed followed Jared's chosen position.

The road eventually became less well-traveled. It widened and thinned as the army move on. Jared stalked onward, listening and watching closely for the enemies that lurk. The platoon followed in formation. The sun beat down on the warriors who marched. Although it was more comfortable than the brush, the open road made it seem ten degrees hotter, and all the men felt the added heat as they advanced. The road—better described as a small path— suddenly forked. Again, Jared gives the silent command to stop. Crouched on one knee, he considers his options. To his left, the path seems to widen in a clearing ahead. To his right, the path seems to thicken and turn hard left. This, he concludes, most likely leads to the path to his left. Jared stands and wipes the sweat off his forehead with a bandana draped he wears around his neck. For a split second he can hear an instruction he gave Aaron in his head. *Your whole life you will choose your own path*, his mind's recorder says to Aaron.

Jared returns the sweat-soaked bandana around his neck. He looks up toward the beating sun and sighs. This quiet thought of his only brother floods his mind with the love he feels for Aaron. He tightly closes and opens his eyes as if to erase this thought that is unproductive for war. Sweat squeezes out of the sides of his eyes as if he had just wrung out a soaked dishcloth. He lowers his head and sniffles hard, taking one half step to toward the path to his left. The sound of the heated jungle is abruptly interrupted with one loud thudded CRACK.

The captain almost instantaneously grabs the front of Reed's vest and burrows to the ground. Both men tumble to a lying position. All the men on the path scurry and bunker to the would-be drainage ditch off the side of the road.. Bolts and safeties are clicking as men hunker and prepare for gunfire. The captain is well aware that someone is hit. A bullet suddenly stopping makes a *thud* sound when entering a human's body. A miss whistles and carries without the defining *thud*.

The captain raises his head and waves his arm like a one-armed umpire motioning safe. Reed's heart is pounding out of his young veteran chest. He too raises his head to look at the men around him. When his eyes focus on Jared lying face down in the path ahead, the young green-horned vet shows why the captain likes the newcomers to the brush by his side.

"Jared!" he yells in a quite whisper while exploding to his feet.

"God Dimmitt Reed!" the captain quietly shouts. "Get over here!"

Young David Reed forgets. Forgets all he was taught about gunfire in basic training. Forgets all of his Cambodian jungle war drills for when a comrade has fallen. Forgets his weapon lying beside the captain, who is stewing in its anger. Forgets the instructions the captain repeated in his ear earlier that day.

"Do *not*. I repeat soldier. *Do not* separate yourself from this radio attached to your back!" the captain had barked.

As the young David Reed ran to the aid of a fallen grunt, he stripped the heavy radio from his back and ran to Jared's side.

Compassion and instincts. The two things the army can never retrain in a man. You're not a bad solider if you care. But as the military training will try to brainwash you into believing, you put every solider at risk when you have careless compassion. Young David did not take to the brainwashing lessons his army instructed. He simply falls prey to the instincts he was born with. He's not a bad solider; today he just simply forgets.

The captain barks in a whisper for the rest of his company to hold their fire as well as their positions. He draws his own weapon, looks skyward, and waits for what he believes will be the sound of another shot. He's convinced it's a lone sniper somewhere in the thick brush, perhaps in a tree stand atop the jungle floor, and he is also certain that the forgetful Reed will undoubtedly be the next victim his platoon will lose. He steadies his rifle and awaits the sniper's muzzle flash.

Reed skids to his knees and turns Jared to his back.

"Jared!" He exclaims.

"Oh Jesus, Jared talk to me," he continues to say.

The sniper's bullet had found Jared's chest. Blood was leaking steadily and pumping with every beat of Jared's heart. As David ripped at the G.I. shirt to get a better look, Jared coughed both blood and pain.

"Jared can you hear me?" Reed pleaded in panic.

Dazed but regaining consciousness, Jared speaks.

"Aaron?" Jared asks.

"Hold still Buddy. Needles is on his way." Reed said. He was of course referring to Billy Needleman, the company's medic. With his hand trying feverishly to stop the flowing blood, he looks with darting eyes for Needles' much-needed help.

"Medic!" He shouts in the direction of the bunkered group.

"Don't worry Jared, help is on the way," he says, turning both his face and attention to the dying solider that lies before him.

Jared is both weak and dazed from the events at hand. In his mind, he hears both the sounds of the reality war and his imagination war in his thoughts. His eyes blink twice as much as they need to, and his lower body is starting to be flooded with warmth. His eyes focus on the compassionate Reed before him.

"What happe..." he begins to say as he coughs and spatters a mouthful of blood.

"Don't talk Jared, save your strength," Reed pleads.

Again, Reed turns to the group just a few hundred feet away.

"Needles get the fuck up here!" He barks.

A shiver comes over Jared, and for the first time he feels death's door. He tries desperately to wet his lips with saliva but does not feel either his tongue or anything cold and wet in his mouth.

"Aaron," he mutters. "Aaron... I'm scared."

Slipping in and out of consciousness, Jared's mind takes him back to his hiding place the day of Aaron's unfortunate birthday.

"Thank you Jared," Aaron said, pausing only for a moment for those words to settle before lunging forward into Jared's arms. The impact nearly forced Jared over, as the two boys feverishly hugged one another. Jared patted Aaron's back seconds before they separated from their emotional exchange.

"You're welcome, Bud. I knew you'd love it," he said, sniffling and wiping at his nose and face. "Now, do you want to play army?" He asked.

"Yep!" Aaron exclaimed, jerking upward in an excited halfhearted jump.

"Careful, you don't want to hit your hea…" Jarred suddenly stopped. He pressed his index finger against his lips, quietly shushing and whispering when he spoke.

"What was that?" he asked, turning his head slightly sideways, trying to exaggerate his power to hear.

"I didn't hear nuffin," Aaron said, confused from his brother's actions.

"I think its communists," he whispered.

"Communists?" Aaron replies.

Jared places his index finger across his lips. The shhh sound most would have made at this point is unnecessary between these two boys. He crawls to the edge of his hiding palace. He takes the very same finger he used to instruct silence and pushes open a vent leading to the Mills' half-finished basement. The vent, old grease-covered fan, and flapper unit were originally above the kitchen stove. The day the contractors enclosed the breezeway and constructed the garage, Butch insisted he keep the old vent for his own use. The contractor was used to this kind of irrational behavior. Homeowners always seem to think the items that find their way to the nearby dumpster are eventually rummaged through by the building crew and kept.

"Hey, I want to keep that!" Butch had said, pointing to a wheelbarrow full of junk heading to the nearby dumpster.

Although he had no real plans for the greasy vent that day, he would later install it in his unfinished basement near his would-be bar.

Jared, with a push of his index finger, can look directly into the family basement.

Light from the basement illuminates the secret place like a striped flashlight. Aaron's face is washed with the striped light, and his pupils dilate to adjust. His jaw drops ever so slightly in amazement as his imagination begins to explode.

"What is it Jared?" he whispers, biting gently with curiosity at his lower lip.

Jared turns to look at his private G.I. and points with his other finger to a broken Daisy BB gun lying to Aaron's right. The BB guns innards were completely removed when it found its way in the Van-Dyne's trash and eventually to Jared's treasure.

"Hand me that weapon, Solider," Jared said, using his make-believe general's voice.

Aaron quickly scurries across the dirt floor and obeys the order at hand. He is comforted by this tone of voice. A moment ago, he was neither sure nor unsure if the threat of danger was real or not. Handing the broken gun to Jared, Aaron chuckles and says, "Jared, I was, I think maybe I was scared."

"No time for that now Solider. Gather your men," again pointing in the direction of piles and piles of other people's trash. The general continued to say, "We'll have to make an ambush attack on the communist camp," he concluded.

Aaron begins to rummage through the junk scattered about the secret place. As he picked up the little plastic green army men, he was still thinking about being scared. Jared's mind, however, is in full gear. His imagination of the make-believe war at hand is running on all eight cylinders. As Aaron searches for his army men, he narrates to both himself and Jared his every thought.

"I don't like being scared. I was scared before, but it's not like being scared now. Mom said I should not be scared. But I think I'm scared sometimes. Jared is never scared. Dad said only babies are scared. I'm not a baby. Jared do you know what I do when I'm scared?" Aaron mumbled softly on and on.

"All I have to do..."

It's of no use. Jared is too far gone in the war in his imagination. He vaguely can hear his younger brother go on and on as he plays out his war for their entertainment. But he cannot specifically catch what the young solider is rambling about now, lying on his deathbed somewhere in jungles of Vietnam.

Needles eventually makes his way to Reed and Jared. He begins to apply pressure and clean gauze to Jared's wound. Jared is in and out of consciousness.

Traveling from the make-believe war in his secret place to the real war where he lays and dies.

"Aaron, what?" He mutters quietly.

Reed leans close to Jared's mouth to hear.

"Hold on Jared, everything is going to be all right," he says.

"I'm scared, Aaron," Jared mutters.

"Don't be scared, Jared," The young Reed says softly.

In Jared 's mind, he hears Aaron's voice. He hears him go on and on about being scared. He can barely make out what Aaron has said. "Dad said baby..."

"Aaron, I can't hear. "Jared, now nearly non-audibly, whispers.

"Hold on! Oh Jesus, Needles," Reed pleads.

"You know what I do, Jared?" Aaron's voice repeats in the belly of Jared's dying thoughts.

"What? What do I do Aaron?" Jared pleads to the young Reed before him.

"What do you do?" Reed asks in confusion.

Barely audible now, Jared whispers in David's ear.

"Aaron... what do I do when I'm scared?" He pleads.

David Reed feels both the dying man's plea for an answer and the finality of the young man's life. He realizes that Jared will not live and at the same time understands he is deep in his own thoughts, carrying out a conversation with someone he loves and looks to for answers. The light bulb of a newly born idea comes to Reed as Jared dies before him, and as this idea hits, he is sure Jared has breathed his last breath. In desperation, David Reed whispers in Jared's ear.

"Jared, it's Aaron. Jared please wake up. Jared what did I tell you to do about being scared?" David said with tears pouring down his face.

Jared gulps and spits air and blood for the last time. His lips are barely moving when his final thoughts and concerns are that of the only brother he ever had. Reed leans in for what is certain to be his last words.

David repeats, pretending to be Aaron. "What did I tell you to do when you're scared?"

"I don't know..."Jared said. "I didn't listen."

Jared regrets.

Chapter 8

(Malisa's Theory)

In October of 1984, Aaron was ready—or so he thought—for his first marathon. Aaron has been running now for over fifteen years. His start was shortly after Jared's death. However, it wasn't until he graduated from high school that he took his running seriously. Seriously, of course, as a standard as only Aaron considers. The track team at his local school knew of the mileages he logged, and the track coach at the local school tried repeatedly to coax Aaron into joining the team. Aaron's times were certainly not blistering by no means; the coach just knew of this young man's commitment to the art of running. Commitment was any coaches biggest challenge when it came to high schoolers. His and the coach's motivation for Aaron to run for him was a selfish act. But so was Aaron's. Aaron ran because Jared said to do so. Jared was right. Running after his death helped Aaron cope with the loss. The more he ran, the more he copped. The more he coped, the more Aaron held tight to the elder brother's lessons. The more he held tight to the lessons, the further and further away he and Butch became. Had Jared never died, he would have instructed his eager student to honor his father and show respect—something Jared tried so desperately to do time and time again. But Jared died when Aaron's heart was filled with contempt for Butch that day in the bus terminal. This was the last instruction Jared had given by mouth to the eager student. This instruction held much more weight than anything Aaron could recall or read that was written in the Vietnam letters. Thus, un-wittedly, Jared put a wedge between father and son that he would never be aware of. Jared would have never done this knowingly, regardless of the relationship he and Butch had or didn't have. For Jared knew the bond between father and son was very special, regardless of if he himself did not share such a bond. Once, when Aaron and Jared were together, and Butch interrupted their play time with barking instructions, Aaron said out loud some derogatory remarks about Butch for Jared to hear. It was the summer of 1967. The Mamas and The Papas enjoyed a number one slot with their song "Words of Love." Ralph Nader publishes a book about car safety practices that will change the car industry forever, and in Western New York temperatures soar to an all-time high. Aaron and Jared are playing catch in the backyard. Neither followed baseball; however, both like to play catch and would pretend a third player was caught in a hot box situation. In a nut shell, this meant the speed at which they throw the baseball back and forth was accelerated, and Jared narrated. Aaron is only seven years young, thus Jared—ten years his senior—needs to be cautious about how hard he throws to him. Butch steps outside for a smoke and watches these boys play for only a moment before speaking.

"Keep your eye on the ball, Aaron," he barks, lighting a cigarette and coughing from the first drag. This of course means nothing to Butch, but it is the only phrase he knows when talking baseball. Jared stops his narration and slows the tempo down a bit. Aaron is intent on throwing out the make-believe runner and shouts, "Where is he Jared?' questioning the position of the would-be runner. Jared nods to Aaron and starts to narrate once more for his brother's sake. "He is caught in the middle, heading for you… Hold the ball! *Run* towards me!" Jared says. Aaron, like a faithful student, does exactly as Jared instructs. Butch watches on but is confused by the boy's game. Truck drivers rarely paid any attention to sports—especially those that required an imagination to partake in—and Butch was no exception. "He's running back to me, Aaron. Throw it hard," Jared barks. Aaron throws a hard strike back to his older brother as Jared exclaims, "He's *out*! Excellent job, Bud," Jared said. Excitement as well as pride fills the afternoon air until moments later when Butch speaks.

"Oh no, no, no… He's safe!" Butch unleashes. He understands less about this foolish game than anyone on the planet; however, what he does understand

is to disagree with Jared in front of Aaron every chance he gets. "Daaaaad…
shut up!" Aaron interjects. "Oh, I'm sorry Son. I saw the entire thing from
here and that guy, the base runner guy, he was safe." Butch said. Jared smiles
from Aaron's instruction to insist Butch shut up. A smile forms on Jared's face
as Butch looks on to see if Jared will challenge him. Jared however only cares
for Aaron. Being right or wrong because Butch disagrees is something Jared
stopped trying to win many years ago. The smile on Jared's face however is
enough to insult the insecure truck-driving, beer-drinking, filter-less smoking,
over-weight-and-soon-to-have-a-heart-attack Butch. "What?!" Butch screams
between inhales of carcinogens he pays happily for. "You have something to
say to me Jared?" He barks.

"No Butch," Jared answers. "Like you said, he was out." His tone was sarcastic and under his breath as he was smiling at the foolishness of this make-
believe play. Jared waits for only a half second at what he knows will follow.
"No way!" Aaron screams and Butch's attention switches from a smirking Jared
to an irate Aaron. Butch, for the love of what he considered all his adult life
regardless of what was before him now, looks at his *only* son, Aaron. He sees
and hears the seven-year-old debate and his frustration over what Butch himself had started. Aaron looks at his father with disgust. Aaron kicks at the turf
and scowls at the non-umpire's decision that played out before him. Jared on
the other hand, is laughing hysterically on the inside. He holds the ball and
waits for the Aaron and Butch exchange to resolve. Butch waves his cigarette-
holding hand and just says, "Ahhhh." indicating that they are both nuts, and
that he is not even sure why he came out here in the first place, waving his
hand like a make-believe, high-five-missing wave. Butch flings his half-smoked
cancer stick in the lawn and turns to walk away in disgust. Aaron puts up his
mitt and states to Jared, "Throw me the ball!" More of a command than a
statement or request. Jared tosses the stitched, hard ball to Aaron and waits
for the back door to completely shut with Butch's exit. When the silent play
from brother returns without narration, Aaron speaks. "Dad's a jerk!" Aaron
says with confidence that Jared will undoubtedly agree. The statement is more
as a matter of fact than an observation that seems painstakingly true. Jared
pauses and thinks before responding. Jared was always very good at thinking

before speaking and to an extent can thank Butch for this trait. He looks at Aaron as the ball reaches his mitt. Aaron returns the throw, and Jared holds the ball before he speaks or tosses it back.

"Aaron, Butc…." He stops midsentence to correct what he wants to say. "*Dad* is your dad, and you need to not talk to him that way." Aaron looks at Jared with bewilderment in his eyes. Aaron is not a fool—never was, never will be. He knows as well as Malisa that Butch is always hard on Jared. Butch is always disagreeing with the eldest son. Butch rides Jared hard, and if anyone in the Mills family knows this fact, it is Jared himself. So Aaron's confusion about what Jared is instructing is warranted. "Look," Jared continues, seeing the confusion in Aaron's eyes. "You can disagree with Dad, you can tell him to his face he is wrong, but hear me Aaron… *Never* tell Dad to shut up." Jared's words are that of the teacher he has always been to his younger brother. Before Jared returns the baseball to Aaron's awaiting mitt, he holds his arm up as to ready his throw and asks, "Do *you* understand me?" Aaron knows all too well when the general is speaking in this commanding tone. "Yes Jared, but I thought… " Aaron said with desire to debate in his voice. Jared quickly interrupts. "No buts. Let Dad say what Dad wants to say." Then Jared's eyes said, "Agreed?" without actually saying the word. Aaron shakes his head to indicate yes, and Jared throws him the hard ball. The snap in the glove resumes play and Jared again starts to narrate the imaginary runner caught in the hot box. This incident paints Jared in a very favorable light. However, Jared has a hidden, more sinister plan in his instructions to the young Aaron. Jared knows all too well that if you willfully let Butch speak, he will show his hand at being the fool. Aaron, Jared knows, is not a fool. Jared also knows that if he bad-mouths Butch in front of Aaron, Aaron will instinctively defend Butch. Thus, Jared learned long ago to let the fool speak. The rope you give Butch is always just long enough for him to hang himself. There is no honor in what Jared had just done—only deception. However, for Aaron, the rue will go unnoticed just as the pending theory Malisa is about to share.

From day one, Malisa and Nora shared a sister-sister-in-law relationship that was more like sister to sister. Nora trusted Malisa, and the decision for her to watch over Kevin while Aaron and her drove to Washington for the upcoming marathon was a no brainer. Malisa is ten years Nora's senior, but the closeness they share is like twins from the same womb. Malisa is divorced and has two children of her own. The divorce fortunately was applicable from both parties. However, Nora was very supportive and helpful when Malisa needed her most. Malisa's children Dianne and Sean adjusted well after the pair split. Dianne was the eldest of the two but only by a year and some twelve days. Kevin is a mere seven and eight years younger than his cousins, thus even their relationships are close despite these many years. Spending the four days it will take for the upcoming trip together will be a breeze for the single parent Malisa, Aaron's only sister.

The wind is howling, and it is bitter and cold the day Malisa and the kids show to pick up Kevin. Kevin is ready and packed, rushing outside when the cargo van pulls into the driveway. "Hold on a second their Mister," Nora said. "They're coming inside for a visit before you go." He spins and returns to the warm house as the minivan pulls to a complete stop. Malisa and the kids laugh at Kevin and wave as he struggles with sack in hand to get back inside. When the doors finally close behind all three temporary guests, Aaron, Nora, Kevin, Malisa, Dianne and Sean all share hugs, rotating from one another like a crude display of synchronized swimmers who will undoubtably lose their pending competition. Laughs and giggles are exchanged as this ugly display plays out. Aaron is the first to speak. "How was the drive? Looks nasty out there," Aaron asks. Malisa replies. "Looks worse than it actually is. Roads are clear. Snow is mostly blowing and drifting off the main roads." The weather is something all northerners talk about. It is the topic of conversation at every family meal. Unlike southerners, where food takes center stage, a northerner speaks only of either how hot it is or was and how cold it got or will become. Or as in this case, the driving conditions as it relates to the root topic of weather. Nora interjects. "I hate to travel in this stuff, but the weather south of us in Washington is supposed to be clear for the marathon." Malisa, looking at Nora as she speaks, turns to her younger brother and says, "So little brother, are you ready for this big running challenge?" Malisa does not really follow the sport but is well aware that the marathon, the 26.2 mile run, is the Super Bowl for the non-competitive weekend jogger. "Well," Arron replies. "We shall see." Nora steps in. "He has been running and training for this for a long time, so I would think he is ready." Nora looks at her loving husband and smiles a prideful glare at her man. Next, Malisa does something she is both known for and has done her entire life. Without any hesitation or delay, she jumps right to the point of something she has been dying to ask since the planning stages of the trip were born. "So, are you going to the wall while you're in town there?" She states as she is still just now removing he coat. The kids ran off upstairs to see Kevin's room and do what all kids do. Aaron moves in close to his older sister and helps her remove the winter coat like a complete gentleman. He looks at Nora and smiles. The smile is clear to both Nora and Aaron because of the conversation that took place between them just about a half hour ago.

Nora and Aaron are in the kitchen. Kevin is upstairs deciding on what toys are appropriate for the four-night stay with his cousin. Aaron and Nora are sitting at the kitchen table as Aaron looks at a map. Nora repeats that she wished they had gotten a trip ticket, something her friend Dawn suggested they needed to make the drive to DC. Aaron disagreed because they did not pay for the service, and it would not be ethical for them to use the service through Dawn, something she pays for.

"Ya know Aaron," Nora repeats. "Everyone does it." Aaron looks up from the map and tilts his head, then smiles. He sticks out his tongue, and the two giggle silently at the exchange. "So," Aaron said, changing the subject as quickly as it was birthed. "I bet you a million dollars the first words out of my sister's mouth is about the wall."

The wall, of course, is the Vietnam Memorial wall. The wall covers some two acres of park space and is visited by thousands of people each year. From afar, the wall looks like beautiful reflective marble or granite slats with a mirrored finish that reflect the sun's rays. However, the closer you get as you walk the deliberate path, the stone's surface begin to reveal the over fifty-some-thousand names. The names, of course, are the brave men and women that served and died in Vietnam/South Asia. Phonebook-like books as thick as a loaf of bread are perched on pedestals where you can look up a person's name alphabetically and it will give you the name's location. Three-inch-by-twelve-inch-thin see-though paper and stubbed pencils or crayons are also available so a visitor can rub a soldier's name off the wall. Every year thousands of flowers, gifts, pictures, and letters are left near fallen soldiers' names.

Nora, flipping through a *Cosmopolitan* magazine without looking up, answers, "No way." She continues. "Am I ever going to take *that* bet. I know Malisa all too well to think for a minute she will not ask. Oh, and by the way." She looks up and finishes. "*You* don't have a million dollars."

Aaron looks at his sister and smiles. He loves her as much as a brother can love a sister, and he simply says, "Of course." Malisa, stunned at the callous reply, goes on. "Really Aaron, I thought for a minute it might be too much?" Aaron is silent but listens to his sister go on. "I never knew any two brothers as close as you and Jared. My thought was, with the marathon being your first that maybe, just maybe, you might think it would not be wise to be so emotional before such a big challenge." She pauses for a moment to see if this last statement will spark any kind of reply of emotion from Aaron. It won't, but Nora chimes in. "Well, the marathon I would think is mostly physical, don't you think Honey?" Nora injects. "What emotions could possibly be too much from the wall visit to keep you from running your first marathon?" Aaron looks slowly at both and thinks before he speaks. As he has aged, he has inherited this trait that Jared was so good at. Aaron had already thought long and hard about this trip, the wall, the marathon, and all that these two spectators all had drummed up. He felt neither anger nor contempt for them, regardless of his thought, *Do either of you think for a minute I have not considered any of this?!* Aaron of course would never say such a thing to either of the woman he loves. The words he states next tells both, without actually saying so, that he has given this matter some thought. After he speaks, the matter is put to bed, so to speak. "I think the day after, or even after the marathon itself is run, might be an appropriate time to visit the wall." Aaron said. His tone and confidence assure both woman that he is the alfa male. Thoughts and desires about the trip and what will take place, like all of Aaron's affairs, have been thought out. No need to worry Gals, Aaron Mills is on the case. After his statement, there is a pause in the room. The children continue to play upstairs without a sound, and the three stand in the kitchen for a moment without a word. Aarons words still hang in the air when Malisa adds "Amazing how close you and Jared were, and if truth be told, you probably weren't even real brothers." Malisa said this as a matter of fact, and this statement takes Aaron off guard more than the inquiry about the wall visit. Nora's eyes bulge as she makes an obvious effort not to look at her husband as she makes her way to the fridge. "Anyone want something to drink?" Nora asks, hoping the statement is lost in the question she asks. For the first time since the wall inquiry, Aaron looks confused. Up until that point, he was in complete control. He spins the thought of what his elder sister just said as he asks, "What are you talking about?"

"Oh, please Aaron." Malisa continues. "Did you really think Dad disliked Jared that much because he was simply the oldest?"

"Dad was hard on Jared. I won't deny that," Aaron rebutted. "But what are you talking about?" Aaron's eyes say, *explain yourself Malisa*.

"Oh, come on Aaron!" Malisa continues. "Do the math, Man! Mom and Dad met and got married in May. They had Jared in November. That is only six months. Last I checked, it takes nine months to make a baby!"

Aaron stands and thinks with a clear and present light bulb above his head. Nora has heard this argument before from Malisa and knows all the finite details of her case. She knows she questioned Gloria on several occasions. She knows she has challenged and even caught Gloria in a lie on some other occasions. And she knows and agrees with Malisa and her theory that Jared in fact was not Butch's son. When no one answered the drink request question, Nora injected, "So, how was Butch hard on Jared?" Nora said hoping this would both change the subject and help her husband cope with the theory at hand. Malisa looks at Nora and then back to Aaron, struggling with what she had said. "Aaron, think about," Malisa says quietly. "Mom was pregnant when she met Dad. Do the math. Therefore, he hated Jared. This is why he loved us so much more. Jared was not his son."

The emotions that flood Aaron at this very moment are like a tsunami that overruns a sleeping city. Everything in its wake is destroyed and no one is the wiser. Aaron's mind works faster and is sharper than most. He immediately starts to ponder this theory and within seconds can conclude its falsehoods or validate its facts. He hears Jared's words in his mind teaching him about what it means to have a father and son relationship. He remembers the look on

Jared's face when looking at Butch and how it changed the older it got. Then Aaron thinks about Dad and why Jared even referred to Dad as Butch in the first place. Did Jared know he wasn't his biological father? Aaron wonders. Then Aaron again is in the bus terminal when Jared would travel off to war. Butch is wrong, Jared had said. Why would he say that? With all these thoughts swirling in Aaron's mind, the only thing he can think to do is answer his loving wife's question that still hangs in the kitchen air.

"One way Butch... Dad, was hard on Jared was cherry pit pie," Aaron states, looking at Malisa with neither a smile or a frown, only the look of a confused yet confirmed witness in a jury box who just made up his mind of the defendant's guilt.

Malisa for the first time sees pain in her younger brother's eyes. It was not her intent, however. Malisa only knows to speak of that which is on her mind openly and directly. But as with in the past, with this personality trait she can never escape, she now sees it has hurt rather than simply questioned. "Yes!" she exclaims about the great example," Malisa continues. "Cherry pit pie of course."

Nora listen as Aaron and Malisa explain the rules as well as the rue Butch played on Jared all those years after they picked and Gloria baked all those pies. Aaron did not tell Malisa or his loving wife of the pit he saved year after year and the very pit he gave Jared that fateful morning in the Rochester bus terminal that turned out to have no luck at all. He did however in a way agree that Malisa was right in her theory, and that was enough for both his sister and his wife. The children ran downstairs shortly after, and Malisa and the children drove away leaving Nora and Aaron to sleep, wake early, and head to Washington for the upcoming marathon.

No one spoke of the theory after the bomb was dropped. Nora, when removing her makeup standing at the master bed room's bath mirror, considered asking Aaron about what Malisa had said and then let the matter go in her mind. She thought, "He has enough to contend with running that distance and seeing the wall... Why did Malisa choose this moment to add her theory?" she wondered.

Sleep came fast for both. However, Aaron dreamed of Jared and wondered if the dream was his own thoughts or if Jared in some spirt-driven way had injected his own opinion into Malisa's theory.

Aaron, around age six, walks through an open, winter wheat field in his REM-stated dream. The clouds overhead move faster than any clouds ever moved in reality. The sound of a baby's cry is heard somewhere in the distance as Aaron walks almost in slow motion. Aaron glides the palms of his hands atop the winter wheat stems a full month from harvest. They are stiff and green with no seedlings atop there thresh. In the distance ahead, he sees Jared in full uniform standing with a smile on his face. In the dream Aaron knows Jared is dead so seeing him is a bit confusing but at the same time so pleasurable and real. Aaron even asks Jared without words, "Are you still dead?" Jared just shakes his head up and down to confirm what Aaron had just thought. Aaron walks in slow motion as the baby cries in the back ground of the dream and Jared stands and waits. In a flash of no dream reason, Aaron is now full grown, twenty-something plus, standing before a baby that lies in the winter wheat field on its back crying. He bends down to pick up the newborn child and cradles him in his arms. Somehow, he knows it is Jared. The baby whines and in a dream-like way he hears the baby's thoughts. The thoughts he hears are in the voice of the teacher Jared. "I've always been just a child and in need of a family and love." The dream-Jared's voice speaks as Aaron comforts the dream-baby crying in his arms. An alarming buzzer sounds in the winter wheat field before the child fades the stop-thinking crying voice. Time to get up, as reality rushes in. Time to run a marathon.

The drive goes without a hitch. Aaron and Nora make the nearly four-hundred-mile trip in less than eight hours. The plan to get checked in and enjoy a relaxing stay before the race was well thought out. The reservations that were made months in advance assured the Mills couple of a lovely place to stay close to the starting line and near all of Washington's most visited tourist attractions. After dinner, Aaron suggests they check out some of the Smithsonian museums that are free to walk through. Nora loves the idea. Sitting in the car all those hours on the road and limited walking after that had both feeling stiff and antsy. Even though Aaron will need a good night's sleep before the race starting gun sounds, Nora feels that if Aaron wants to walk around, then so be it. Most of the museums are south of the restaurant and the hotel they are staying at. However, Aaron fears that since it is already 4:03 P.M., these will in all likelihood close at either 5:00 or 5:30 P.M. So Aaron suggests they walk north to the only two he feels might be closer and stay open later. He, of course, is right. The American Art Museum is open until 7:00 P.M. and even though this museum is chosen at random, it displays something Aaron and Nora will marvel over all their married adult life. The Game Fish.

Nora said, "Well this is such a lovely idea, Sir Aaron. Are you sure walking this evening won't hinder your performance tomorrow?"

"The only thing that might hinder my performance tomorrow," Aaron continues. "Is all that bread I ate with that pasta."

Carb-loading the night before a marathon was something Aaron had read to do in *Runner's World* magazine, a magazine he subscribed to and read faithfully monthly. He even conversed with a friend, Drew Mule, who told him that at the New York City Marathon they encourage all runners to partake in the tavern on the greens pre-run pasta dinner, something Drew had done and recommended when he himself ran The New York City Marathon. Drew was the runner's runner in Aaron's mind. He was a longtime friend Aaron looked up too, as well as a co-worker he always enjoyed.

"Oh my God," Nora said, looking just inside the museum's doors. Stairs that seemed to go on forever cascaded before her. "Look at those stairs!" she concluded.

Aaron sprints to the top with neither a breath or concern. "Come on Honey!" he exclaims. "Time's a wasting."

Nora, however, is less than physically fit. Her ankles already hurt from the mile-and-a-half walk getting to the museum, and she was not about to sprint to the top of the stairs regardless of her marathoner husband's enthusiasm. "Time can wait for my fat butt to get there," Nora states as she uses the hand rail to carefully walk up the stairs before her. They walk through the many rooms looking at paintings and statues, pretending to critique art and have a knowledge of anything artful. Nora, even after several minutes, is still out of breath from all the stairs. When they turn the corner from one room to another, it hits them both square in the mouth.

"Oh my God!" Aaron starts to say as Nora is quick to finish.

"Look at this!" she says as Aaron points to the plastic Marlin-looking trophy fish that hangs on the wall before them. A plastic fish made of all gameboard pieces from hundreds of gameboard games is assembled and hanging before them as they gaze in wild wonder. Some ten-feet-long, or as Nora would state, "I think it is actual size Aaron." They were in total amazement. No greater piece of art will be seen or appreciated from these two redneck Western New York hillbilly farmers during the entire Washington trip. Also, had they had a camera to prove this wonderful masterpiece even existed, they would have told countless stories to family and friends of this moment. Unfortunately, this is not either the time and era in which cameras were so readily carried and photo opportunities were given. However, The Game Fish lived. Dice, Monopoly pieces, the game of Life pieces, checkers, chess, dominos and even a plastic doll's arm were all assembled in the shape of a great Marlin fish, decorating and constructing the fish itself. It was both beautiful and offensive, with a poetic beauty only a few that observed it could appreciate. To a degree, it was out of place in this museum, but to some I guess it was considered art. For Aaron and Nora, it capped the ending to a perfect trip before the emotions of Aaron's first ever marathon and of course the trip to the Vietnam wall. Aaron was wise to wait after the run to visit the wall. Even he could not predict how it would affect him. Nora would see things in her husband she did not think were possible. Aaron lost all composure and self-control. But… Nora did not blame him one bit.

The next morning Aaron awoke a couple of hours before he had to make his way to the starting line. Nora could have slept in but wanted to be awake when Aaron had to leave the hotel room. They kissed and held one another longer than most couples that morning, and Aaron had an idea.

"After the race," he said. "They will have large balloons with letters on them telling family members to meet the runners near the appropriate letter of the runner's last name." Aaron continued. "Let's meet under the balloon Z," he said. "There cannot be too many people with the last name beginning with that letter," he concluded. Nora agreed, kissing her husband goodbye.

The start of the Washington Marathon in the fall of 1984 had two aspects that Aaron had not anticipated. One was the starting gun. It was a canon fired by a General Norman Schwarzkopf Jr. The fact that the general was to eventually lead troops in one of the greatest military victories of all time in the Gulf

War was not the significance to the starting gun that Aaron would forever remember. What Aaron recalls is how loud the sound of the canon explosion was and the repercussion in his chest he had felt after the explosion, which was some hundreds of yards away. Aaron thought of the Civil War and all the men that had fought and died during the battle of North and South. This one blast, and all he felt took him to a place in Gettysburg or the battle of Antietam. Aaron thought surely the blast for the starting gun was a blank. What did it feel like to be fired upon when a live round was shot? he questioned. The other unanticipated event was a television talk show host would make this marathon a spectacle for her own televised event. For Aaron even thought, this second event did in fact take place during his first marathon. He really didn't notice much of the event other than on one occasion seeing some television lights on the other side of a grassed park across from where he ran. If it wasn't for Nora telling Aaron of Oprah Winfrey running her first marathon this very same day, Aaron probably would have never even known. Aaron knew of this popular host but that was about his extent of it. Nora and he did not watch her show or know much about her. The television they had was only rabbit ears and a crude antenna atop the family's home roof. Still, for Nora, the woman running by as the crowd screamed around her for a brief moment made her spectator role a little more exciting.

Aaron, meanwhile was running the course that snaked its way around Washington's streets. At one point the only thing separating him running north and the return runners running south was orange cones in the middle of the road. The illusion for Aaron and probably many other runners was that they had the feeling that it was a short distance between the two sides of the cones. Nothing could be further from the truth. By the time Aaron was on the other side of the cones with runners running toward him was in fact a full hour later. When this occurred, Aaron thought, *Of course, I should have recognized the speed of the oncoming runners when I was on the other side.* Only now, looking at the slower runners, does he realize this.

Mile after mile, the race goes on. Somewhere around mile twelve or thirteen, someone on the road next to him states that the building to the left is the Pentagon. Aaron had seen this five-sided shaped building before from an aerial view on the news. What amazed him as he ran around it was that the building was so big that from the ground you could not tell the adjoining walls' angles were not ninety degrees. Five-sided yes, but so big one could not tell, thought Aaron as the miles logged on and on.

Dehydration and thought processes started to effect Aaron in two distinct ways. One was a large cramp that developed in his right thigh muscles somewhere around mile twenty. The other was he had a hard time doing simple math equations. The thigh muscle he recognized from some of his long training runs. He knew from both reading and training that any time a muscle starts to cramp it is nine times out of ten a lack of fluids. In this case, water. He drank, even though he was full, at least a cup full at each and every water station the course provided. He was shocked at the starting spot that these stations began at mile three but decided to load up and drink regardless of the regularity. At mile twenty-two he made a catastrophic math error. In his mind, when he closed in at the mile marker (a large plywood triangle sign of sort that read the numbers 22), in his mind he thought, *Only three miles to go. You can do this Aaron. It's like a short jog around the block at home.* His mind lies. True, the distance around the block at the Mills' home was three miles to the tenth. Not true was the math required to add three and twenty-two and get twenty-six. For three very long painful miles, Aaron believes it is simply a jog around the block at home. He is doing the pace of an eleven-minute mile at this point and he is also considering that this is the very last marathon he will ever run. All marathons do this to runners. There is simply no preparation to this distance that cannot cause this thought process if the race is in fact "run." What do I mean? Jogging is simply running without a purpose. However, running is to get from one point, point-A, to another point, point-B, as fast as you can. Start to finish when running should cause you pain. Start to finish when jogging should be enjoyable and a decent work out. Aaron is a runner; the goal is to get to the finish line as fast as *he* can. Every runner and their ability is different, and this means every time when a runner finishes is also different. There is no disrespect or lack of honor for any runner in the runners' world that finishes his or her fastest time, even if they do not win. Aaron's first-ever marathon will forever mark his time-to-beat time. He has run a good race.

His end-time will be four hours, forty-four minutes, and forty-two seconds. He will forever wish he was two seconds slower, just for the conversation piece of 4:44:44. However, now as he approaches the triangle plywood sign that reads a large spray-painted "25," he realizes his error. Aaron thinks, *22 plus 3 is 25—not 26*, and his shoulders drop nearly to the pavement. Beneath it, his feet seems to torture him with every step. What a confidence-crushing moment. Another mile, which at this point feels like ten miles. The crowd around him on the street's sides thickens, and if not for this, he latter would think, he could have never finished. People he would never know cheer him on. Signs for loved ones drape the side streets and people urge everyone to keep going, "You are almost done!" They scream. Aaron reads a sign that states they are proud of him, but he is still an ass hole. He chuckles at this ridiculous sign, and it gives him hope. He looks for Nora in the crowd but is unable to find her as the last thousand yards come to a close. He sees the timer clock in the distance as it ticks down, and his heart is filled with pride. He didn't even know if he was capable to finish, and even if he did, his best guess was his time was under five hours. As his heart swelled with the knowledge that he will in fact finish, on his feet, looking like a runner, he thinks, *I crushed it!* Aaron smiles the "runner's high" smile. *Not only did I finish, I did it in four hours and less that forty-five minutes!* He crosses the finish line and tears start to run down his face as he pumps his fists in the air. To the world right now in this moment, Aaron Mills screams in his head, *Fuck you! Fuck you*, he thinks to Malisa and her theory. *Fuck you*, he thinks to Butch and treating Jared like shit. *Fuck you Oprah Winfrey and your stupid attempt to share with the world your stupid pathetic jog around Washington while your cameras film every step. Fuck you twenty-six miles and fuck you Vietnam wall.* All these harsh, yet flooding emotions flood Aaron as he crosses the finish line with both pride and hate. Someone wraps his shivering body with a silver melamine blanket. Water and Gatorade is offered, as well as Power-bars, and people are repeatedly getting in Aaron's face asking if he feels all right. Aaron walks the sectioned-off finish-line course like cattle in a well-thought-out hall heading to the slaughterhouse. His legs quiver from the task, and he shivers and walks, thinking now only of Nora and the worries she might be feeling waiting as his mind reminds him of their plan. Hate escapes his thoughts as fast as they consumed them. His tears start to dry as he analyzes what he thought crossing the finish line. Common sense and rational thinking seep in as Aaron becomes more the Aaron we know with each passing step. He walks, as a runner to his left looks as though he might pass out. Oddly, no other runners attempt to help, but medical staff is on him well before he would have hit the ground. It occurs to Aaron just then that he is being closely watched. Hundreds of volunteers line the sides of the cattle path on this side of the fence. Thousands more it seem are on the other side of the fence with encouraging words, clapping hands, and holding signs that read they are proud. When the fenced area stops on both sides, all runners flood into a common area where family and friends await them. Large balloons are staggered throughout the large grassy area with jumbo-sized letters on them. As Aaron snakes his way through the crowd looking for the letter "Z," it is clear that he was not alone in making this meeting place a better choice than his real last name initial. For starters, the balloon read, "WXYZ" and not simply the letter "Z." But also, this was the end of the area where family and friends could meet, as well as the largest exit from the park. Hundreds of people, both runners and spectators, speckled this area, and just as Aaron thought finding Nora would be impossible, Nora screamed, "Aaron!, Aaron, I'm here!" while yelling and waving her arms. The two embraced and Aaron again felt tears swelling up in his eyes. Nora too felt the emotion of the trip and task at hand and made a conscious effort not to speak. The noise and crowd around them holding one another felt silent for only them. What in reality was nearly twenty seconds felt like five minutes. Aaron was exhausted both physically and emotionally. Nora could feel her running man's limp body during the embrace. Aaron speaks first. "Under five hours. four hours and forty some minutes," he said. Nothing but pride and the feeling of accomplishment in his crackling voice. Nora replies, "I was worried. I didn't see you and thought maybe you had run on by and were waiting for me. I'm so sorry I missed you crossing, Honey."

"Oh, Baby I'm glad you didn't wait. We would still be looking for one another," Aaron said. And no truer words would be spoken. The number of people after Aaron had finished was nearly as larger than the finishers before him. The difference being, these runners were slower, having way more fun at times, and needing far more medical attention. The cattle fenced area bottled up and stopped for nearly an hour.

Aaron and Nora walked hand-in-hand back to their hotel. Aaron's legs began to stiffen as lactic acid began to seep deep into his muscles. Walking was the best thing to slow this process down, but it would come nevertheless. A very hot bath and some food will finish out the day as the two would talk about what they saw and experienced, one as a first-time marathoner, the other as a first-time marathoner spectator. This bond and what was shared would forever be theirs. Regardless of what's to come for these two individuals and their uncertain future that neither could predict, the marathon and their memories were this married couples own shared, loving time. Tomorrow will change with what's to come at the Vietnam, wall, but today was theirs and theirs alone.

The next morning, Aaron could hardly walk. He had stiffened up during the night and walking downstairs to the continental breakfast was comical to watch. Nora excused herself when laughing but both found it funny, and Aaron could only laugh at how silly he had to look. Pushing through the pain and stiffness and walking as much as possible is really the only way to get those stiff muscles back in working order. "Are you sure you want to walk the Vietnam Memorial?" Nora asks, filling herself with scrambled eggs and jelly toast. "Of course," Aaron replies, eating more or at the very least as much as Nora for the first time in a very long time. "It's several blocks, Aaron," Nora interjects, questioning with concern and remembering the stairs he had just tried to navigate about twenty minutes ago.

"Nora, it will be fine," Aaron continues. "Walking is the best thing. Besides, taking a cab just doesn't seem right." Aaron of course is exactly correct. The memorial was designed for foot traffic, as with most of Washington's memorials and parks. Something Nora might not have considered but Aaron did was that walking a slow pace toward the memorial would give him time to prepare. It would be foolish to say this will be harder than the miles run yesterday; however, this will not be easy either. Aaron has been thinking and preparing mentally for the experience, and with doing so, has thought about Jared a lot these past few weeks leading up to the marathon. Back home packing for the trip, Aaron quietly took down the shoe box in the upper corner of the closet that held the twenty-two letters Jared wrote to Aaron so long ago. He didn't open any but thumbed through the envelopes, recalling each letter inside them almost word for word as he hears Jared's voice in his head.

"Be strong and think," Jared said.

"Never run to get away. Run to understand," Jared said.

The last letter hurts Aaron's mind and heart the most when his thumb hits it, and he recalls.

"Can't wait to see you soon," Jared said.

The walk started off cool and damp for Nora and Aaron, and the clouds turned from a muddy gray to a muddy color as a very light rain began to fall. The people on the streets and in the parks were up from the marathon the day before and limping men and women or simply slow walkers could be spotted all around. In the distance they could see the wall as the city sounds began to fade into the background of Aaron's thoughts. The closer and closer they got, the names began to appear on the giant slabs, and the overwhelming number of names sinks in very quickly. A hush among the crowd is apparent, and if people do speak, they whisper to one another. Hands find their way to gasping mouths as you walk by visitors, some standing or touching a name they know. Nora slows and lets Aaron lead as they both look at all the names on the wall. Aaron's lower lip quivers as his eyes begin to swell with tears yet again. He would have never predicted he would cry yesterday after the pride he had after finishing the marathon, but today he knew tears would fall, and fall down his cheeks they do, slowly mixed with the misting rain that will turn to a sprinkle soon. The book to look up names sits open on the pedestal at both ends of the wall. Aaron and Nora walk up to the very thick book and thumb what they assumed would be alphabetical in order. The names are not listed alphabetically but rather chronologically by date of death or missing in action, beginning and ending in the center where the two walls meet. Though the wall is shaped somewhat like wings, one stretching towards the Washington Monument, while the other points towards the Lincoln Memorial, it reads like a circle with the name of the first official American casualty at the top of the east panel beneath the date 1959. The names then continue down the east wing, make an invisible circle of sorts around, then begin again at the far end of the west wing. It then concludes at the center with the date 1975. Only if there were more than one casualty in any one particular day are those names are listed in alphabetical order.

Nora reads the instructions and rubs Aaron's back before asking. "Honey, when did Jared die?" She states softly, "The book is set up by dates and then alphabetically," being cautious to say, "Date of death."

Aaron shakes his head from side to side as if to wipe the cobwebs from his emotions and thoughts. "Uhmm, it was 1969. I think in the fall of '69," Aaron said. Nora thumbs through the pages and finds what they are looking for. Jared Neal Mills, location panel 15W line 87.

Nora and Aaron walk to the wall and read the panel numbers and letters at the bottom of each panel. Aaron's heart races as they count the lines to find his brother's name. There in the misting Washington rain between Jim Allen Eggleston and Danny Lee Grimshaw was the very fine chiseled out name of Jared Neal Mills.

Aaron touches the name and explodes with tears. Nora comforts her man as only she knows how, rubbing his back and tearing herself. Aaron's quivering lactic-acid-filled legs give way as he first bends at the waist and then falls to his knees. He leans against the stone wall as passersby try not to look and feel his pain. Flowers and letters are at his quickly soaking pants as the clouds open and the rain starts to fall even heavier. Umbrellas open as tourists run for cover. In the distance, the thunder roars, and for a very brief moment it is only Aaron on his knees and Nora standing beside him at the wall. Lighting flashes miles away as thunder follows with a roar once more. Aaron stands and then he and Nora hold one another up, looking at Jared's name. When they finally turn to walk away, Aaron explodes in tears once more. He loved his brother so much. He still misses him even after all these years, and he thinks, *Malisa can have her theory. Jared was my brother, and I don't care what anyone says.*

The next day they drive back to New York with the tears long dried as well as their rain-soaked clothes. Most of the drive is silent, and if they speak at all, it's light chit-chat and no word of the wall or Jared. However, as sudden as the falling rains at yesterday's wall, Aaron speaks seemingly out of nowhere. "There is a shoe box in my closet on the top shelf. If something ever happened to me would you give it to Malisa please?" Aaron pauses for a moment and then before Nora can ask what's inside it, said, "It's letters from Jared, from Vietnam."

"Of course, Honey." Nora replies. "But nothing is going to happen to you," she states with absolute certainty.

"Promise?" Aaron asks.

"Yes, of course I promise," Nora said.

Aaron of course cares little if at all that Malisa receives these letters Jared wrote. His plan is to write a list in the event of his untimely demise, along with insurance papers Nora will need. He will put this list and papers in this box, knowing Nora will surely look inside it before giving it to Malisa. The idea comes to him when he thinks back to how unprepared he himself was when Jared died. He wants only for his wife and son to never suffer, but regardless of the plan he has put in place, they surely do so suffer.

Aaron then tells Nora what he thought yesterday and saying this out loud feels good as he drives.

"I don't care what Malisa said about her theory. Jared was our brother regardless," Aaron said.

Nora shakes her head up and down slowly as she looks at Aaron as he drives. Aaron's eyes never leave the road, but he smiles a sinister smile, knowing all too well what Nora will say next as well as the plan he just put into motion.

"I agree," Nora said. "I really believe Aaron, you are right."

Chapter 9

(House of Tears)

The months that followed Aaron's death ticked bye one painful minute at a time. A grandfather clock that stood in the foyer of the house of tears reminded Nora of her pain. On the quarter hour, this gift Aaron had given her and the attachment she had to it caused her remorse to surface. Time after pain-ticking time. A friend who Nora confided in about the grief this chiming clock caused her said, "Why not simply silence the chimes?" Only now can Nora truly understand that the chimes that rang her heartbreaking tune were all in her head and heart; that running from what is inside you is a fatal attempt of emotional suicide. Night after sleepless night, Nora lied awake in bed crying over the only true love she had ever had, and now he was gone. Night after night, staring at a darkened stucco ceiling, peace eluded her. Sleep only came in short bursts followed by violent awakenings of reality. For Nora, looking back at the months that followed the loss of Aaron and all he had meant to her, she is clueless about how she even survived. *A lifelong Christian with even God's help,* she now thinks, *would have had trouble comprehending what I was forced to endure.* But survive she did, and she did it all in those first few months all alone and without God's help—or so she had once thought. But here she stands, nearly four years to the day, with all her memories organized and labeled in the back of her mind. A whisper of her past catches her off guard, and without warning for no apparent reason she feels pain once again. It's odd how the sorrowful thoughts will flood the reservoir of normal thinking even after all these years. The water fills slowly and unexpectedly, and before you know it all the sandbags you stacked or the channels you constructed to handle the inevitable flooding memories crash and overflow once again. Saturated and drowning, time and time again you relive the troubled waters in which you had previously swam. Each breath gets you closer to the healing, higher shore. Each flood pours, farther and farther between storms. She often wonders why God did what he did. She longs for Aaron's logic to explain what she feels. She laughs at this silly thought, now believing he never knew what she really felt, that she as well as others hold tight to their own thoughts and emotions, regardless of what we show to be true on the outside. Only her and her God understands her, and the void in her heart she filled with Aaron's love was good but temporary. But still, she misses his thoughts on the things she will never understand. Only a fading voice of an Aaron she once knew can sound in Nora's head. The events that lead to her salvation are truly some of God's most miraculous of works. How did he take a once devoted atheist and change her into a believer with such faith? Nora, in her feeble little human mind, has traced the chain of events to a man she met at a local grocery store, but somehow in her heart she knows it was God's plan from the point of her creation. He knew that from her birth and for many years she would turn her back on his love and ignore the quiet sounds of his presence. It was only when she had lost everything she believed in that she would listen to God, and he used a simple man named Phillip Moore to guide her in her hearing.

Eating was something Nora did very little of nine weeks after Aaron's death. But Kevin was still a growing boy and the mundane task of grocery shopping had to be done whether Nora liked it or not. She didn't like going out, or more accurately, she didn't like driving. She could tell her concentration was lacking, and after making some turns or passing through an intersection, she often could not recall if she had stopped or observed the traffic lights and laws. Several times in the years that followed she was either in an accident or in what air-traffic controllers call a "near miss." But shop that day she did, and in aisle two (boxed cereals and dry goods), Phillip spoke.

"I can't believe how much cereal has gone up in price these past years," he said.

Nora twitched a passing smile and said nothing.

"Seriously is it me?" he asked. "I can remember when this box was fifty-five cents." Phillip was holding the smallest of frosted flakes boxes available with Tony the Tiger looking happier than any real tiger would ever look eating a sugar-coated flake.

Still no sound from Nora, but Phillip did manage to get eye contact and her attention.

"Am I showing my age by saying that?" he chuckled.

"Ah no," Nora replied. She felt no threat. The aura Phillip projected was that of an older married man with no hidden agenda. His conversation was simply polite and non-threatening. He was neither "hitting" on her nor wanting anything in return. It was this casual air that held Nora's attention. Too many times women feel this silent air of lust from the hunter men. Too many times the prey will recoil in disgust when happily married or not married men want the lustful attention. But there was none of that here. Tensionless attention followed by conversation without plans.

"You look familiar. Do you go to Saint Anthony's on Old Norcross?" Phillip inquired.

"Church?" Nora answered. Her face as well as her expression said everything about her attendance habits.

"No," she continued. "I don't go to church… well." Her voice trailed, slowing silently as she hesitated in speaking. Her eyes dropped and looked down and to the left as if to show shame in what she had just said. But shame was nowhere to be found in what Nora was feeling. She simply has learned that the topic of faith, religion, God and what she did or did not believe, was better left unspoken. Although she desired the conversation with this gentle, kind man, she was disappointed that it so quickly turned to a topic she neither wanted nor needed to have, or so she thought. So in all of a quarter second— a micro split moment of history that will neither return or be repeated—all of what Nora has been and will become changed when God used Philip to intervene. And the "well" she had spoken of was a grain of sand of evidence on a beach of tears, when she was reminded that the last church and funeral hall she stepped foot into was to bury her dead husband just nine short weeks ago.

This too was seen in her eyes, and Phillip felt he had inadvertently stumbled onto some painful threads.

"I'm sorry I didn't mean too..." Phillip quietly said.

"No, it's all right," Nora interrupted. "It's just, I lost my husband, and..." Her eyes again begin their familiar dance of death.

"He was killed, going for a run..." She slowly continued. Again looking down. Again not feeling shame.

"Not the young man on Route-33? Oh my... I am so sorry. I read about that," Phillips left hand covers his mouth in disbelief.

Nora immediately hears Aaron's voice inside her head. "Philip," it whispers. "Is left-handed."

Nora simply nods a slow yes as the pool of today's tears begins to fill the sockets of her eyes.

She had hated the grocery store experience all on its own. The music that played in the background intended to add to a pleasant shopping experience had often left her crying without Phillip's help. And as ridiculous as it may sound, certain products she and Aaron had purchased together or made a comment on also reminded her of the one she lost. So today, already in aisle two of all places, she begins to cry yet again. Phillip says nothing as Nora stands and struggles. Driving to the store, she had promised herself she would not cry until frozen foods (aisle nine) or at the very least paper goods (aisle eight). But here she stood in aisle two, struggling to hold back the tears directly in front of a man she had never met. All these thoughts, the driving promise, the non-threatening Phillip Moore, the frosted-fucking-flakes, and of course another moment in her world without Aaron crashed her peaceful mind and heart with pain.

Phillip, with his Christian heart, could stand and do nothing no more. His own heart had swelled with both love and pain for the women he had never met who stood before him. Slowly he edged forward, and with Tony in his left hand, he hugged Nora at the very moment she lost all her composure and control. Nora leaned heavily on Phillip as the dam broke. Her breathing was choppy and erratic. Her chest filled and contracted as the emotion and tears poured out. A full minute of lost control in a world that is consumed with so much pain and suffering overwhelmed her. As the minute begins to slowly pass and as the control and awareness of the reality she was in opened, a thought that she would later never be absolutely sure was her own tickled her mind. A request really, and she will never be sure of its origin or source. A thought she has no recollection of ever having before, or at the very least, for a very long time. When the music and the volume of the world around her were slowly turning up the thought (a request really) that changed everything was soft and comforting when comprehended.

"God please…" is what Nora heard somewhere deep inside her mind or heart.

Was this an undocumented moment of telekinesis believed by those who believe in the paranormal? Because at that very moment, Nora "heard" the whisper plea. Phillip was doing what good Christians do—praying. The prayer that he held in his mind as he held Nora in his arms was, "Please God help this poor woman." Or was this God himself in a moment of intervention opening a sliver of hope to a painful plea? A believer will choose his or her rationale and reasons based on their own experiences and what they have allowed themselves to be taught. Those who believe in the paranormal believe that they can read the unspoken lines of reality through their own power of thought and mind. The Christian believes that all things are from God and that anything supernatural or unspoken is his will and his power alone. With this freedom of choice comes the world's greatest irony of ironies mankind has ever known. The creator gives the creation the freedom to choose. The creation chooses to disbelieve in the creator. Irony.

Nora was a living, breathing example of this irony for nearly twenty-five years. She has wrestled with this moment in her past in her mind several times. She has prayed for an explanation since her salvation to the God she now loves and needs. She simply can't get past his unconditional love that allowed such freedom of disbelief for so very long. She was there, she had thought. She knows the thought, voice, or feeling she can't explain when hope entered her heart that day. With her plea for help, she knows God in his mercy and grace stepped in. She also knows what she herself would have said when she disbelieved if someone had told her this story of the touch of hope from the hand of God. She is able to argue what was or was not real in her head because of the extremes she has lived and is now living. "And yet…" she has prayed and wept. "You were with me all along, patiently waiting for me to humbly ask."

Phillip walked and shopped with Nora the remainder of the time they spent in the grocery store. Jokes were exchanged in aisle eight (paper goods) when Nora loaded her cart with Kleenex tissues. As they stood in the check-out line, Philip invited Nora to his Sunday worship.

"I would love for you to join me and my Rose at church on Sunday," he said. His eyes and heart sent nothing but care and concern for a friend he had met just one short hour ago. Nora knew she needed something. There was no end to the pain and sleepless nights if she didn't open her heart up to people that cared for her, and the clock would continue to chime in the house of tears when she returned home. She wondered, *for how long?*

"Okay Phillip," she replied. "You have been very kind."

The service Nora first attended was like no other she had ever encountered. She had very few memories of the times she sat in church and daydreamed as a child. She only remembers wanting it to end as fast as humanly possible. Her father was something she also remembered during those years of youth. He seemed to know every word, every line, every turn of his big, black-leathered, bounded Bible's pages. He listened and drank each and every word the preacher spoke. Nora could hardly keep her eyelids from closing, but Father couldn't miss a word or blink in fear of doing so. But this church was different. The music was full and joyful. The colors that draped the walls and the people were bright and inviting. When the preacher finally spoke, the message and words cut fast to Nora's heart. She would later think, *He was speaking directly to me,* in amazement and disbelief. It was those words, songs, and colors that kept Nora coming back. Nora even looked forward to each and every Sunday as the weeks passed. Phillip was a volunteer, so days of sitting with him and his wife Rose was far and few between. As the services passed one by one, the days turned to weeks, and the weeks turned to months, Nora began to question her own understanding of what she held to be true. Her mind was now open to the idea that she really didn't know every fucking thing. She could have never in a million years known she would be a widow.

She could have never predicted in a trillion years that she would be attending church. But more than all that, Nora's heart had softened. Nora felt empathy for people around her now. She wondered if they too had experienced or were experiencing the pain of a lost loved and were having to function and do the daily activities regardless of the loss. She had an angry interaction with a woman at a Quickie-Mart check-out line, and in the past, heated words would have been exchanged. Hate for one another would have prevailed. But Nora simply stepped aside and let the woman pass. In her mind, this seemed so ridiculously unimportant when considering the empty house she will go home to and the husband she will miss all night long. *The clock will chime later as it chimes this very minute I stand in line. Who fucking cares*, Nora thought.

In the week to follow, with these uncaring thoughts in the back of her mind, the church handout that week included some programs the church offered its congregation. As Nora sat in her seat she chose every week and waited for the service to begin with the pleasantry, smiles, and nods that fellow seat-seekers around showed as they got settled in, she read of a recently widowed class that was about to begin at the church on Wednesday nights. Just as with the whisper she might or might not have heard in the grocery, she feels or hears that this is something she is meant to attend. The voice of God is so clear at the exact moment we hear it. It is only later we question if this is something we ourselves conjured up in our head. Or, if we had indeed "heard" anything at all. As Nora sits as the music for the service begins, she is without doubt that this Wednesday night class is for her.

Kevin slops up his dinner with hardly a word. Nora grilled pork chops and opened and then heated some canned corn. As with most dinner nights as of late, Nora simply pushes her food around her plate until Kevin's done and tries to unlock her nine-year-old boy's world from his mouth that he's filling.

"How is swimming going?" Nora asks.

"Hmm...?" Kevin responds. He either didn't hear the question or didn't understand his mother's recent concern about his swimming world.

"Swimming? I asked how your swimming is going?" Nora repeats.

"Uhhh," Kevin swallows his mouthful of chops and continues to answer. "Good, I love it. You wanna come? Tonight, to practice I mean?"

Before Aaron's death, Nora came to at least half of Kevin's meets as well as practices. The goal was two-fold in Nora's mind. She knew her husband very well. He enjoyed his alone time. Also, like a good mom, she knew her son very well. Even though around his fellow swimmers Kevin would laugh, ignore, or sometimes even make fun of his mom in the stands around, Kevin liked Nora there watching him. Nora knew, like all good moms know: *My son needs me to watch and my husband needs me to give him space*, and like a good mom, she did both with one single, unselfish sweep. Aaron would use this alone time to run. Guilt-free, after-work, no-one-home time to run. This unspoken predeath Aaron time was something Nora herself orchestrated. Mother did this all her adult life. Seemingly without thought, mother kept the family working and living in shared space and parallel times. If any of us would stop and really think about this for one second, we could only conclude these actions were random or by chance. However, this was mother's genius, like secretly moving chess pieces across the board, only to find out too late—checkmate.

"I'm sorry Honey," Nora replied. "I have something at the church tonight. In fact, for the next nine weeks every Wednesday I will be at the church from 7:00 to 9:00 P.M."

A pause filled the dining room. For Nora, it was if time itself stood still. A fly near a windowsill stopped midflight, its wings flapped, and then slowed to a stop. The furnace micro-seconds to combust froze for a split second regardless of the thermostats reading to ignite. Outside, miles above the Mills' family home, a rain drop that was to form and fall at that very moment paused in its cloud as Nora's words hung in the dining space air.

"Cool," Kevin replies, stabbing the last pork chop from the plate knowing all too well that Mom would not be eating it.

The first night at the widow's Wednesday night church function was very uncomfortable for Nora. About thirteen people, both male and female, showed up. An elderly couple, who Nora would later learn have been happily married now for some thirty-two years, facilitated the class. At first this struck Nora as odd. How, she thought, can two people who have never experienced a spouse's death lead a class of people who have experienced a spouse's death? But that, as well as the uncomfortableness, explained itself as the night progressed. God was the centerpiece in this class. Thus, loss and what Nora experiences really is not the topic. Also, the loss for the married facilitators was for their only son, who was killed when a firetruck tipped over and crushed him. It was Nora's open mind that held her tongue this first night. When she looks back on that first night and what followed, Nora now understands that it was God himself that held that tongue and Nora and her mind had little if anything to do with it. Introductions and a general structure to what was to come the next eight weeks was discussed. A book was a suggested purchase, and the topic of inability to "buy" it for the measly ten dollars was also discussed. Nora paid the ten dollars asked for the book she thought she would never read like a lemming handing over the keys to the city. Money for Nora was not an issue. Aaron made sure of that. But she did come to understand that not everyone was as thoughtful or prepared as Aaron when it came to the unpredictable or unforeseen events. Some in her class were clearly more uncomfortable with being asked to purchase a book than the topic of God as the center of our loss and how to deal with it. The very first page of the seemingly meaningless book changed Nora's life forever.

Kevin was only two and spoke very few meaningful sentences that either Nora or Aaron could understand. The day was sunny, and Kevin stumbled and hobbled across the family lawn as Nora and Aaron watched with delight.

"We need a sandbox, I think, for the boy. What do you think, Hun?" Aaron asked.

"A sandbox would be fine," Nora replied.

"Yep, all good boys need a box of sand I believe," Aaron said.

"You keep thinking, Aaron. That's what you're good at," Nora said jokingly to her loving husband.

Aaron also looks at the old barn, looks back at his son playing and walking in the freshly cut grass, and then back at the old barn.

"Oh, I sense a tone of sarcasm from my dear wife," Aaron replied.

"Oh, you know I'm kidding," Nora said with a look of love and softness in her voice. "You are the nucleus of our family. Without *you* we are simply eons floating in space," Nora finished.

Only pure love in their eyes passed to one another after those simple words were spoken. Aaron knew what Nora meant and agreed. He was the nucleus. Nora knew what she said, and the universe knew it to be true as well. Aaron was the center to this perfect family they had built. Even now when the thoughts of knocking down the old barn are a seedling starting to grow in his mind's garden, he would labor his entire short life to see that it was always well kept. Nora also knew of this labor of love and her statement on that day was revisited in her mind after the very first page of the seemingly meaningless book she felt forced to purchase.

Nora read the first page as the elderly facilitators continued to speak. Her mind flips back and forth from the church group to the nucleus conversation her and Aaron had had years ago.

"When you make a person as a nucleus to your world, if that person leaves or dies, your world will explode."

"However, when you make God your nucleus, he will never leave you, and thus, your world will never explode."

Nora read this in disbelief. Like a sound we do not hear all around, Nora became silent as she heard a deafening sound inside her head. She rereads the words in disbelief, and nothing outside of her was real. Her mind spun backwards in time to that day when Kevin played and Aaron suggested the box of sand. She flipped over and over the words inside her head that were spoken with no one around but her and her new family. *How could God know even when I didn't believe he existed?* she thought. How could he see what these words would mean to me so many years in the future? Or did he? Is this a random event? Is this a coincidence I cannot explain? Nora's mind was drunk with thought. She resettles these thoughts in a silent torture as the people around her go about their widow meeting. *What else does this meaningless book have to say,* she hears? A prayer follows. What Christians refer to as the sinner's prayer. A confession, if you will, of your own unrighteousness and God's forgiveness. Nora reads this prayer in her head silently to herself. Church as of late, the open mindedness of her own consciousness, and the idea that she understands fucking nothing is filling her mind and heart. After the meeting, she exchanged pleasantries with a few of the members, recalls none of their names, and goes home. The drive was like a dream, and like so many miles before this one after Aaron's death, she has no clue how she safely returns home. The next day she opened the book and reread all she had digested the night before. Her thoughts were similar from the night before, and the only thing she could think to do was actually pray that fateful prayer. So she did. Day two. Then day three. Then day four, all came and went with these hollow words prayed by a former atheist. A prayer from a book that she never wanted with words that connected both time and space from years past. After day six, she knew that reading these words was just that—reading.

Day Seven

Kevin was hungry, and all that Nora had without a much-unwanted run to the store was hot dogs. Kevin was never a huge fan of hot dogs, but if they grilled them—something Aaron did regularly—Kevin never complained. This, Nora thought, had more to do with Dad cooking Kevin's next meal than the food itself. In any event, Nora fired up the grill and began the task of cooking Kevin's dogs. The day was sunny with cumulus clouds overhead. The smell of the grill, the hot dog cooking, and just life without the man she had loved for so very long, set in. There were days she could never explain and thoughts that provoked tears she had not a clue from where they came. This was one of those days. As the hot dogs fizzled and needed to be turned, she cried. The tears that day where as painful as she had ever felt or wept. How lost she was, she thought. There was no hope or end to this trying pain. Her tears filled her eyes to the point of making her visionless. In complete desperation, she muttered the prayer she had read six days straight, but this time she meant every word. "Oh Father," she cried. "Please forgive me of my sins," she wept. "I am not worthy of your grace." Her shoulders felt heavy. Her body weight was nearly too much to bear, "Please help me. I am so sorry and lost."

As Nora looked to the clouds, a bird flew overhead and the backdrop was the cumulus clouds. Just then, as if a clear piece of thin filament was pealed from a piece of plexiglass, the entire sky became clearer. Before the bird was visible, however, at that exact moment when the pealing occurred, Nora's heart flipped inside out and regained its beating pulse. The clouds were clearer, the bird in flight was crystal clear, and the world itself changed from the vantage point of Nora's eyes and her heartbeat, the same but very different. Nora stood in disbelief. *Something had just happened. But what?* she thought. By the time her conscious mind could even begin to understand the clarity and beating heart, she realized the tears had stopped. She stood at the grill's edge and wondered what in the world had just happened to her. The task of mother kicked in. The hot dogs were done, and she brought them inside to her waiting son.

Kevin said, "What's with you?" looking at Nora with hot dogs plated in in hand.

"What?" Nora questioned with a look of disbelief.

"You look different," Kevin said.

Nora was different. From that day forward, Nora came to believe and know with all certainty that she was saved. Only many years later did she come to realize that she was one of the elect. Phillip Moore, in aisle two, was destiny. The sandbox idea and her nucleus description were prewritten. God had a plan all along. The only soul who did not know what was to come was Nora herself. But now, even in all her pain, she is okay with that fact. When God is in your world and has a plan, you might feel and be in pain, but his plan is for *his* glory, not yours. If God wanted to glorify Nora, he could, and Aaron would have never died that fateful running day. A child would never be still-born. A criminal would never rape or steal. The unjust would never profit. However, glory be to God and the highest, and as a result, Nora Mills is now saved. However, it's still a house of tears.

Chapter 10

(Letters, Lists & the Thing We Write.)

A couple weeks have passed, and the pain in Aaron's legs from running his first marathon is finally starting to dissipate. Since returning home, Aaron wanted to continue with his plan to prepare or at least ensure that in the unlikely event of his early demise, Nora and Kevin would be okay. He started by calling an insurance agent for some life insurance. Then when that was all set, he began to think about the letter he would leave and the instructions for Nora, as well as what to put in the letter. When it was completed, he created a list. Nora would understand this to mean that the items on the list needed to be done in chronological order. However, that was never Aaron's intention.

Misunderstandings of what we think was meant from piles of letters, pictures, notes and belongings from loved ones that pass on are inevitable. They're gone and asking what someone meant or did not mean is impossible. The finality of these questions we have, and the inability to ask them is so permanent that it causes us pain. Forever hurts. There is little comfort when forever sets in. The passing of the people we love can reveal itself in the strangest of ways. When Aaron died, for example, Nora noticed that there was never any ice in the freezer's ice container. When Jared left for good, Aaron noticed his bedroom was far messier than before, and items he looked for regardless of where he left them were strangely in the places they were expected to be. Getting the daily mail fell on Kevin's shoulders after Dad, died and we wondered without connecting the dots, *How did mom get the mail before?* But as these iceless cubes, straightened-up bedrooms, or mail-fetched items work themselves out, the haunting loss—whether realized or unnoticed—adds to the pain that we suffer. Consciously we know they are gone. Unconsciously we learn just how far they were intertwined in the fabric of our lives.

Aaron decides to re-read some, if not all the letters Jared had left him (depending on what time allowed). Nora and Kevin are at a swimming practice on this particular Saturday morning, and although Aaron would normally would go for a run, he finds himself upstairs in his bed room with a shoe box full of Jared's letters, notes, pictures, and belongings. When he takes the box down from the top shelf, he thinks, *My brother's entire life minus the memories are in this stupid shoe box.* Tick tock, the pain clock begins to move. Inside are the letters from Vietnam, the tin's entire contents—including a dead spider— and the empty money envelope. There were sixty-five undated journal entries, including the error on the day Aaron was shown the hiding spot for the first time when his birthday was assassinated. Also, there was the one letter he truly needed to read, the one that instructed Aaron on what to do in the event Jared did not return home.

> *If you are reading this I have instructed you to find this treasure. The only reason I can think of for why I would tell you about this is I am not ever going to come back for this myself. The only person I can think I would ever tell is you, Aaron. So please listen carefully. I will miss you. You are and always will be my brother, my only brother I will forever love. Try not to be sad and remember all we have done and how we lived as brothers. You are an amazing person Aaron, and you have given me hope when at times I'd seen none in my life. The items in this treasure meant something to me at one time but now writing this letter to you I know and understand it was YOU, you all along that meant everything to me and it is you that is my true treasure. Take the money it is yours now, buy yourself that Walkman radio you wanted. Remember Butch is your*

dad, but he does not understand us. Mom will always help you so when you need it lean on her. I love you Aaron, be good.

~Love Jared.

Sitting on the bed's edge after the re-read of the letter, Aaron has a thought between the tears that swell in his eyes. Tick tock, the pain clock continues to move. "I cannot believe I never picked up on this before," Aaron thinks. "The Walkman radio…" he continues in his mind between the tears that will soon fall. "The Walkman was something I wanted right before Jared would leave on that bus. That means this letter was written in 1968. Jared was at least eighteen years old."

Aaron's mind began to race with that possibility. Aaron had thought up to this moment that the tin must have been buried when Jared was just a teen, maybe thirteen or fourteen years old. It was Jared's handwriting that Aaron would think gave this away. Also, as Jared got older, he even told Aaron that he could no longer fit comfortably under the breezeway, thus the hiding place was for Aaron to have and enjoy now. Jared, Aaron thought, was an early teen when that conversation took place. How then did Jared get under the breezeway and bury that tin when he was such a large, young solider preparing himself for war? Tick tock.

Aaron notices something else this time as he held this letter in his hand. This paper has not yellowed as much as all the other handwritten notes from the tin. Also, strangely he is just noticing that the ink from this letter is black, and as he rummages through the rest of the tin's letters and journal entries, he sees that the ink is all blue. Aaron can now see after all these years that Jared must have written this right before he left for Vietnam. Aaron also can see that the letter is more about his feelings and love he has for Aaron than instructions on what to do in the event Jared never returns. Tick tock. The tears begin to fall.

The time flew by as Aaron re-reads and ponders all the shoe box contains. As he is straightening and filling the shoe box with its contents, he hears the car pull into the driveway. Nora and Keven have returned home, and Aaron will move quickly from bedroom to shower. Time flew by so fast in Aaron's haze to digest and travel down memory lane. He wipes his tears and runs the shower water, stepping inside. He hears the screen and then large wooden front door open as the house comes alive once more with the entire family home. The shower will hide his tears, and the warm water will comfort his body. However, his thought and purpose to reread Jared's belongings and the conclusions he now sees in his mind's eye have him frozen in thought. More important that the instruction letter left and the timing when Jared did so was that the letter covered more information on his thoughts and feeling than on what to do when gone. *We see what we want to see at times,* Aaron thinks. For years, Aaron saw and highlighted in his mind that Butch did not understand Jared and me. Also, the money he spent on the Walkman after Jared's death when mother took him to the store to purchase it was just as Jared had said in the goodbye letter. *Mom will always help you.* Gloria did just that. She later would lie to her husband about how Aaron was able to purchase the Walkman and where the money for such an expense had come from. She also instructed Butch to never to question Aaron on how or where he got it, and this was one motherly rule to her husband that Butch followed.

As the water runs down the body of the healing marathoner, the pain clock continues to tick. His letter to Nora must be more about how much he loved her and will miss her than about what she needs to do, as Aaron had previously thought. Just like Aaron, Nora will focus more on the list and instructions Aaron will give in his letter than on the emotions he tries to convey in words and handwritten print. Someday Nora will only see what Aaron focused on saying, just as Aaron's showering time now focuses on what Jared was saying all along. But for years, like Aaron, Nora will see what she thinks Aaron wants her to see. In the shower, the alarm clock's pain tick-tock rings, and Aaron pulls himself together with a deep breath and concluding thought. *The letter needs to be about love, just like Jared's.*

The days that followed the hospital visit and the hate that fills Nora's heart for this man that in her mind killed her husband—life and only love—are as dark a day anyone person will ever live. Her salvation has not come as of yet. That chiming grandfather clock, although still chiming at this early stage of mourning, is not heard either by the recent widowed wife. The near miss driving accidents or traveled roads are still to come. Nora sits on the bedroom's bed in the very spot Aaron did that Saturday morning when he drew all those conclusions to Jared about what to write. Malisa and the kids are on their way to bring uneaten food for Nora and Kevin that all loving family members bring after a death. Nora recalls Aaron's instruction to give the shoe box filled with Jared's letters to Malisa, and she thinks now is as good a time as any. She knows and understands that Malisa is also hurting, but in all honesty, in her own world of pain she thinks, who cares? She is unaware of what is in the box and opens it to check it is the correct shoe box to give Malisa just as Aaron had predicted she would do. This will not be Nora's last cry. In fact, this will be one of many, many more to come. It might very well be, but it is very hard to tell if this will be her most painful, her most uncontrollable, her most suicidal cry, when she finds in that box her only reason to live and continue to press on. The shoe box on the top shelf of the closet is one of three shoe boxes up there. She knows for certain without checking that the black box is the dress shoes Aaron hardly wears. This leaves two to choose from; she has never opened or wondered what was inside them. As she picks one and opens it on the bed's edge, she sees a letter addressed to her. In Aaron's poor handwriting, the envelope simply says, "For Nora's eyes only." Nora reads this and picks up the letter. Her mind is dizzy with wonder as she looks at the next item in the box she cradles. MetLife Insurance policy papers. She reads this too and again wonders almost out loud, *what in the world is this?* Sliding the box and policy alongside her, she slowly opens the letter in her right hand. The bed creaks from her weight, and the box nearly slides off to the floor before she catches it just in time. She thinks of her weight, as she always does in these moments. The box, she would think even in all her grief, would not move if she was thinner. What she does not realize that what is to come is that she will get thinner. Much thinner, as the weeks turn to months during her mourning of her loss. The box sits securely behind her on the bed, a task not as easy as one would think for the obese. She slowly opens the letter and begins to read

> *Dear precious Nora, I'm so sorry I am not with you and that this journey you are to embark will be alone and terrifying.*

After the one simple line, Nora stops and thinks. *Aaron knows me so well, even from his grave he knows how scared and alone I am feeling.* She starts to weep. Not cry— weep, from so much grief. Her head feels as though it weighs a ton. Her eyes fill with tears and trying to read anything at this point is pointless. She breathes choppy, gasping breaths and tries to continue. The waterfalls of tears take over, and she realizes by connecting the dots that Aaron has made sure she and Kevin would be all right. The MetLife policy and the letter with instructions she had glanced at all come flooding in simultaneously and she misses her hero now more than ever. How will she go forward? How will she take control of a family when Aaron was the nucleus? *Her and Kevin were in Aaron's world, not the other way around,* she thinks. Weeping turns to full-fledged tears and hysterical crying on the bed's side. She falls to her heavy side on the bed's edge and the box behind her spills its remainder of contents on her back side. She cries until a much-need nap takes over her consciousness. Lucky for Nora, Keven is staying with his friends tonight. As hard as it has been on Nora, Kevin needed some friend time, so she agreed to a sleep over. Malisa would come with the kids to stay and see Kevin as well, but Nora in her grief cannot think that far ahead. So she agreed for Kevin to spend the night with his friend Scott, and she also agreed for Malisa and the kids to stop by to comfort and feed them both. Now crying hysterically on the bed as sleep finds her from emotional exhaustion, she cares not. Somewhere in her mind, she utters the phrase, *Sue me.*

Nora is walking in a city that has no lights or sound. She has never been here before, she thinks, and in this dreamworld she is lying on her bed with letters askew all around her enormous body. She is thin in the dream, and in a way that can only be described in the logic of a dream world, she somehow knows it is the distant future. Alleyways are dark and uninviting in her dream walk through the darkened future city. The moon is the only light that exposes her path as she walks in slow motion. Shadows from her peripheral vision duck to cover if she turns to look. People see her walking and are curious to see the thin Nora survive her scary future without her husband. A shadow off in the distance in front of her stands, and the figure this silhouette mimics is Aaron.

In her dream, she thinks it must be him and starts to walk just a few steps faster. The image never moves, but as she continues to pick up her pace in this darkened dream city street, the image never gets any closer. She trots, and still the silhouette remains the same size and shape. She runs, and still the silhouette remains the same. She is sprinting full speed now and the alleyways and darkened streets are flashing beside her faster than she runs, in a flickering fashion like those old eight-millimeter projector films. In an instant, she is standing in front of the darkened image of the dream Aaron figure, and as times flashes still, and the light hits this man's face, it is Dwayne Cunningham.

In the real-world bedroom in a flash, Nora awakes from the dream. Stunned and sweating, the abrupt awakening startles her, and she breaths deeply. The afternoon light has faded, and for a moment she is confused as to her whereabouts and the time. She wonders in an instant, *How long did I sleep?* Her mouth is dry, and she drooled a small puddle of saliva on the bedsheet. She sits upright trying to gather her thoughts, and as she does so the doorbell rings.

Malisa and the kids stand at the door for a moment after the ring and begin to open the screen door. Upstairs Nora gathers the bed's belongings and quickly deciphers what is meant for her and which of the letters are meant for Malisa. Stuffing the insurance policy papers as well as the unread letter for Nora's eyes only into the nightstand's only drawer, Nora stands and straightens her bedsheet-sized dress. As Malisa and the kids open the large wooden front door, Nora walks downstairs.

"Nora are you home? Are you okay?" Malisa yells as the large door slowly swings open.

Nora is slow to answer as she walks the stairs down leading to the foyer and the slowly opening door. "I'm coming, Malisa," she answers and for a minute considers the question, "Am I okay?"

Nora thinks for a second and answers in her mind even quicker. *No, I'm not fucking okay! In fact, I'm far fucking from being okay. Truth be told, I want to die! I have lost my one and only love, and I really don't think I can continue. Life and all it is right now means fucking nothing, and I don't give a shit if you too are feeling what I am feeling even though I doubt very much my loss is remotely understandable to anyone at this point except me.*

There are five stages to loss, and all five will show their ugly face more than once and in no particular order or frequency. What Nora just felt after her much needed rest is anger. This feeling, unfortunately for Malisa and the children, will not leave her anytime soon. She feels fat, she feels at loss, and she feels anger right when Malisa and the kids walk in her house. When she reaches the bottom of the stairs and faces the door, Malisa sees hate in her eyes and cowards from the face to face exchange. "Uh… I'm sorry Honey, is this a bad time?" she states, slowly stopping her entrance with the children, nearly stepping on her heals as she slows her entry. Nora does not mean to look so angry or eyeball her sister-in-law with such hate. She is still reeling from her dream, and the last thing she had seen as she was violently awakened was not the face she expected to see. As fast as the anger comes, the anger leaves Nora and her face. She now in a split second feels for Malisa and the kids and what they too have lost. The five emotions of grief—anger, denial, bargaining, depression and acceptance—will haunt Nora, much like they haunt all of us when the bomb of loss explodes near us. Or in the case of Nora and the ones that loved Aaron, on us. The stronger the love, the more devastating the loss. In the days to come, all who knew and loved Aaron at one point or another will wish they never did. The wish is only to avoid such pain. However, pain knows no boundaries, it has no friends, and it will hunt and kill whoever it pleases. In time, if you have not yet been its victim…you soon will be.

Malisa and the kids visit Nora for about two hours. The stay, as well as all the food they brought, was pleasant, and tears were shared as they comforted and hugged one another to cope. When they left the house, was still and silent. Nora stood in the doorway as the minivan drove away. Malisa was grateful for the box of letters. However, other than a brief look inside, most would go unread. Malisa was no reader. In fact, Aaron and Jared had made fun of her for never opening a book when she went to school. The brothers mocked their sister, but Malisa got the last laugh. She graduated every elementary school grade, every middle school class, and high school without ever reading anything. Her method was simple. Pay attention in class and ask friends that did read the books that were assigned what the story or topic was all about. Then on reports or tests, she faked it. Regardless of her past and non-reading habits as a single mother of two, Jared's letters and small items that are left in the shoe box will now sit in Malisa's linen closet's top shelf.

Nora watches as the van gets smaller and smaller in the horizon. She is thinking of the letter she started to read and is mustering up the strength to go finish it. Like a zombie without a purpose, she slowly walks upstairs and opens the nightstand's top drawer. Again she pauses, taking in a deep breath and like the dead watching a van drive out of sight, she stands and stares at the hand-written letter. It reads:

> *Dear precious Nora. I'm so sorry I am not with you and that this journey you are to embark will be alone and terrifying. But my love for you and Kevin is not over even though I am gone. You have meant the world to me my dear sweet love. I can only imagine as I write these words what you must be feeling and going through. It is my desire to ease your loss not with this letter because I know all too well that this letter hurts so much when first read. In time the pain will go away my dear and this very letter you will cling to and re-read a thousand times over. There are things honey that need doing that for the sake of care I have planned for you and our son. The insurance policy has a number you can call, and they will guide you in the process. My wish is that you stay in the farmhouse and resist the urge to sell it or leave…*

Aaron knows that a very large pull to grieving the loss of someone is to run from yourself. He did this as a boy after Jared's death when day after day he went on his runs. As he ran, he dreamed of not returning home. Home, in his mind, was where all the tears and pain from Jared's death festered. In his mind, he would think that if he simply never returned he would heal from the loss. Many widows make this error and move or sell the home they shared with the passing of their spouse. Unfortunately to do so too soon brings a feeling of regret, and it won't replace the grief they are trying to avoid. Regret adds to the pain and mourning they are experiencing. It is another tragedy on top of one that only delays the true healing process. Divorcees also feel and make this same mistake. When the marriage is over, there is a desire to run from all the pain, but there is a real danger to making some very large decisions or changes to try and avoid the suffering, like selling the house, buying a new car, or moving out of state play out in the hurting mind and heart. Aaron knows all of this, and that is why he made this his very first request as both a wish and instruction on what to do first.

Nora reads, and tears once more fill the sockets of her eyes, once again making it difficult to keep reading. The list of to-dos' in the letter that she will misunderstand as something she needs to do in order are becoming more and more difficult to read, not just because of the tears that fill her eyes but because Aaron's handwriting is getting progressively worse and harder to decipher. This is something Nora and Aaron have joked about in the past. Also, Aaron cannot spell very well, also something they both also joked about in the past. Growing up, Jared tried and tries to help his brother in both his handwriting skills and with his difficulty to spell words correctly. However, try as he might, the more Aaron tried to write clearly, the worse his handwriting became. The more Jared tried to help his brother spell correctly, the more Aaron's spellings seemed to get worse. In the end, Jared concluded that it simply is what it is. Scolding, praising when well done or correct, or even instructing Aaron to draw the letters instead of writing them did not work. The boy, now a man, has and had his entire short, life, terrible hand writing and spelling abilities. Things could be worse. Nora knows this all too well this very moment.

Pounds then stops. Pounds then stops. A very large piece to a handwritten puzzle is finally solved as the water washes over Nora's hands as she stands at the kitchen sink. Four years have passed since that fateful day that changed Nora and Kevin's world forever. Four years to complete Aaron's to-do list and finally know every word he wrote, decipher every misspelled word and understand each and every phrase. She would have never guessed it would have taken that long, but this is what healing looks like in the real world. Movies at times would have us believe that healing or moving on takes place in the time the film moves from start to finish. Directors even use words that flash on the screen telling the viewer that a set of years have passed. Still, subconsciously this is interpreted by the watching audience that all is well in about two hours. Justice, It can seep into our consciousness that justice, healing, and a solved murder mystery, fairness only takes the time we watch from start to finish. It is why we watch. The story loops and concludes, making us feel closure and justice. However, in the real world, this is only a facade. Real healing in the world we live in takes many years, and sometimes we really never do heal. Nora in these past four years did in fact experience all the stages of grief that most will suffer. After her salvation, she tried to bargain with God. She prayed and prayed, asking for just five minutes of not thinking about her loss if she attends church every Sunday. She begged God to help her forget, and if he did, she would volunteer her time to help others. She pleaded with him a thousand times in prayer to hurt Dwyane as much as Dwyane has hurt her. When her prayers fell silent to these requests, she slowly learned over time that asking for anything when you really don't know what you need is pointless. It took years, however Nora learned that the key to a successful prayer life is to ask God to show you what he wants from you and give me the strength to do it. God is not a vending machine to bargain with and give us what we want. Nora has come to believe that God wants us to trust him in knowing what we need and guide us in the path he has cherry-picked for us. There will be seeds along the way. The game will have losers and winners, and deception is a very real possibility. However, when you can finally get to the point of trusting your heavenly Father, pain and to suffering might never stop, but for Nora the tears did. Her crutch was now to lean on him—not Aaron or the list or anything else of this world. Aaron was right when he wrote that she would grow to re-read the letter he left her and the words he wrote. Aaron was right when he wrote that she would treasure the letter and almost idolize it as gospel. Nora has grown and come to accept that the letter's lists and the things we write have value and can help us heal or move on but to cling to them or worship them brings the dangers of never moving on or healing. The day Jim finished her siding and Nora inadvertently decoded Aaron's list as she cried for the last time, did something else that day. She decided to never read the letter again. She didn't need too. It was God's plan all along and she was okay with that.

Chapter 11

(A Rare Blood Run, Sirens & Tears)

Nora chops onions at the counter's edge as the chicken cordon bleu bakes in the gas oven. She cries from the chopping vapers that reach her eye, mindful of the baking chicken beside her. In the background she can hear the living room television's sound of the animated television show Rugrats that Kevin is not really watching. He tinkers with his massive collection of Legos in front of the blaring TV but is not interested in these either. A young boy's imagination is running wild at these after school times. Nora's tears fall as she reaches for a paper towel to wipe her face. Aaron has gone for a long run and had left more than an hour ago. His timing on returning should coincide with Nora's dinner plans. However, Aaron rarely ate much after a long run. He did however make it a point to sit at the family dinner table and pretend to eat, if only for Kevin and Nora's sake. Nora was well aware of this common habit and never challenged or questioned her husband when it came to this. She knew Aaron would be very hungry a couple hours after the long run and would consume all the leftovers that would not be left over at all. As Nora chopped and diced, another distant sound other than the TV can be heard. Sirens, very far away, begin getting closer and fill the air outside the Mills family farm. This time of the year, the windows are always wide open. There is never a need for air conditioning in Western New York. Thus, late summer, early fall days mean no need to heat or cool the large family house. The cool breeze coming in the windows, the smell of the chicken baking, and mother crying fake onion tears is all that is happing in the Mills' family house as Aaron runs.

Aaron is on Route-33 on a rhythmic, event-less run. He is about nine miles in and is heading to an exaggerated fork in the road that will lead him to another two miles heading home. Griswall road was named after the farm family that lived on the road back in the 1800's. It crossed Route-33 like a very sharply written "V." There it would lead Aaron back to an intersection that was the Mills family house's road perched on a hill. Nearly every time Aaron reaches this fork in the road, he is reminded of a story he heard from the locals about the name change of the road. Apparently, the road was originally named Caswell road. The Caswell's had a dairy farm on this road, as did the Griswall's. Back in the day, as they say, the family with the most kin folks earned the right to have the road named after their family. This was the Caswell's until time, a dying and not very well-run farm, as well as the deaths of many Caswell's naturally occurred. Father Griswall, after counting the number of his family members living on the road compared to the number of Caswell's on the road, went to the courthouse to get the named changed. This struck Aaron as comical behavior, and he would imagine an old farmer waiting and counting out the days before he could strike the courthouse clerk. The man who told Aaron this story only told it maybe three times. Aaron, however, told everyone. Every time Aaron told this tale, Nora would roll her eyes at Aaron; these was some of the few times she would do so. She loved her husband very much, but even love has its limits when you've heard your spouse tell a story over a hundred times.

Before the onion tears fall and the sirens screams get closer and closer to the Mills family farm, air Aaron approaches an intersection some mile-and-a-half before Griswall Road. He was more than a tenth of a mile from the intersection and in "the zone," not thinking or breathing much. A fit runner in the zone can get in a rhythm that seems effortless. It is still a workout but just conditioned from many miles previously logged. In a flash that seemed unreal and movie-like, a car heading in the same direction as Aaron but on the right-hand side of the road (Aaron is running against traffic on the left) zooms by. Microseconds before the intersection, a milk truck makes a right turn heading away from the speeding car and the running Aaron. The driver of the speeding car unsuccessfully tries to swerve out of the way of the much slower truck pulling out and slams into its rear in an explosion of fuel, milk, and metal. The impact and sound jerks and goes through Aarons chest on the other side of the road just a couple hundred yards away. As the two twisted-metal vehicles that just collided come to a stop, another car—a 1988 Monte Carlo with a pissed-off drug dealer and a lying little weasel named Snot—screech to an unsuccessful stop and slam into the back of the heavily leaking milk truck just to the right of the other car. This is a huge forty thousand gallon holding milk truck that visits the nearby dairy farms to transport the fresh milk for processing. Again, metal hitting metal, screeching, twisted, crashing sounds explode in the air as Aaron is just digesting the first crash. Snot is hurled through the windshield and skids to an instant death a hundred feet on the gravel side of Route-33. The drug dealers' fate is much the same, however, his bloody, riddled body is half in and half out of the windshield as he clings to life for the next few seconds. The second impact awakens Dwayne, seat-belted into the stolen car. His head has violently hit the steering wheel twice, first on his own impact with the heavy milk truck and secondly when the Monte Carlo clipped it to a stop. Dazed and confused with a face now dripping with blood, he reaches with his right hand and unbuckles the seat belt that saved his life. His left hand is still gripping the 9-millimeter hand gun he stole two nights before from the now-dead drug dealer who had been chasing him. Unaware of the car that also crashed into the milk truck, Dwayne is in fight or flight in this heart-racing, stunned moment. In his head, he is still being chased. However, now he thinks the chase will go on foot and that he'd better be more accurate at shooting the stolen pistol if he plans to survive. As Dwayne is fumbling for the seat belt, dazed and confused, three things outside the twisted wreck are happening. One: The owner of the small convenient store located at this intersection is franticly calling 911. He can see Snot's dead body not moving and staining the gravel on the side of the road leading to his gas pumps. Two: The milk truck driver, unhurt but shaken, is like Dwayne unfastening his seat belt and getting ready to exit the vehicle. Three: Aaron makes a fateful decision to help. Aaron slows his run to a jog as he looks both ways, cautiously crossing Route-33. As he gets to the center of the road, Dwayne (now unbuckled) pushes open the driver's-side door that was stuck upon the impact. Dwayne's vision is blood-soaked and blurred, and when he sees the helpful Aaron approaching, he instinctively draws his weapon and shoots. Three shots ring out, and one strikes Aaron in the chest. Dwayne continues to pull the empty gun's trigger, stumbling in confusion and heading straight for Aaron. Dwayne still thinks the person coming toward him means him harm, and Aaron, in disbelief of what has just happened, falls to his knees on the double-yellow line of the road. He grabs at his chest with his left hand and looks directly in the eyes of the approaching Dwayne. Dwayne wipes his face with his left arm, still holding the now empty pistol, to tries to look clearly at the man kneeling some twelve feet before him. Staggering still closer, Aaron falls face first on to the road as blood both internally and externally starts to fall. Dwayne wipes feverishly at the fallen man but begins to lose both consciousness and eye sight. Now just a few feet from Aaron, Dwayne collapses on the yellow line of the same road just a few short feet from Aaron. Both men are unconscious. Both men are bleeding terribly. Both men are clinging to life as the sirens far off in the distance start to ring. The milk truck driver exits his vehicle and is trying to comprehend if he indeed heard gun shots fired. When he walks up on the two men lying in the road, other cars slow and some stop to avoid the accident before them. He looks down on the two men, and in complete bewilderment, sees something his mind will never understand. Two men lying on the road face down in nearly the exact position. One with blue running shorts on, the other with blue jeans on. One is holding a gun with his left hand. The other is holding his chest under his lifeless body with his right hand. The arm of the gunned hand has a Coke-sized birth mark, almost a perfect circle where a tattoo would be. The left arm of the fallen runner has the same. As the police cars and ambulances arrive to the scene, the milk truck driver stands staring at the men that even look somewhat similar.

Nora is now getting worried. It has been much too long for Aaron to be gone, and the food she has prepared is out of the oven and waiting. The sirens that screamed by the house twenty minutes ago have her thinking. The possibilities she considers scare her as she paces in the kitchen thinking of what to do. Looking out the kitchen window, she can see Route-33 from atop the farmhouse hill. Dusk has some cars at this hour with their lights on, and she can see brake lights through the horizon before her on the road, as traffic is backed up. Odd, she thinks about this occurrence, but she did hear sirens. Across the street she can see her neighbor's truck pulling in the driveway coming from the opposite direction as the traffic route. This would be the direction Aaron would have run had the horrible events had not occurred. Nora heads for the front door.

"Kevin, honey, stay here I'm going to go speak with John across the street," she said, walking briskly out the front door. As she pushes the screen door open, she yells to John Sand who is exiting his truck.

"John!" Nora politely screams, waving her hand to get his attention. She scurries across the stone driveway as John turns and walks toward her. As they meet near the road's edge, Nora asks, 'What's going on out there?"

I don't know. I think maybe there was an accident at the crossroads I think where that convenient store is on Route thirty-33," John said. "There was a police car making traffic get off 33 at Griswall Road."

Nora breaths heavily and puts her hand to her soon to be trembling mouth. She looks at John and says, "Aaron's not back from his run. I'm getting worried."

"Oh, my Nora…" John interjects. For a split second he considers the unthinkable as Nora with her tone and sixth sense introduces it into the conversation. He continues with, "I'm sure he's all right Nora. Maybe he is just watching and seeing what is going on out there and that is why he's not back yet."

"Maybe, I think I'll call the police. Is Jenny home? Can she watch Kevin if I need to run out?" Nora asks. Jenny is the eldest of the Sand's girls and will pass the torch to her younger sister Becky in the years to come.

"Of course," John said as Nora walks briskly back to her house to grab the phone.

The call to the police station and the 911 operator will play out like a dream. The following drive to the Buffalo General will also be dream-like for Nora, as well as the hectic emergency room entrance and what is to follow. In Nora's mind, she plays back all the questions the operator asked after a long pause on hold. Her womanly instincts told Nora that the operator knew more than she was telling, and why was she asking about Aaron so specifically? Rushing into the emergency room entrance, she heads for the only unoccupied front desk. She leans as much as she can into a small opening in the glass window that can be closed with another piece of glass on a track.

"Hello!" Nora loudly speaks into the small, hectically cluttered office space.

A run-down receptionist that looks both overworked and tired comes to the window from a back room around the corner.

"Can I help you?" she states, with a tone and concern that shows no emotions or concern with the customer of sorts before her.

"My husband, Aaron Mills was brought in here I was told by the police a little bit ago," Nora said franticly as she stares with panic and unblinking eyes at the run-down receptionist before her.

"Okay Ma'am, please have a seat, and I will call you when I know something," the receptionist said, pointing with her eyes to the many plastic-seated chairs in the waiting area behind Nora.

Nora franticly says "What?!" and turns to look at the many seated people in the room behind her. All these people waiting, some with bleeding bandages and worried looks on their faces had gone unnoticed by Nora as she rushed in. Faces and concerns with worry about loved ones or bleeding, and seated friends and family, all with a look no different than the one Nora now has. This worn-down receptionist has seen these faces for all of her six years sitting at this desk. She doesn't mean to not show a faceless, uncaring stare when looking and dealing with emergency room patients and family. The dead eyes of concern and the seemingly uncaring heart is something that cannot be avoided at times. The longer one works at this desk, the more often the dead eyes stare. The next words out of the dead-eyes face had been said a thousand times.

"Please, Ma'am…" pointing to the chairs behind Nora. "Have a seat. I will call you."

In the belly of this same hospital, on the same floor, Aaron lies on a gurney. Beside him on a similar gurney is Dwayne, and both are clinging to life and have hospital staff rushing around them in a large emergency room. Doctors evaluate the wounded and decide in a heartbeat where they need to go, what happens, and who will see all the patients next. It's like a controlled tornado blowing in a circular fashion with cries for help and orders being barked out military-style to the buzzing staff. Patients that need blood are tested for type, and a course, action is decided almost as quickly. Information on these emergency room patients is collected as fast as humanly possible, but in some cases, the nearly fatally hurt go unnamed for hours or sometimes days. Sadly, some die in this room without a name. Like the dead-eyed receptionist this fact takes its toll on the staff and doctors. For Aaron, the blood loss is severe and unfortunately his blood is the rarest of all types. AB-negative is less than one percent of the population and in short supply at Buffalo General. To make matters even worse, another emergency room patient was tested and in need of the same blood type just a few short curtained emergency room stalls away. As the shouts for blood needed are ringing out in the emergency room from one stall, the doctor about to shout the same hears this, walks out briskly, and calls out.

"Doctor McKenna!" the doctor inquires. "Did you just ask for AB-negative?"

McKenna exits the curtain space where Aaron lies. He looks over at Doctor Page and answers. "Yes, what's up?" The two walk toward one another and begin to share what they are trying to diagnose in each of their spaces.

Nora squeezes into the waiting room plastic chair unaware of the emergency room doctor's discussion several hundred yards away on the same floor. The seat to her left is empty. However, to her right a small child sits weeping as the apparent mother to the child holds a bloody towel to the child's head two seats to the right. At best guess, the child fell from his bike and hit his head. This is a thought Nora will not have. Her focus is all on Aaron and where as well as how her husband is doing. More people rush into the automatic sliding doors and the dead-eye receptionist instructs these people in the same way Nora was instructed. The same concerns and confused looks are spilled into this emergency waiting area like a rerun sitcom we have all seen a million times. For what seemed like eternity, Nora waited, unable to shift in the tight plastic seat due to her size. Finally, after twenty or so minutes, her name is called by "Dead-eyes," and she explodes from her seat to the glass window.

"Sister Ann will help you from this point forward Mrs. Mills," she says as she motions with her hand to the small nun standing to Nora's right. Nora stands for a brief second looking down at the much shorter Nun and nods her head to indicate yes. The two walk off to the receptionist's right and disappear down an adjacent hallway.

Tow trucks, sirens, and flashing police cars litter Route-33 as cleanup of the unbelievably violent accident from over an hour ago takes place. Yellow police blankets are draped over two corpses at the scene. A detective assigned to the case is speaking with the first responders as the morgue's hearse pulls up. The detective is given information about the stolen car and accident number one as well as information about car number two and the owner, who now decorates the hood and windshield with his remains. A police officer directs traffic as best he can as the cleanup unfolds. Another police officer informs the detective of the milk truck driver's statement of a possible shooting at the scene, that a pedestrian out for a jog might be the victim of the shooting, and that both shooter and victim were rushed to the hospital. They stood at the blood-stained yellow lines the two rushed men once laid on. Police radios from ambulance drivers and 911 operators add to the case's information as the detective scratches on a note pad what he believes took place. In a matter-of-fact voice, he reads to the police officers standing near him what he wrote.

Car number one hits milk rig. Car number two hits car number one and same rig. Car number two perps are ejected and die on impact. Car number one's perp exits the vehicle and shoots the jogger here in the road. Both are rushed to BGH." He reads it as if it is fact, looking at the police officers for confirmation with a question on his face.

They all shake their heads to confirm that what was read is accurate, as one adds, "Uhm... The driver also said he thought the two were related. Sir. He, Jerry Fidanza, is very shaken up from this. Apparently, his wife died at this very intersection some twenty years ago."

"The two?" the detective adds. "What two?"

"The driver of the stolen car and the jogger, Sir," the officer answered. "Apparently the milk truck driver said they looked alike and had the same tattoo or birth mark on their arms."

"Hmmm..." the detective said as he scribbles this seemingly unusual point in his notepad.

The detective leaves the scene and heads for Buffalo General Hospital to see if he can add more information to the case at hand. Names with the who, what, and why's that all detective search for are needed in this case, as with many. More question in this case will be unanswered however—even after some names and facts are filled in. The one looming unanswered question of course will be how is it that two unrelated men with the same rare blood type and birthmarks end up on the road, side-by-side, clinging to life?

When the detective reaches the hospital, a decision has been made. Nora signs a form that gives the hospital permission to harvest organs from her now deceased husband. The hospital will use said organs to save the life of the life-long thug Dwayne Cunningham. Saving lives is the doctors oath, and they care not for the good or the bad in the decision-making process. That said, they are unaware of the good in Aaron or the very bad in Dwayne and only consider the percentage of survival facts that help them save one or the other. The actions they take are to save both before any decision to harvest organs from one or the other. A database of potential recipients of organs was checked, but in the case of hearts, lungs, and livers, a blood-type match is absolutely necessary. The odds of this blood type and needed organ is a small miracle in Dwayne's case as he was rushed to emergency surgery on the fifth floor. His chest was badly bruised, and his heart was beginning to fail from the impact he endured from the second car. His head was also hit badly from the first collision and the second incision. This forced trauma to his brain will cause him blindness the rest of his life. Fortunately, or so it seemed, the strong same blood-type available in Aaron Mills' heart is a perfect match. Unfortunately for Dwayne, it would have been better for him if he had died. The blindness and his fear of the dark all his life will drive him speechless and insane. He was tortured by the demons in his head he created every time the lights went out. No nightlight will save him now. His future with a strong beating heart transplant will ensure a long, tortured life in an institution for the criminally insane. Doctors "saved" him, but only the shell of a man lives now. A shell of a man living in a darkened hell within his mind. Doty, Nora, the detective, psychiatrists, and doctors will never know the hell that Dwayne lives with in his screaming mind. If Doty knew, she probably wouldn't care much anyway. If

Nora knew, she might feel pity more than the hate for him that she will feel in her future mourning. If the detective knew, he might reconsider what the grandma—a lying old woman—tried to tell him about who this young man was. Doty actually went to the police station after reading in the paper what had taken place, looking for some sort of reward for providing information. The veteran detective quickly took her to be a con artist and didn't believe a word she said. He also never told her the whereabouts of the man she claimed to be her grandson, regardless of her insisting it was the truth—but with no proof. After the meeting with this detective, Doty would later scavenge what little Dwayne's room had in it. She will conclude that regardless of where Dwayne is, it is certain he is not coming back.

Being lost is such a dark place. Nora's pending darkness is the loss of her loving husband. The new widow tries to cope with all that will follow in a reality she cares not to digest. Dwayne's demons, so very real in his mind, are also dark and torturous. All suffer with pain and loss that seems like such a waste. It is so terribly hard to find the blessings in the darkness of lost love— lost love for another or lost loved for light of sight. It takes years of healing for Nora to see even a sliver of blessings from the death of her only true love. In this tragic fact, maybe even more tragic is that Dwayne will never find any blessing at all. There is so much unjust pain in a world broken by sin that God tried to avoid. Adam and Eve had one rule God asked that they follow. Do not eat of *that* tree or the knowledge of good and evil you will know. Pain in this world today is the results of these two not following this rule. One rule, not the ten that most would answer if asked what how many the Bible speaks of.

Nora and Dwayne, seemingly disconnected from past events, mourn and weep. One with true tears of sorrow the other with tortured thoughts of fear in a mind gone mad. Pity and empathy from people around them will not mean much to either in the weeks that followed that fateful day or rare blood run. Those sirens and tears will flicker and fade in time but leave a permanent mark on the lives of so many. Poor Kevin will be fatherless. Malisa has now lost two brothers and a dad. Nora is a widow and feels as though she will never love again. A rare blood run, sirens, and tears is all that is left from that day.

Chapter 12

(Salvation's Myth)

A month and a half has passed since Nora's world crashed and burned in the Buffalo General Hospital she now stands before. In her sleepless nights, she remembers the kind compassion a young nurse showed her in the mourning room with the lime green wallpaper where she grieved. Although hurt, confused, and without direction in life after Aaron's death, she still feels a thank you is in order for the staff—and in particular nurse Dena for showing such compassion. She walks inside, and the flood of emotions from that day come rushing back. The reception desk is quiet and clean as she approaches, unlike the emergency room entrance she ran into more than a month before. Two administration people are behind the half-mooned-shaped desk, and both say "Can I help you?" in unison and then turn and giggle to one another—a dialogue these two employees shared on more than one occasion. The elder of the two receptionists takes the lead and continues. "Sorry, can I help you?" she states again with the emphasis on the word "I."

"Uhm, yes," Nora said. "I'm looking for a young nurse named Dena Fidanza. She was so helpful and compassionate when my husband passed away here about a month ago, and I would really love to just…simply thank her." Nora's eyes drop to the floor midway through her sentence. It is not shame that draws her head downward. It is pain. Speaking the words "husband passed" hurts beyond words. She hates those words, and they hang all too long in the air around her even when she is not the one speaking them. They hung at the funeral parlor in whispers from family and friends. They hung when the MetLife Insurance man spoke to them before her benefits would begin, and they hang now from her own lips trying to give thanks. "Thanks," Nora thinks sarcastically to a God she does not believe in at this moment. "Thanks for taking my only true love away from me."

"Oh, my Dear I am so sorry," the receptionist replied. "What was that name again?"

"Uhm, Dena Fidanza," Nora said, this time with more clarity in her tone and affliction. Her eyes and head return to the horizontal position.

The receptionist clicks and tatters computer keys with her freshly polished nails. She reads a large bulky, outdated monitor with the image of the hospital's logo that is burnt onto the screen regardless of whether the computer blinks and thinks or shows a different Dos image. The system is completely outdated, but the one thing it can do well is search all the hospital's employee's names and position titles.

"I'm not showing an Dena Fidanza in my database," the receptionist states. "Are you sure about the last name?" she politely asks.

"Yes, I'm certain," Nora replies. "I had her nametag pressed against my face for at least ten minutes."

"Name tag?" the receptionist questions. "Ma'am, we don't use name tags."

Nora looks as confused as the politely speaking receptionist before her. The youngest of the two receptionist walks a couple of steps in the direction of the two talking women.

"Well do you have any Dena's that work here?" Nora asks, getting a bit frustrated from what she perceives as a simple request.

"Yes, we have three. One is a doctor, Donavan. Two work in the cafeteria, Carr and Wooton, I show no nurse with that name at all at this hospital." The polite receptionist insists that this is factual, pointing to her computer screen, which is of course unseen by the frustrated Nora.

"Well I know she was with me, and I know for a fact she had a name tag," Nora continues. "She had a paper hat and a striped red and white nurse's gown or dress. She held me while I wept in a room that had that ugly lime green wall paper. I know she was with me…" Nora reaches for her forehead as she struggles to gain composure and keep from crying from recalling that fateful day. She is nearing tears when the younger of the two receptionist speaks up.

Carol," she asks, looking at the older of the two receptionists. "Didn't we used to have candy stripers in this hospital? Ya know, volunteers that wanted to become nurses?" she states. "Do we still have that program? Maybe she was a volunteer and is not in the computer."

"Lisa," Carol replies in disgust. "This hospital has not had candy stripers since the 1950's!"

The three women just stand there in disbelief as those words hang in the air like the smell of burnt toast long after the breakfast plates are cleared.

Nora walks away slowly with her back now facing the receptionists, the elder Carol and younger Lisa. Her mind is numb, and she has not the strength to question or research and try to comprehend the possibilities of that day in the lime-green wallpapered room. Carol and Lisa say not a word as Lisa holds her hand to her mouth in disbelief. Both women feel the pain and grief Nora is showing as she slowly walks away. The weight of life is nearly too heavy to bear. Nora digests all the words she just heard as her mind flips and flops like a goldfish soon to be suffocated outside of its nearby bowl.

No one here by that name, Nora hears in her soon to be weeping mind.

"Not since the 1950's," she said, whispering thoughts to herself and waiting for the tears of pain to flow once more.

She is drunk with thought as she walks like a zombie to her car. This day will pass like so many after her husband's last breath here on earth, a day she will hardly recall until many weeks, months, and even years later. She will always wonder how she survived. Unsaved in these weeks after Aaron's death, she will forever wonder how she made it at all. She does not believe in God, but in an irrational way she blames him just the same. How can it be his fault if he doesn't exist? Nora asks all these unanswered questions intertwined with the statements the receptionists said. How can a person that does not exist comfort her in the wallpapered mourning room? All of it, the questions and the statements of facts to non-existent hospital personnel, all come crashing in as Nora sits in her car in the hospital parking lot. It is too much to bear and digest as the tears once more flood down her face. She hasn't eaten in days, and this contributes to confusion and depression. Pain from love lost is a pain like no other. As she weeps in her car before turning the ignition key, she has another thought that she hates. "I would not wish this feeling on even my most-hated enemy," she concludes in her mind. As she tries to gain control of herself before the drive home, this thought even includes the man who now has Aaron's beating heart. She hates that man for what he did to her and wishes with all her own heart that he was dead. But that said, she still thinks that the pain she is feeling at this moment should not be felt by any one person. *Not a-one that this hate-filled world has should endure what she now feels,* she thinks *Not even Dwayne fucking Cunningham*, she concludes as she turns the ignition and starts her car. Tomorrow she needs to go grocery shopping, so as she drives home, she tries to think out a list of needs without thinking about some phantom nurse or non-existent God.

Phillip and his wife Rose are driving to Nora and Kevin's farmhouse with fresh-baked cookies on a plastic tray wrapped with a clear cellophane top. Rose was not much for baking but did so from time to time in her fifty-plus year marriage to her adoring husband Phillip. They drive past the grocery store where Philip and Nora met that fateful day in aisle two near the Frosted fucking Flakes. It has been nearly six months since that day and Nora's salvation as well as the weeks she has spent in the widows recovery class at church. She has grown in spirt and shrunk in dress size since last seen by either Rose or Phillip, and the dinner and fellowship she has planned is appreciated and needed for these Christians.

Nora is preparing dinner when the Moore's car pulls into the stone driveway. She sets the knife she was using next to the cutting board and diced carrots she will add to the tossed salad. Kevin is upstairs in his bedroom and peaks outside his window when the car pulls in. He will not need to be called to come greet the guests, but mother will yell for him to come down just the same.

"Kevin!" Nora yells as she walks toward the front door.

"Coming!" he returns as he has already left his room heading downstairs. At ten years young, he is a good boy and listens to his mother more now than ever after his father's passing. He rumbles down the wooden stairs faster than gravity would spill water. When he reaches the bottom, Nora is by his side as they walk together to the large front door. Nora ruffles his jet-black hair and smiles as she drops her hand down the back of his neck and to his thin, muscle-growing back. She pushes the screen door open and meets Philip and Rose under the front porch.

"Hello! So good to see you," Philip says as they all exchange greetings, hug, and hellos. "My goodness," Philip continues. "Nora you have lost a lot of weight!"

Rose lovingly slaps at her husband and tells him to "hush with that."

"What?" he responds. "Can't a man compliment a young, beautiful lady anymore?"

Nora and Kevin smile at the old married couple's playful exchange as Nora says, "Why thank you Philip. Yes I have lost some weight."

Rose interrupts, "It's never appropriate to speak of a women's weight."

Philip adds, "Not even when it's a compliment?"

Rose responds, "You know the rules, Mister!"

All four make their way into the kitchen and talk, joke, and laugh as dinner is prepared and served on the large walnut table. Philip teases Kevin with corny old man jokes as the two women talk about the weather and the best way to prepare a roasted chicken. When the stretching bellies of full stomachs reach capacity, Kevin asks if he can be excused.

"Yes Sir, you may." Nora nods her head at his plate, and the young boy takes his plate to the sink.

Afterwards Kevin runs back upstairs and returns to doing what ten-year-old boys do in their bedroom after a dinner with three adults.

Rose is the first to change the subject of pleasantries with concern and love in her voice.

"How are you my Dear?" she asks, reaching out her hand to hold Nora's, as all at the dining table knew what the weight of that question implied.

"I'm okay," Nora said and takes a deep breath and continues. "There are good days and bad days. There are times when I am very much alone." Just as those words leave her lips, the grandfather clock in the other room chimes on the quarter-hour. Nora smiles at this before continuing. "There are times when I really hate that clock." She adds, "Aaron gave it to me as a gift, and when it chimes, and I hear it… well, you understand." Rose squeezes Nora's hand as Philip nods his head up and down to confirm what was said.

"I am so thankful Aaron had the presence of mind to ensure Kevin and I would be okay financially with a life insurance policy. There as some in my group who not only have to deal with a loss but have to worry about their next meal," Nora sadly states.

The three talk, cry some dry tears, digest a good meal, and Philip says a prayer of thanks and healing before the three start the cleanup process. Busy hands cleaning and good conversation with loved friends can heal a broken heart. Of course, this is only temporary. With the dishes dried and put away and the after-dinner coffee brewing in the Mr. Coffee coffeemaker, they head back to the now-cleaned dining room table and sit once again in the same seats they had eaten in. Nora smiles inside herself because she hears Aaron say in her mind that this is an unusual habit we all do. He goes on to say that he sees this at conference meetings all the time. Twenty or so people will be in a meeting at work, and they will leave the meeting for a break. No one will leave any items on the table when the break ends, but if they return to continue the meeting, all will instinctively return to the same seats. Nora remembers this conversation as three return to their seats. She takes a deep breath and said, "I went and seen him."

Philip was pulling out his chair to sit down and stopped. Rose was already seated with Nora, and there was a pause in the room as the words floated like ash, weightless in a stagnant air. Neither Philip nor Rose needed to ask who exactly Nora went to see. Both knew it was Dwayne, the man responsible for Aaron's death, and the very same man that now has Aaron's beating heart in his healing chest.

Rose put her right hand to her mouth as if to keep the ash from floating in. Her words were soft and quiet, almost a whisper or something she was embarrassed to say out loud.

"My God Nora, Sweet Jesus…" she whispered, shaking her head from side to side, slowly indicating a nonverbal no.

"Rose, let her speak," Philip added to the ash air, much in the way Rose corrected Philip an hour ago when he brought up Nora's weight loss.

"I had to," Nora continued, looking back and forth to both of the guests that paused in silence. "I wanted to see him. I had no idea if I was going to say anything. I just needed to…I don't know why…just needed to see him." Her statement was like a question but not. Apologetic with no remorse or feeling of guilt.

"Did you speak with him?" Philip asked.

"No, he didn't even know I was in the room," Nora continued. "As I walked up, a nurse was just leaving. The hospital room door opened, and I stepped inside as it closed behind me. I stood with my back to the door for what felt like twenty minutes. I was memorized by him lying there just a couple of feet away from me. I couldn't really tell if he was sleeping… or maybe dreaming. He shook his head and quietly moaned a lot while I stared at his face. He was in a lot of pain, I could tell. When I snapped out of my gaze, I looked and listened to the heart monitor at his bedside. I watched as that line thingy danced up and down with his heart beat…My Aaron's heartbeat. He looked a lot like Aaron, just… I don't know… a harder face 'ya know?" Nora trailed off in her speech as she looked through the table before her with a thou-sand-mile stare. There was not a sound to be heard for miles. The ash air was heavy, thick, and in need of a cool breeze. None would follow, only more words from the widow's mouth telling a story of standing bedside of the man that killed her husband.

"I won't lie to you," she slowly spoke and continued. "There was hate in my heart as I watched the heart machine bleeping. I wished… no… prayed God would make it stop right then and there as I watched him die…"

"Nora Honey" Rose interrupts. Philip gives the "shut your trap" stare that his wife has seen a hundred times. Rose does so just this once.

"I know I prayed for forgiveness to take over my thoughts and heart for this man," Nora begins to tear up. "I know that hate in my heart only hurts me and separates me from my heavenly Father." Her voice now cracks and holds back true heartfelt tears. "I… I can't Philip… I can't forgive him." She pleads with tear-filled eyes. She looks back and forth to Rosa and Philip with begging eyes. Her eyes scream, *Please let me hate him. Please explain how this unjust, filthy, lying, scum can live when my good husband had to die. How can this*

177

glorify God, Rose!? Her face, tears, and eyes scream. *Tell me damn it!* the voice only in her head demands.

Nora's speech is now labored as she tries to continue. "It felt like I was in there a long time, but it was probably only five or maybe ten minutes." The pauses between what she will say these next few minutes are longer and what she says is more deliberate and clearer.

"I wondered standing there if I could... just... ya know, unplug something," Nora slowly spoke. "I thought if God won't do the right thing here than... maybe... I should? But he moaned again in pain and his left arm.... His left arm slid out from under the bed sheet." Nora again gathers her thoughts and wipes the tears that are slowly falling down her face. She sniffles in a watered-down helping of nose drippings and continues.

"His arm... His arm had the exact same birthmark as Aaron."

If this scene was a movie, cue the dramatic orchestra now. Da da da dumm. But it's not a movie, and the reality that is sinking into the three sitting at the large walnut table will produce far more questions than answers.

More crying, hugs, prayers and coffee would finish out the Moore's visit. All kinds of theories and conclusions were drawn as to how is it possible that this man no one ever met or knew had the Aaron's same rare blood-type and Coke-can-sized birth mark on his left bicep. Also, he even looked like Aaron as well. Or as Nora described it, harder. The doctors, the helpful detective, Nora, and now the married couple Philip and Rose Moore will never know how any of this could be. More importantly, poor Nora will never know how this apparently unjust thing whereby she becomes a widow and the scum of the earth lives on happily ever after can only be in her mind, salvation's myth. She will also never know the hell and fear Dwayne will forever live with in with total darkness from the injury to his head that blinded him.

The room Nora sits in has muffled the sounds of the hectic goings on of the emergency room entrance. A nun walked her to this tiny room with two non-matching cushioned sofas down the hall from the emergency noise. Nora kept asking how her husband was doing as the tiny nun of less than five-feet tall looked at her with sympathetic eyes.

Nora stops and grabs the nun's arm, demanding an answer as they stand in the hall leading to the lime-green room. "Listen to me," Nora demands. "How is my husband? Where are you taking me?"

The short nun has been in this very situation a hundred times. A frozen moment of time where she has to decide if she will wait to drop the nuclear bomb on the unsuspected city or rip the pull cord at this very moment in the hallway and drop the said bomb. Fortunately, she is very experienced with delivering bad news. History has taught her that if she spills the beans here, about twenty-feet from the lime green papered room door, she knows she might have to help carry a week-kneed Nora Mills, and judging by Nora's size compared to the tiny nun, this was a task that would probably prove impossible.

"Please Honey, come this way," The tiny nun said. Her eyes pleaded with Nora. They were sad, drooping eyes, and her face held years of sharing disappointing truths. Nora never sees what the old nun had always hoped people would see when she spoke these words. She would even walk people to this doorway as family members were crying inside and stood pleading with only sad eyes that the person she walked to the door way with would simply put two and two together. *Can't you hear what is going on right inside this room?* she would think, even after the family member she had guided asks once again the status of the loved one's condition. This anomaly played out nearly every day for the old nun. However, this time there was no crying family members in the lime-green room. This time, Nora will think the nun is bringing her to the bedside of her healing husband. This time, the only person in this tiny room is an administrative supervisor that will ask for consent to use Aaron's organs for transplant. Aaron was an organ donor. However, with the wife on site, the hospital still needs consent from next of kin.

"Honey, please sit down." The nun says as they enter the tiny, stale room and look at the supervisor's blank, staring face.

"Who is this? Why am I here?" Nora pleads as her breathing becomes labored and choppy. "Is someone going to tell me what is going on? Where is my husband?" Nora demands.

What unfolds next is just a blur really. Nora has little memory of the first ten minutes of being in that room. Somehow, she is not even sure how, but she ends up on one of the leather non-matching sofas. Somewhere in a dream-like state, she hears the words that her husband has died. A racing, beating, broken heart and mumbled words of a tiny nun and an administrator's request are just blurred dreams Nora will black out her entire life. Her world has just exploded. She is no longer a loving wife. In one carefully dropped and placed nuclear fucking bomb she is now the grieving widow. When the two try to comfort her, she feels nothing. Tears blur her vision more than the memories she will have in that room from this day. She vaguely recalls signing the supervisor's form, and truth be told, you could have asked her to sign her own death warrant and she would have done so. Her heart is broken. Her world is shattered like a cold, pointless icicle on a winter's day breaking free from a gutter's edge smashing to the ground that no one sees or hears. She has no sense of time as she lays and cries in the lime-green room. The door opens and closes without her lifting her heavy head to see who is coming or going. Sounds cascade in and out of the tiny room each time, but for Nora it goes unheard. The couch's armrest, which her face is pressed against, is wet and snot-covered. She can feel someone sit beside her but has not the concern, care, or strength to lift her heavy head to look and see. She feels the touch of a concerned someone gently rubbing her back and the tears flow even harder when she realizes someone else is mourning as well. She feels love and concern from the gentle touch. Nora tries to sit upright to have a look at who it is that sits beside her. As she does, the helping hands of her new couch companion help her to do so. As Nora sits upright, she hears a gentle voice whisper, "I am so sorry, Nora."

Nora looks at a young, blond color haired nurse with a paper hat and striped garment. Her smile is inviting, yet sorrow-filled for Nora's pain and loss. Her legs are crossed as she reaches for Nora's hands to comfort and hold. Nora just stares at the young nurse and oddly notices white stockings on her legs and hospital white shoes, looking her up and down. A small name tag is pinned to the young girl's dress that reads, "Dena Fidanza" in script and a very small phrase underneath the name Nora cannot read with her tear-filled eyes.

As their eyes meet, Dena whispers something almost without her lips moving. Nora is never sure what she really said. Dena either said, "He is all right," or "She'll be all right." Somehow in Nora's mind, she knows this either to mean that she was telling Nora that Aaron is all right or that she was telling Aaron that Nora will be all right. However, as the whispered words are comprehended in Nora's brokenhearted mind, she falls face-first into the welcoming chest of the young Dena Fidanza. Tears again burst from her eyes, and the pain resumes as Nora's face presses against the name tag of the young beautiful nurse. She feels as though she will never be all right as she contemplates the two different possibilities she is never sure she just heard. What felt like hours were mere minutes as she cried on the young name-tagged chest. Again, she has no clear concept of time or clarity on how long this takes place.

Shock with extreme trauma can cause the most unusual things to happen that can really never be explained. Nora hears the door of the room open once more as Malisa enters the room with the tiny nun behind her. Nora is face down on the leather couch now, alone and in complete shock. Malisa, crying from the news she now is trying to digest herself, lunges at her sister-in-law paralyzed with pain on the couch. More tears follow. More memory-less time in a lime-green wallpapered room are shared. How anyone ever got home and cried themselves to sleep that night, no one really can say how. But exit the hospital they did that night, and while they did, elsewhere in the belly of the Buffalo General Hospital, a detective and two doctors are discussing what no one can understand. Two men nearly identical in age with the same, rarest of blood-types, seemingly unrelated. One desperately in need of surgery to save his life, one less than a few short minutes from death. A matching donor for Dwayne in a process that usually takes months is his salvation. Salvation's myth.

Today is release day for Dwayne. The hospital has cleared the speechless criminal to be transported to a mental facility some seventy miles away in Rochester, New York. His prognosis is healthy from the heart transplant. However, his mental state no one is really clear about. Dwayne, although able to speak, has not done so since coming out of surgery sixteen weeks ago. A heavy woman claiming to be his grandmother tried to fill in the gaps to the unknown man's history; however, the detective that handled the interview did not trust a word the elderly woman had said. A psychologist has deemed Dwayne unfit mentally for prison or even to stand trial for the alleged murder of Aaron Mills. The state really has no other choice than to lock him away and commit him until he can at least speak without the violent outbursts the blind man screams as he randomly explodes with from time to time between sleep. He is healthy and young. However, no one knows but Dwayne the torturous fear that is crippling his thoughts day after day. Fearing the dark all his life and now deemed blind for life from his head injury in the crash is beyond cruel and unusual punishment. How Dwayne got here started after leaving Doty in her unsuccessful creeping to skim some fast cash.

Dwayne eats some poor man's stew right from the pot off the stove. Doty is sitting in the living room watching afternoon shows and flipping through stacks of stolen magazines. When and if she does venture out, she is sure to stop in the local laundromats, hair salons, and doctor waiting rooms, if only for the purpose of stealing magazines. She has no use for a laundromat. She washes, cuts and styles her own graying hair. And she feel that all doctors are scam artists, much like herself, just with a framed degree on the wall. Dwayne continues to shovel in stew, neither bothering to sit or bowl a helping. The tiny kitchen and small countertop space is cluttered and semi-clean. Doty as of late spends less and less time cleaning or cooking in the kitchen because most goes uneaten. No words are shared between the two living roommates of sorts, and truth be told, if either knew this was the last time they would even see one another, words would still not be shared. Dwayne spending the night and day here is as random as the lies they rarely communicate to one another now anyway. Dwayne looks through the doorway that leads to Doty and the back of her chair in the living room with TV a blaring. He has a thought as he shovels in another mouthful of stew.

Think I'll find a place of my own without Nanny, he thinks. *Maybe head back to D.C.* His idea is not sparked because of any growing mature obligation to be responsible for himself. The thought is a selfish one altogether, much like Doty's earlier thought to hatch a scam to rid her of the violent gun-carrying thug Dwayne. No, being responsible is not what Dwayne is thinking at all as he stares at the back of Doty's head as she flips her stolen magazines. His thought is simple. She is getting older and looking like she may need help getting on soon. He has neither the desire nor care to do any helping of that sort. With his last table spoon shovel of Doty's stew in his gullet, he dismisses the idea and walks out the door. Doty, never looking at the magazine in her lap or watching the TV show before her, listens for the wooden door to close. As usual, Dwayne will make no effort to lock the door as he leaves, and Doty slowly lifts herself to walk to the kitchen to do so herself. She stands for a moment and looks at the contents that are eaten from the stew. She ponders her plan on filling the next batch with sleeping pills and waits for the hungry Dwayne to consume it. Not enough to kill him. Oh no, she only needs him to sleep soundly when he returns home from a night of crime long enough for her to pack and slip away. She thinks this will work best for both of them and starts to think about how she will steal the pills needed.

Dwayne leaves the apartment complex and hits the city streets. It's about five o'clock and the street life begins to wake as the daily workers create traffic for the ride home. Across the street sitting in a heavily-tinted 1988 Monte Carlo parked by a broken parking meter, two more of Buffalo's finest thugs watch as Dwayne walks down the street.

Snot, sitting in the passenger seat, slaps at the driver of the three-year-old car and says, "That's him! That's fucking Dwayne Cunningham!" while he points and fingers Dwayne for execution.

The drug dealing driver starts the car and slowly starts to follow Dwayne. Traffic in the city is a bitch. However, when you are an asshole, drug dealing thug and you cut someone off in traffic, most let it be. This takes place several times during the slow following of Dwayne as he walks the city street. The traffic is thick, and in spite of the rudeness of a would-be drive-by shooter, Dwayne slips out of sight—but only by pure luck.

"Fuck!" Snot screams as they lose sight of the intended target. "Okay okay okay…He is probably heading over to my cousins Cheeto's house over near that Deli."

"What fucking deli?" the would-be assassin barks. "Hay! Did your fucking cousin help this prick rob me?"

"No no na Man… Cheeto's cool. He don't do shit like that bro," Snot replies, lying through every gap in his rotting, crack-pipe-smoking teeth.

"Cause if I find out that fucker stole from me, I'll shoot that mother fucker too."

"No Man, it's cool… It's cool," Snot adds, then instructs him to drive to the corner of Badcock Street and Seneca Street—the deli that is a favorite hangout spot for Dwayne and his friends when planning their nightly activities.

There are times that when walking and cutting through yards, back alleys, and empty lots in a dying city like Buffalo and its surrounding neighborhoods, it is faster to walk than to drive a car. This is one of those times.

Dwayne enters the deli and gets the same glaring look the store owner shoots each and every time he enters.

"All I want is change to use the phone out there," he says before the owner has a chance to run him off. He hold up a five-dollar bill in his left hand and points using his thumb with his right. He looks like a hitchhiker flagging for a ride, and he is willing to pay.

The storeowner hands over the change, and Dwayne as promised, heads outside to use the phone. When he opens the deli door, a car pulls up and the driver quickly jumps from the driver's side door onto the curb right in front of Dwayne. He leaves the car running in an attempt to simply run inside for some smokes. The two exchange a look common on the streets of a hardened city. Both faces read, "What the fuck are you looking at?"

Just as the face insults are hurled at one another, shots ring out. Dwayne, as well as the soon-to-lose-his-running-car man in need of cigarettes, dive for cover. Dwayne into the running car, the man now wishing he didn't smoke, flat on the pavement in front of the deli.

The running car is Dwayne's salvation.

Salvation's myth.

With the dishes done and the last tears dry, Nora walks upstairs to the nightstand near her bed. The list Aaron had handwritten to ensure his family would be all right is in her hand. She reaches to the lamp on the nightstand and turns the spindle to the on position. The afternoon light from outside is just not enough for Nora to read the list for what could be the thousandth time. She holds it in her hand, and the thought of Aaron knowing she would do so makes her smile. *God*, she thinks, *I miss him, and he was such a blessing.* Her smile is genuine and pure. She looks over the list and reads the terribly handwritten two-word phrase in parenthesis after "get the house vinyl sided so you will never need to paint." She reads what she now knows because of the rambling Jim Leary: "*Low Maintenance.*"

A smile purer than the last returns to her loving face. She asks herself a rhetorical question aloud to no one in her bed room. "How on earth, Aaron Mills, was someone to know what that said? Oh... and ya spelled maintenance wrong!" She shakes her head with a fading smile and returns the note to the nightstand drawer. She adds to what she said with the thought, *You never could spell could ya?*

Nora is okay with fact her husband could hardly spell, like she is okay in her heart after the passing of Aaron these past five years. Obviously, she would have preferred he did not have to die, but she wonders if he had not, would she have ever found the Lord? There are times that had passed in the mourning process when she hated him for leaving her. Sadly, there are times to come as well when all the emotions that followed those dark years will return. Yes, even hate. There were more times in those dark years that she blamed herself, and sadly there are more times to come when she will again. Yes, blame. But she is saved now, and God is on her side. She knows and believes this to be true, and she cares not if any one human ever believed her about this ever again. She can't even remember the days when she was a nonbeliever, but she knows they existed. Her heart aches at this at times more than the loss of her one and only true love. In the years to come, Nora will struggle with the gift of salvation and grace God has given her. She will forever feel unworthy of such grace, knowing in the back of her mind the person she use to be and the sinful nature that still lurks inside her. But Nora is so thankful for her salvation, and just like when she judged her self-worth through the eyes of the mirror by all her fat...still Aaron truly loved her. She feels God had something to do with this. God, in all her disbelief, did the same. Strangely she credits Aaron for having something to do with this. Thus, her own salvation and all that she has learned can lie to her like that reflective glass mirror. Nora has come to believe that salvation is not the end of her life's struggles, questions, doubts or convictions—it is merely the beginning.

Salvation's Myth.

Epilogue

(Graduating an Understanding Love)

For most of the parents and students at Kevin's school, the class of 2000 was seen as a very big deal. Kevin, now eighteen and a senior himself, thinks this is ridiculous. He is so much like his father Aaron, Nora can hardly believe what she hears and sees in him. Kevin was nine years young when his dad perished, but the DNA that mapped his being was all Aaron.

"Kevin!" Nora screams up the oak staircase. "Are you almost ready?" Kevin stands before the mirror that is attached to the back of his bedroom door. He is nearly too tall for the image to reflect if he did not stand far enough back in his room to allow the mirror to reflect his full image. Again he looks at the cap and gown he will wear in a short hour or so at the high school gymnasium for his graduation. As he stands and looks at his own image, an Aaron thought he has all his own emerges. *Every mirror is sold used*, he concludes in his mind, just as his mother's yell reaches his ears.

"Yeah Mom, I'll be down in a minute!" he yells back. The drive to the school was uneventful. On Route-33, the spot where Aaron and Dwayne laid on the pavement's center double-yellow lines those fateful years ago are driven over without nearly a passing thought. "A passing" thought, defined by almost no thought at all. However, the reason it was neither passing nor not given was for Nora always thought about at that moment and spot when driving over it. She would never tell Kevin, even when asked, where exactly dad got shot. Mother spared Kevin that information, so as to spare him the pain each and every time he drove to school. However, Nora would never forget. One-time she had thought of putting some flowers or a cross on the road's edge near what she drives over on the way to graduation. Nora had seen this practice in the past few years and asked a friend why someone did it. Dawn, Nora's friend said she heard that this is common thing among the Mexicans and what they believe. According to Dawn, the Mexicans think that is the spot the soul made its way to heaven. So they mark the spot in remembrance of the loved one's passing. 'Why?" Dawn asked. "Are you thinking of doing this on Route-33?"

"No," Nora replied. "I wasn't thinking that at all." Nora noticed in the months and years after the loss of her husband that any questions or comments she made were naturally assumed to be connected to Aaron's death. Regardless of if they were or not, Nora always lied in her reply. If she was thinking of Aaron when asked, she would always say no. If she wasn't thinking of Aaron, she would lie and say yes. Her behavior in this regard was analyzed by her own critiquing mind. This conclusion is not set in stone, mind you, but for now she thinks it is because she wants her memories of Aaron and the love they shared to be hers alone. Telling someone or letting others into her heart seemed like her feelings are being shared. Nora has no desire to release or share even a sliver of what Aaron had given her to anyone.

As they near the school, the traffic begins to slow as the graduating class of only about a hundred students thickens the road. The small Western New York farming community where Kevin attended school was well-run and modern. The buildings and soccer fields that dressed the five full acers of government space were well-kept. The elementary and middle schools were in one large building. The swimming pool and high school was in the other. It was in this bigger building, in the gymnasium, that the graduation ceremony would take place. Parking took some time as the cars line the drive in. "Wow, more people here than I would have thought," Nora comments. "It must be because it's the year 2000." She injects with a smirk on her face, knowing all too well what's to follow.

"Oh pleeeeasse…" Kevin chokes in response. "We didn't do anything to warrant some special attention to the year we graduate," He continues. Nora smiles with delight as her only son barks what she would consider an Aaron thought process. What Kevin had said is so true. The year you graduate is like a theory Aaron had about birthdays, Nora thought. Aaron hated the idea we celebrate the day we were born like we had anything to do with that day at all. Kevin is doing the same with the graduating year. Mom sees father in son when these "Aaron moments" are revealed. She happily provokes these theories just to see her husband's spirit in Kevin live on. "Well, I think it's nice," Nora states. "I like the way they trimmed the grass in the front of the school lawn." The groundskeepers scalped the turf into "2000" for the occasion. "Fine," Kevin responds in rebuttal. "But I think it's stupid."

Inside an hour later, the ceremony goes off without a hitch. Kevin took his place in line as they called the names of all the students on a makeshift stage. In the stands, proud parents' videotaped the event on camcorders that will be watched in the years to come. Some students tried to do something out of the ordinary, but Kevin simply took his diploma, shook the principal's hand, and walked off. Nora did not record this event. Aaron was the camcorder operator, and honestly, even had mother attempted to record this event, the footage would have been painful to try to watch. Not because of the content. No, painful because mother's skill in shooting events was terrible. Once Aaron would run a ten-kilometer road race and made the unfortunate error of trying to instruct Nora on recording his finish. The race was the largest around and close enough for the family to attend. The Rochester Lilac 10K. The Lilac festival was a week-and-a-half long event in the city of Rochester. The 10K event started the weekend off with a bang, and the weather and date of the event were centered around the blooming lilacs the city donned in Highland Park. Nora and Kevin had accompanied Aaron in many road-race events. It was good family together time. However, Aaron thought that standing around and waiting for him to run by must not have been much of a spectator sport for his loved ones. So for one of the events, he suggested Nora record the event. Aaron loved to record family events. Thus, he thought Nora would also love the task at hand. Nothing could be further from the truth. Nora vaguely knew how the camcorder worked. Worse yet, to focus on anything or pan then zoom was way over Mother's head. When the Lilac 10K was run and the footage was viewed later that day, it was clear to Aaron that any future recording attempts by Nora would be a waste of time. Nora actually continued to clap as she tried to record Aaron running by her and Kevin toward the finish line. This made the footage jiggle and jump repeatedly out of focus and contain the amplified sound of clapping so close to the recorder's microphone—impossible to watch, let alone enjoy. After that experience, it was clear Nora had no business even trying to film anything, and after Aaron passed, the only person to play with the camcorder again was Kevin and his friend Scott.

When all the students had received their diplomas, the crowd clapped for a full minute. The principal made a brief announcement that refreshments would be served and thanked everyone for coming. Nora waiting her turn in the bleachers and tried to make her way down to her son. As she wormed her way past the proudest of parents (along with herself), she excused herself when bumping into the back of a stocky man. "Oh, I'm so sorry," Nora apologetically said. The man just nodded as Nora passed by with a smile that was both warm and somewhat recognizable. A few seconds later, a gentle tap on Nora's shoulder was followed by the same man asking, "How is that siding holding up for you Mrs. Mills?" Standing before Nora was none other than Jim Leary. Nora turned and looked at Jim but had not even a whisker of a clue who this man was. Jim had lost more than a hundred pounds since the time he sided her house, another fifty after that since he had stood on her porch rambling on and on, and still ten more on top of that when he returned that Friday to explain the warranty on the maintenance-free installation.

"It's me, Jim Leary. I sided your house… what, seven or so some years ago I guess?" Nora now, after hearing Jim's voice, recognized the name but not the person. "I've lost some weight," he continued. "I don't blame you for not knowing who I am."

"Jim!" Nora explodes. "How good to see you!" Nora's head tilts to the side as her voice, look, and tone gaze at the man while trying to reconcile the tremendous difference in his appearance. Jim simply smiles as Nora continues. "Well I guess *you* did lose some weight! My God, how are you? Do you have a student graduating here this afternoon?"

"Uhm, no, my sister does. I thought I would just come and show my niece some support. She is the one that graduated," Jim replies. He continues as the crowd and noise of the gymnasium increases around them. "So, no trouble with the installation or the siding, I assume?" Jim states.

"No, of course not Jim. None at all," Nora said.

The small talk continued with increased volume due to the crowd and noise until Kevin came to Nora's back. "Ma!" Kevin screamed. "I'm going to ride home with Keith'er and Scott, okay?" Nora excuses herself from Jim's attention and turns.

"Hold on a second, Mister, let me look at you," Nora replies. Kevin tilts his head to the side and stands at attention. A half smiles emerges on his young face. Mother and son share a loving look that only mothers and sons share. Her eyes say it all. "I am so proud of you is never heard or spoken," but surrounds all that can preserve this moment. Nora spins and steps aside to her right, placing her motherly, proud hand on Kevin's shoulder and introduces Kevin to Jim Leary. "Jim!" Nora screams over the deafening gym acoustics. "This is my son, Kevin. Kevin do you remember Jim?" As Nora turns from Jim to Kevin, Kevin quickly reaches out his hand to shake. Jim startled by this young man's quickness to do so, brings his hand up slowly to meet Kevin's for the custom between men.

Jim's face lights up and while shaking the young man's hand says, "I remember *you*. Uuu... why, you were no taller than a mailbox, as I recall" All three giggle and smirk as Nora answers Kevin approaching question.

"Yes, sure no problem. You can go with Keith and Scott. Just be home by ten, okay?" Kevin nods his head and looks directly into Jim's eyes.

"It was very nice to meet you. Ah, see you again Mr. Leary," he says, nods, and then turns and disappears into the crowd. Again, the sounds in the gymnasium slowly increase.

Jim is immediately impressed with both the politeness of the eighteen-year-old young man and the eye contact he had made. He tells Nora this with both pride and a complimentary tone that Nora had done a wonderful job in her parenting. Jim was aware when the siding was being installed that Nora was widowed and had even had a short encounter with Aaron before his death. He did not know for certain that it was Aaron, but after meeting Kevin and the eye contact and handshake, he now was certain. Then, some not-so polite teens were mocking a much fatter Jim Leary as he pumped gas at the local gas pump. Jim could hear the rude remarks from afar and pretended to not do so or be amused. On the adjacent pump among the rude teens was a tall, slender, jet-black-haired man pumping his own gas that day. As Jim finished and pulled away, he saw this man approach the boys at the pump. First as his truck turned, he viewed the exchange without hearing a word through his opened window and using only his peripheral vision to "not" look. However, after he turned to get on the street, he observed the exchange more from his rearview mirror. Jim never would know what the man said to the kids who mocked him that day. But he could tell from the kids' and the man's body language that they were getting scolded for their insensitivity toward him. The car this man drove was the very same car in the driveway at Nora's house when his siding job began. Jim had seen this car around town after the gas-pumping insults were slung. He wondered who the young jet-black haired man was and what was said but never had a chance to approach this individual. As Kevin walks away and Nora turns to Jim once more, Jim smiles with such confidence to who defended him that for the first time, Nora is attracted to another man. Confidence is the key, gentleman. All woman are drawn to the alpha male. It is the security they seek in the confident man. All confident men thrive on the woman's approval of what they hold to be true. A Tammy Wynette song reminds a woman to stand by her man. Sound advice from a silly 1968 one-hit wonder. However, it is all too true. Jim and Nora talk as they leave the gym's noise. Both listen to one another as they speak and dance the getting-to-know-you blues.

Before they part ways, Nora asks Jim if needs to say goodbye to his sister and niece. "No," Jim replied. I'll see them when I get home. They live next door to me. So does my mother. One lives to the left, mom lives to the right. We're a close family."

Again, Nora is drawn to this man in a way she has not felt in a very long time. Nora's understanding of what love is has evolved. Love was and at times is still pain. Love is forgiveness, even though this is something Nora struggles with, especially while dealing with her emotions toward Dwayne. She thinks that forgiveness will elude her when it comes to Dwyane and what he did, but she also believes hate without forgiveness keeps her prisoner to what she knows she needs to let go. Someone told her once that hate for another was like drinking poison and expecting the one you hate to die. Nora has drunk her share of the poison for Dwyane. Dwyane, trapped in his own nightmare, never gives Nora a second thought. She prayed to forgive him out of an obligation to her faith and Lord. However, hate returns at times, and the poison repeatedly kills her soul, even after all these years. Nora tries to fill her heart with the understanding of love. She concluded long ago that love is the most powerful force. That this gift of love from God is just that—a gift. God is not love. Love is something he created, like you and me—a gift. Sometimes the gift for others through us. Sometimes the gift of us for others.

Nora nods as Jim works up the courage to speak not of his family and living conditions, but to question and risk. They stand some four or five feet from one another in a moment that soon will be filled with uncomfortable silence. Risk is always present when we seek the attention of others. The hunter man seeks the woman prey. The woman can defend or accept the approaching advance. Men, even the most confident of them of all, are fearful for the potential rejection. However, they will pursue the woman game just the same.

"Nora," Jim pauses. "Would you like to have pie with me sometime?"

"Pie?" Nora replies.

"Yes," Jim continues. "There is a restaurant in town named Bones. Have you heard of it?"

"Yes…" Nora interrupts, slowly nodding her head up and down as tiny blood vessels in her cheeks start to fill.

"Well the food is not very good, but they have wonderful cherry pie," Jim adds with his clear intentions and every card showing risk.

"Cherry pie, you say?" Nora smiles. Her eyes and her body language as she brushes the hair from the side of her face back, says that she would love to go. The blushing vessels are now filled but unnoticed by the hunter Jim Leary.

"Yeah, pie, uhm, cherry is the best," Jim concludes.

"I would like that, Jim." Nora said as she turns and walks away.

Jim bounces forward to follow Nora with delight. He catches up alongside her as they walk to the parked cars. Nora willfully gives Jim permission as well as her number to call. Jim stands and watches as Nora drives away. Jim feels good. Nora feels good. Simultaneously, as one drives away and the other stands and watches, they both have the exact same thought. *I sure could go for some pie right now*, as their stomachs growl with anticipation and delight.

The End

Special thanks to my favorite ex-wife for the wonderful book cover design. If you agree, she can be reached at: *dusk2dawndesign@att.net*

CPSIA information can be obtained
at www.ICGtesting.com
Printed in the USA
BVHW040541210619
551437BV00027BA/193/P